A Most Peculiar Courtship

The Daring Damsels
Book 3

Mihwa Lee

ARE YOU SIGNED UP FOR DRAGONBLADE'S BLOG?

You'll get the latest news and information on exclusive giveaways, exclusive excerpts, coming releases, sales, free books, cover reveals and more.

Check out our complete list of authors, too!

No spam, no junk. That's a promise!

Sign Up Here

www.dragonbladepublishing.com

Dearest Reader;

Thank you for your support of a small press. At Dragonblade Publishing, we strive to bring you the highest quality Historical Romance from some of the best authors in the business. Without your support, there is no 'us', so we sincerely hope you adore these stories and find some new favorite authors along the way.

Happy Reading!

CEO, Dragonblade Publishing

**Additional Dragonblade books by
Author Mihwa Lee**

The Daring Damsels
Touched by a Traitor (Book 1)
A Literary Liaison (Book 2)
A Most Peculiar Courtship (Book 3)

THE DEVIL HIMSELF

THE *METROPOLITAN REVIEW'S* printing office hummed with activity even at this late hour, the massive press clanking rhythmically as Amelia traced her finger beneath the lines of her latest editorial. "'While Lord Byron's poetic merits cannot be disputed, one must question the posthumous deification of a man whose moral compass pointed decidedly hellward.' Yes, that should do nicely," she murmured, making a small mark with her pencil.

WHOOSH. BANG!

The back door crashed open with such force that she jumped. Charles Eldem Bartholomew Hereford, the Marquess of Hereford, practically fell through the doorway, his dark hair wild and chest heaving beneath a half-unbuttoned shirt that had clearly begun the day in a much finer state.

"Pardon the intrusion," he gasped, those aristocratic features looking rakish and apologetic at once. His eyes darted around the cramped room, searching for cover.

The sound of approaching footsteps and angry shouting from the alley revealed his predicament. The marquess dove behind the printing press where Amelia had been standing, moving with remarkable speed for someone who'd clearly been drinking.

"I say," he whispered urgently, gripping her skirts, "be a dear and pretend I'm not here."

Amelia looked down at his hand tangled in her dress. "My

lord, I assure you my skirts are not public property, regardless of your extensive experience with others that are."

He had the audacity to grin up at her. "Desperate times call for desperate measures, Miss Thornton."

Just then, the back door burst open once more. A gentleman of middle years stood there, face puce with rage, brandishing a silver-tipped walking stick. "Where is he?" he demanded, chest heaving with exertion. "That libertine! That scoundrel!"

The man began searching behind the machines and under the tables, leaving the staff frozen in their stations.

Amelia casually adjusted the paper feed tray, extending it several inches outward so it pressed uncomfortably against the marquess' shoulder, forcing him to contort his tall frame into an even more cramped position. The libertine's eyes narrowed at her.

Becoming frustrated, the pursuer started walking in Amelia's direction, shouting, "Where is he? I know he came this way!"

Amelia reached for loose type, casually scattering the metal letters on the scoundrel himself, creating a trap of noise-making hazards. The Marquess of Hereford, in the meantime, uttered silent threats using language that Amelia was certain would have his marchioness mother washing his mouth with soap.

"Sir," she called to the man while holding Hereford's gaze, "what does this scoundrel look like?"

The pursuer stopped to look under a desk as he said, "He looks like the devil himself! Charming as a man can be but has no qualms about compromising the innocent."

Amelia glared down at the marquess, who was vehemently protesting by shaking his head. Shaking her head in response, Amelia stepped to the side. "Sir, you'll find your quarry attempting to hide behind this machine. Though I would request that if you plan to commit murder, you do so away from the printing press."

The hidden man popped up, his mouth agape. "That's hardly sporting of you, Miss Thornton!"

The gentleman lunged forward, his walking stick whistling through the air as Hereford ducked with impressive agility.

"I may have been more generous had you not hidden in the lady's wash closet at the Duchess of Lancaster's wedding," she exclaimed as the marquess vaulted over the table with surprising grace, scattering her carefully arranged papers. "How many innocent women must you ruin?"

"They were hardly innocent!" he shouted indignantly while being chased around the room by the man with the cane. "I do not dally with ladies of less than five and"—he paused to duck under a table—"twenty!"

"They can still be innocent!" Amelia called after him.

"You have only your character to blame!" he called over his shoulder as he fled toward the front door. "Do mind the leading on that editorial!"

The older gentleman cursed, following his quarry out the door in what was obviously a futile pursuit.

Once the building was devoid of both men, Amelia noticed the scent of Hereford's cologne lingering in the air—something expensive and masculine that made her think of crystal decanters and leatherbound books. She could still feel the phantom pressure of his hands on her skirts.

Despite her irritation, she couldn't help but recall how he had looked in that disheveled state—his fine lawn shirt gaping open to reveal a glimpse of tanned skin and well-defined muscle. Those striking blue eyes had fairly glowed with mischief as he had grinned up at her from his hiding place, dark hair falling to his shoulders and across his forehead in a way that made her fingers itch to brush it back.

What would it be like, she wondered, to be the object of such focused charm? To have those clever hands moving with purpose rather than desperation? At six and twenty, she was well past the age where such thoughts should make her blush, and yet…

"Don't be a fool," she muttered to herself, heading back to the office where Elisha was carefully crafting her review. She'd seen exactly what became of women who fell under the marquess' spell. How many crying ladies had she consoled at literary functions?

Besides, she'd seen the way his lip curled ever so slightly when addressing those he considered beneath him. The way his eyes would slide past her at Hyde Park as though she were just another weed in the garden. No doubt he saw her limp as just another mark against her, assuming he'd even noticed it at all.

A commoner. An invalid. A bluestocking who dared to critique his peers.

"Leading indeed," she scoffed as she stared at the scattered papers on her desk. Still, as she settled back into her chair, she couldn't quite suppress the memory of how gracefully he'd moved, even while fleeing. Or the way his voice had dropped to that intimate whisper, making her skin prickle despite herself.

"Focus," she commanded herself sternly, pulling a fresh sheet of paper toward her. "He is a pompous fool who is determined to be as insufferable as humanly possible," she said, stabbing her pen into the inkwell with more force than necessary.

Elisha Lancaster looked up from her own writing, amusement dancing in her eyes. Though marriage to a duke hadn't diminished her dedication to the *Metropolitan Review*, it had softened some of her sharper edges. "Which insufferable man would this be? Though given the circumstances being whispered about, I suspect Lord Hereford."

"The very same." Amelia attacked her paper with the pen. "A perpetual adolescent who treats life as though it's all some grand game. I've never met anyone so determined to waste their privileges on pure frivolity."

"Hmm." Elisha's noncommittal hum made Amelia glance up. She knew that tone.

"What aren't you telling me?"

"Only that people can surprise you." Elisha set down her pen. "Did you know that Lord Hereford personally funds three orphanages in London's poorest districts? Not through his family's charitable foundation but using his own private funds."

Amelia's pen paused mid-air. "You're joking."

"Not at all. Edgar mentioned it last week. Apparently, Hereford visits regularly to check on the children's welfare. He's particularly invested in their education and insists on qualified teachers and proper books."

"Lord Hereford? The same man who had two widows fighting over him at a ball last Season?"

"The very same." Elisha's smile turned knowing. "He's particularly concerned with the girls' education. Says they shouldn't have to rely on marriage as their only path to security."

Amelia sat back, frowning. The image wouldn't reconcile—the rakish marquess who seemed to spend every waking moment fleeing angry brothers and husbands through terraces and back alleys also spends time with orphans? "There must be some other reason."

"Must there?" Elisha raised an eyebrow. "People can contain contradictions, you know. Look at Edgar. He may seem like the perfect duke now, but you remember what he was like before we married."

"That's different. The Duke of Lancaster always had substance beneath his facade. Lord Hereford is…" Amelia gestured vaguely with her pen.

"Is what? Handsome? Charming? Surprisingly well-versed in printing techniques?" Elisha teased.

"As infuriating as a goose on a mission," Amelia said firmly, ignoring the warmth in her cheeks. "And apparently determined to drive me mad with his… his… everything."

Elisha's smile widened. "Everything?"

"Don't look at me like that. I simply mean he's impossible to categorize. One moment he's causing widows to fight over him at Mr. Dickens' reading, the next he's concerning himself with girls' education, and now you tell me he's some sort of secret philanthropist?"

"Oh, he's still very much a rake," Elisha said cheerfully. "In fact…" She glanced at the door before lowering her voice. "Edgar told me that Hereford and Patrick Adams are now in sole charge of some colorful business ventures."

Amelia leaned forward. "Colorful how?"

"Do you recall I had suspected Edgar of distributing London's more passionate literature?" Elisha's eyes twinkled. "Apparently the salacious business is quite profitable."

Amelia's eyes widened. "You mean to say you were correct in your suspicion? Lord Hereford now publishes those scandalous novels?"

"Among other things."

Amelia slumped back in her chair. "So, he funds orphanages with money from selling scandalous literature."

"Life is full of delicious ironies, isn't it?" Elisha picked up her pen again.

"Ironic for certain. Whether or not it's delicious, I'm unsure." Amelia stared unseeing at her editorial. Her carefully ordered worldview was being rearranged against her will. Lord Hereford—rake, critic, philanthropist, and purveyor of scandalous literature. "I don't suppose he writes any of it himself?"

"Why? Planning to offer him a position at the *Review*?"

"Certainly not!" Amelia grabbed a fresh sheet of paper, determined to focus on work rather than enigmatic marquesses.

Amelia had barely dipped her pen in ink when rapid footsteps approached. Thompson, the assistant editor, burst through the door, slightly breathless.

"This just arrived for you," he said, holding out a folded letter with his expression unusually grave. "It's from Dr. Morrison and apparently urgent."

Amelia's hand froze mid-motion, a drop of ink falling unnoticed onto her fresh page. Dr. Morrison. She hadn't heard that name spoken aloud in years, though she occasionally glimpsed him on London's streets—always hurrying past with averted eyes, as if the sight of her brought him physical pain.

"Dr. Morrison?" She set down her pen with careful deliberation. "I wouldn't have thought he'd remember me after all this time."

"How could he forget?" Elisha said softly, perching on the edge of Amelia's desk. "He spent days treating you, sent you herbal compounds for weeks without charging you anything, then avoided you like the plague, didn't he?" Her eyes held that faraway look, no doubt remembering those dark days when she'd stayed by Amelia's bedside through the worst of it.

Amelia broke the seal with trembling fingers. The handwriting was shaky, nothing like the precise script she remembered from her prescriptions.

"He's dying," she whispered. "He wants to see me. Says he has something important to tell me. What do you suppose he wishes to speak to me about?"

"I cannot imagine what it could be," Elisha admitted. "Perhaps you left an impression on him. Would you like me to come with you?"

Amelia considered it, but something in the letter's tone made her shake her head. "No, thank you. One of us has to stay and finish setting the type for tomorrow's edition."

They embraced, and Amelia felt those same arms that had once lifted her through fever-soaked nights tighten around her. "I'll be fine," she murmured, though her voice wavered. When they finally pulled apart, Amelia saw her own tears mirrored in Elisha's eyes. She pressed a kiss to her friend's cheek, trying to convey in that simple gesture what words could never fully express—thank you for keeping me alive when I'd given up on living.

THE JOURNEY TO Dr. Morrison's home stretched like a fever dream. Through the carriage window, London blurred past, but Amelia saw none of it. Instead, her mind kept returning to the day of the accident, to a pain so intense it had felt like her body was being torn apart.

The carriage stopped before a modest townhouse, its brick facade weathered and windows partially shuttered. A maid led her up a narrow staircase that smelled of camphor and illness, Amelia's wooden leg striking each step with a dull thud.

The man in the bed barely resembled the commanding physician she remembered. Dr. Morrison had collapsed in on himself, his skin stretched paper-thin over prominent bones, his chest rising and falling with visible effort.

His eyes fluttered open at her approach. "Miss Thornton," he wheezed, one trembling hand reaching toward her. "You came. I wasn't sure…"

"Of course I came." She lowered herself carefully into the chair beside his bed. "Though I confess, I was surprised to receive your request."

"I can imagine," he nodded weakly. "I've been living as a coward, afraid to face my past mistakes." A ghost of a smile crossed his lips. "I've followed your career. Like watching my own daughter succeed." His words dissolved into a coughing fit that shook his entire frame. "Which makes what I must tell you all the more difficult."

Something in his tone made Amelia's spine stiffen. "What do you mean?"

He closed his eyes, grief etching deeper lines around his mouth. "Your leg… I could have saved it. Should have saved it. The damage was severe, yes, but not beyond repair. But the factory owners insisted amputation would be quicker, cheaper. Said they wouldn't pay for months of treatment. And I… God help me, I gave in."

The words crashed over Amelia like a wave. The room tilted and spun as their meaning sank in. Her leg, her life, had been decided not by medical necessity but by businessmen's ledgers.

"You chose expediency over your physician's oath?" she heard herself ask.

"I was weak," he whispered, tears tracking down his sunken cheeks. "The factory owners had influence, could have ruined my practice. But that's no excuse." His grip on her hand tightened. "Can you ever forgive me?"

Amelia stared at their joined hands, her mind reeling. All these years she'd blamed herself, believed she should have been more careful. But every painful step, every altered dream, every prejudice she'd endured—all of it had been a choice made by others who thought her expendable.

"Who made this decision?" she asked, fighting to maintain her composure. "Do you know the proprietor's name?"

"I was told there were three proprietors, but I don't know which," he croaked. "The foreman at the time, Moore, sent missives to all three. Only one reply arrived, unsigned." His fingers twisted weakly in the bedsheets. "The letter's in my desk drawer. The key's in the vase."

Moving as if in a dream, Amelia retrieved the key and opened the drawer. Inside lay a folded, yellowed parchment, its edges worn from repeated handling. Her fingers trembled as she unfolded it:

Expediency and economy are key. If recovery more than a month, amputate.

The stark brutality of those twelve words struck her with physical force. This scrap of paper had decided her fate—a calculation that had altered every day of her existence since.

She carefully refolded the letter and slipped it into her reticule. "Thank you for your honesty, Doctor. I hope it brings you peace."

As the door closed behind her, something hardened in Amelia's heart. The nameless proprietors who had deemed her leg expendable were still out there, perhaps still making such calculations about other lives. The familiar ache transformed from memory into purpose, driving her forward with newfound resolve.

MARQUESS IN LEADING STRINGS

THE MARCHIONESS OF Hereford's annual charity fundraiser for the Children's Hospital sparkled with all the precision of a military campaign disguised as a social gathering. Every detail had been arranged to extract maximum donations while maintaining the illusion of intimate exclusivity.

Amelia adjusted her notebook, grateful that her work allowed her to remain on the periphery of the glittering crowd. Her leg was aching after a long day at the printing press, though she'd rather suffer than let it show. She had just settled into a quiet corner to observe when a feminine voice carried across the room.

"Charles, darling, you must let me fix your hair. How do you already look so charmingly disheveled? Perhaps your valet's vision needs to be examined?"

"Mother, please," the Marquess of Hereford said with barely leashed patience as his mother attempted to tame his dark hair. "I assure you I'm perfectly capable of grooming myself."

Amelia couldn't help but laugh at the marchioness' shameless pride in her son who was apparently still in his leading strings. The sound escaped before she could contain it, a brief musical note that drew the attention of both mother and son.

The marchioness turned sharply amid patting her son's cheeks. "I see you find the discussion of my son's virtues amusing, Miss Thornton. Perhaps if you spent more time cultivating feminine graces rather than opinions, you might understand their worth."

"My apologies, your ladyship. I was merely admiring the unconditional love mothers are able to bestow on their children."

Somewhat pacified, Lady Hereford's eyes roamed over Amelia's form while her son observed the exchange with interest. "Why are you lurking around here? I was expecting your brother. The invitation was addressed to the *Metropolitan Review's* proprietor."

"I am the proprietor, my lady." Amelia kept her tone pleasant. "Mr. Thornton, my brother, gifted me full ownership last year."

The marchioness' face performed a fascinating series of expressions, finally settling on barely concealed horror. "A lady journalist? But surely such work isn't… that is to say, a woman?"

An unfamiliar voice interrupted smoothly, "Miss Thornton's background makes her uniquely qualified to report on London's commercial interests." Viscount Norwich joined their group. "I particularly appreciated your recent series on educational reforms, Miss Thornton. Your analysis of the peerage education was very thorough."

The sincerity in his tone made Amelia look at him more closely. They'd greeted each other politely when their paths crossed at Hyde Park but had not spoken. He met her gaze warmly.

"You're familiar with Miss Thornton's work, Lord Norwich?" The marchioness' tone suggested this was hardly a recommendation.

"Indeed. I take pride in informing my peers that the *Review* ought to be required reading among London's business community." He smiled at Hereford. "What say you, Hereford. Wouldn't you agree?"

"Miss Thornton's writings are occasionally worth noting," Hereford drawled, barely glancing in her direction. "Though one must wade through considerable melodrama to find the substance."

Amelia tried not to clench her jaw too visibly. "Perhaps because my observations, like scarecrows, are only noticed when the crows are already feasting on the crops," Amelia replied, her polite smile not quite reaching her eyes.

Norwich's eyes sparkled before addressing Amelia. "Miss Thornton, your piece on medical care in poorer districts struck a particularly personal chord. My late wife..." He stopped, pain briefly crossing his features. "Well, access to proper medical care can make all the difference, can't it?"

"Lord Norwich has been quite generous to the hospital," the marchioness said to Hereford, clearly trying to steer the conversation toward safer waters. "He's introduced many donors to the establishment. Invaluable connections."

Hereford's lips twitched. "More valuable than actual donations, Mother? How fortunate that you'd prefer a rooster over an egg-laying hen."

The marchioness waved this away. "We all help the less fortunate in our own way, dearest. You taking time out of your precious day to be here, for instance. True nobility has different priorities."

Amelia caught Hereford's slight wince at his mother's gushing praise. It was almost endearing how uncomfortable he looked being cast as the philanthropic hero when he'd likely stumbled in here by accident.

"Speaking of philanthropy," Norwich said, "I'd be very interested in hearing more about your observations regarding hospital conditions, Miss Thornton. Perhaps we could discuss it over tea sometime? Purely professional interest, of course."

Something sharp flashed in Hereford's eyes. "Miss Thornton's next article focuses on factory owners who value profits over worker safety. You must have quite the perspective on that topic, Norwich."

Amelia tensed while Norwich's face went slightly pink. *How did the marquess know about her next article?*

As if to read her mind, Hereford's baritone voice added, "The

Duchess of Lancaster mentioned it the other day."

Amelia bristled at his eyes, which seemed to dance with mockery even when he was saying something perfectly appropriate. "I'm conducting a rather extensive investigation into several accidents that occurred at prominent factories over the past few years. The results should illuminate the factory owners' priorities."

She watched Hereford carefully as she spoke, noting how his eyes sharpened even as his mouth curved in a grin.

"Speaking of priorities, I believe the Widow Rutland could benefit from my social obligations." He offered his mother a rakish wink. "Don't wait up, darling Mama."

The marchioness watched her son saunter away with obvious pride. "Such a delightful boy. Though I don't know where he gets his wild streak from."

"Quite the mystery," Amelia murmured, recalling the late Marquess of Hereford's scandalous reputation while noting how Norwich's eyes followed Hereford with something harder than mere social rivalry.

LATER IN THE carriage, reviewing her notes, she found herself dwelling less on the charity's impressive donation total and more on the curious undercurrents she'd observed. Norwich's strange intensity when discussing medical care. Hereford's unexpected animosity beneath his lazy drawl. And most intriguing of all, both men's peculiar reactions to her planned investigation.

She had a feeling there was a much bigger story here than a simple charity fundraiser. She just wasn't sure yet what it was.

The charity event had left Amelia emotionally drained, her usual defenses weakened by the curious undercurrents between Hereford and Norwich. As her borrowed carriage delivered her home, a restlessness seized her that could not be quelled by the prospect of an empty parlor and half-written editorials.

"Driver," she called suddenly, leaning forward before she could reconsider, "take me to Crown Street instead."

"Crown Street, Miss?" The driver's voice carried clear skepticism. "It's nearly dusk, and that's no place for—"

"I'm quite aware of what Crown Street is," she interrupted, her voice betraying none of her trepidation. "Please proceed."

As the carriage turned toward London's industrial quarter, Amelia's determination hardened even as her wooden leg began to throb with memory. Thirteen years since she'd ventured anywhere near that place. Thirteen years of deliberately chosen routes to avoid even glimpsing the brick facade where her life had irrevocably changed.

The setting sun cast long shadows across cobblestones as they approached. Amelia instructed the driver to stop at the corner, a safe distance from the factory gates. "Wait here," she ordered, ignoring his concerned expression. "I won't be long."

The evening air hung heavy with coal smoke and cotton dust, an acrid mixture that instantly transported her back to her fourteen-year-old self. Her stomach clenched as she approached the factory. The familiar silhouette of Crown Street Textiles loomed against the darkening sky, windows still illuminated by gas lamps despite the late hour. The night shift would be starting soon.

Workers streamed from the main entrance—women with kerchiefs covering their hair, children with hollow eyes who looked far older than their years, men with stooped shoulders and coal-stained hands. Amelia stood in the shadows, watching. Did she look so weary at fourteen? So resigned? She couldn't remember.

A man emerged from the side entrance, his portly frame unmistakable even after all these years. Peter Moore, the foreman who had been present during her accident. She would never forget his face hovering above her as she lay trapped in the machinery.

Without conscious decision, she followed at a careful distance, her wooden leg striking the pavement with muffled determination. He entered the Ram's Head, a public house crowded with factory workers spending precious coins on momentary comfort. Amelia took a seat at the bar, keeping her face averted, her hooded cloak concealing her fine clothes.

"Profits are up again this quarter," she heard Moore announce with satisfaction. "The new machines increased output by seventeen percent."

Amelia stared at Moore's profile as his companions raised their glasses and cheered. Sweat gleamed on his brow in the dim light as he pontificated to his friends with a self-satisfied curl of his lip. The memories suddenly pressed against her lungs. With a hand on her chest, Amelia left a coin on the counter and slipped out, the burden of her past choking her. The factory's shadow still loomed, darker and more oppressive than before.

She made her way back to the waiting carriage where the driver helped her inside without comment, though his expression suggested suspicions about her reputation. "Home now, Miss?"

She nodded, her throat too tight for speech.

Amelia sat with the yellowed letter before her. Her fingers traced the cold, clinical words that had sentenced her to a lifetime of adaptation and struggle. Inside her, two voices warred with increasing ferocity. One thirsted for a personal reckoning—to discover which of the owners was responsible and to see his face when she revealed who she was before driving a sword into his heart. She wished to witness the fear in the devil's eyes when he realized his cruelty had returned to haunt him, to make them feel a fraction of the pain and uncertainty she had endured.

Yet the other voice, quieter but no less insistent, reminded her that exposing them publicly through her newspaper would protect countless others from similar fates. This path offered no personal moment of triumph but would keep her safe from the gallows and comfort her with the knowledge that she might prevent others from experiencing the same suffering. As the carriage approached her modest home, Amelia realized the true struggle wasn't between justice and vengeance, but between healing her past wounds and preventing future ones. Perhaps, she thought as she carefully refolded the letter, there might be a way to accomplish both.

CHIMNEY SWEEP OVER A MARQUESS

T HE *METROPOLITAN REVIEW'S* office hummed with activity as Amelia sorted through her notes from the charity fundraiser. The door burst open, and Elisha, Duchess of Lancaster, swept in with familiar confidence.

"I heard Viscount Norwich was paying you particular attention at Hereford's charity event," Elisha announced without preamble, settling into her favorite chair.

"Who told you?" Amelia looked up from her notes.

"Edgar heard it from his secretary. Lord Norwich is apparently quite taken with your articles on reform."

"He was knowledgeable about industrial reform," Amelia said, setting aside her pen.

"Hmmm. I wonder if it's just your writing he's admiring," Elisha added with a knowing smile. "He hasn't courted anyone since his wife died fifteen years ago. He's devoted himself to raising their daughter, but she'll make her debut next Season. Perhaps that's why he's finally showing interest in someone."

Amelia laughed. "If you're suggesting what I think, you're being ridiculous. A man like Lord Norwich wouldn't look twice at an illegitimate daughter of a disgraced viscount."

"You underestimate your appeal. You're intelligent, beautiful, passionate—"

"And a cripple," Amelia cut in. "Not to mention nearly twenty years his junior."

"Men prefer younger women," Elisha countered. "And he's quite handsome for his age. More importantly, he shares your passion for reform. Unless you're interested in a certain rakish marquess…"

"Lord Hereford?" Amelia scoffed. "That spoiled boy who thinks life is one grand game? I'd sooner marry a chimney sweep."

While Elisha laughed at the jest, a messenger arrived with a calling card. Amelia read it, her cheeks warming. "Lord Norwich requests to call on me this afternoon for tea to discuss my articles."

"How providential," Elisha's smile widened. "Would you like me to join you? As chaperone, of course."

"Yes, please," Amelia replied. "Though purely for professional reasons."

"Of course," Elisha stood, smoothing her skirts. "Though you might want to wear that green silk that brings out your eyes. For professional reasons, naturally."

"Out!" Amelia threw a wadded paper at her friend, smiling despite herself.

Elisha paused at the door, her demeanor suddenly serious. "How was your visit with Dr. Morrison? I waited for you as long as I could, but Edgar needed me at home."

Amelia's smile faded. "Enlightening in the worst possible way."

Elisha closed the door and returned to her seat. "Tell me everything."

"He called me there to confess something horrendous," Amelia lowered her voice. "My leg could have been saved. The amputation wasn't necessary."

"What?" Elisha's face paled.

"The factory owners refused to pay for months of treatment. They decided amputation would be more economical." Amelia withdrew the yellowed letter from her desk. "He gave me this."

Elisha read the cold, clinical words silently, her face paling.

"This is monstrous," she whispered. "Does it say who sent it?"

"No signature. Dr. Morrison said the orders came from one of the proprietors, but he never learned which one. The letter went through the foreman first."

"The handwriting is distinctive," Elisha observed. "Someone educated, clearly."

"I need to identify all three owners Morrison mentioned," Amelia said. "I've already confirmed the foreman, Peter Moore, still works at Crown Street. He's now the site manager."

"You shouldn't investigate alone," Elisha cautioned. "That part of London is dangerous."

"Perhaps Lord Norwich's connections could help," Amelia mused. "If he truly supports reform, he might inadvertently provide access to information I couldn't otherwise obtain."

"A strategic alliance with a handsome viscount?" Elisha's lips quirked.

"A professional consultation," Amelia corrected firmly.

⇒⟩⟩⟩⟨⟨⟨⇐

THE AFTERNOON LIGHT slanted through the Review's windows as Amelia served tea in her private office. Lord Norwich accepted a cup from Elisha with gratitude.

"Your articles show remarkable insight into the workhouse system," he said. "One might almost think you had firsthand experience."

"I do," Amelia replied. "I spent my childhood in workhouses after my mother died when I was five."

Surprise flickered across his face. "My sincerest condolences, Miss Thornton. It must have been extremely difficult."

"It taught me valuable lessons about society's inequities," she smiled briefly at Elisha. "The duchess and I met in one such establishment."

"And how did you progress to newspaper editor?" he asked.

"When I injured my leg at fourteen, my brother found me during recovery. I hadn't known I had a brother, also an illegitimate child of the viscount."

"May I ask how the accident occurred?" Norwich held her gaze intently.

"At a textile factory. My leg was caught in one of the machines," she replied steadily. "I don't recall much about that day. The duchess was by my side during my recovery."

The silence that followed was heavy. Norwich had gone very still, his face draining of color.

"My family lost everything when I was young," he said finally, his voice weaker than before. "Our estate, our standing. I began as a clerk in textile factories, watching owners live luxuriously while workers suffered." His fingers tightened almost imperceptibly around his teacup. "I vowed to rebuild what was lost. It took years of sacrifice."

"That explains your interest in reform," Amelia observed, curious about the change in his demeanor, but also moved by his story.

"Yes," Norwich nodded, though something flickered behind his eyes.

The door burst open, interrupting them. Hereford stood there, impeccably dressed, his usual languid expression replaced by something sharper.

"Norwich," he said, ignoring proper greetings. "I saw your carriage. We need to discuss the railway matter."

"Lord Hereford," she said as an icy chill settled inside her, "this is a private meeting."

"My apologies, Miss Thornton, but certain business matters can't wait," he said with a stern expression she hadn't seen before.

"It might be better if I leave," Norwich rose quickly, nearly knocking over his teacup.

"Are you unwell?" Amelia asked. "You've gone quite pale."

"Just a slight headache. Thank you for the tea, and for sharing your story."

They watched him hurry out, his composure notably absent. Hereford's eyes narrowed as he observed the older man's retreat.

"I don't suppose either of you would care to explain what prompted Norwich's color to match that of fresh linens?" Hereford asked.

Before they could respond, Hereford was already gone, following Norwich as if chasing him.

"I believe we've just witnessed something significant," Elisha said thoughtfully.

Amelia stared at her cooling tea, feeling uneasy. "Whatever it may be, I feel troubled."

⤜⟫⟫⟩⟨⟪⟪⤛

HEREFORD CAUGHT UP with Norwich beside his waiting carriage. "Your sudden interest in the *Metropolitan Review*," he began, "I find myself wondering about its timing."

"How fascinating that you're monitoring my reading habits," Norwich replied coolly.

"Reading is one thing. Calling on its proprietor for private tea suggests you're hoping to influence the paper's coverage."

"My interest in Miss Thornton is perfectly legitimate." Norwich's smile didn't reach his eyes. "She's quite remarkable— intelligent, passionate, and surprisingly beautiful despite her... imperfection. Her newspaper provides a useful platform."

Hereford's jaw tightened at Norwich's casual reference to Amelia's limp. "If you're considering adding her to your collection of conquests, I advise against it."

"My collection?" Norwich's eyebrows rose. "That's rich coming from you."

"Miss Thornton is not some opera dancer or bored Society wife. She's a serious woman of substance."

"Precisely what makes her so intriguing," Norwich leaned forward slightly. "Imagine having such a voice of moral authority eating from one's hand. Or should I say, warming one's bed?"

Hereford's hand clenched at his side. "I'm warning you, Norwich. She's not a woman to be trifled with."

"I find myself more intrigued by your reaction," Norwich studied him. "Could it be the lord who tups every lightskirt harbors a tender spot for our Miss Thornton? Or is it merely that you've come to appreciate certain of her… attributes?"

"I respect her work," Hereford hissed. "And I know your methods. You'll use her, damage her reputation, then discard her once you've extracted whatever value she offers."

"How chivalrous," Norwich's tone dripped with amusement. "I wouldn't have expected you to appoint yourself guardian of a commoner's virtue."

"Look elsewhere for dalliance."

"We shall see," Norwich's smile turned calculating. "Miss Thornton has proven quite receptive to my attentions so far. Her newspaper's influence would be most valuable to my interests, not to mention the more personal benefits."

"If you harm her in any way—"

"You'll what?"

Hereford's smile was dangerous. "Let's just say I know things about your business practices that would make fascinating reading in the *Metropolitan Review*."

Norwich's eyes turned icy despite his smirk. "You will not, Hereford. I recognize a kindred spirit when I see one. You wouldn't ruin my reputation when it's tied to our joint venture because you're as insatiable as the rest of us."

Hereford watched the older man embark onto the carriage and pull away, wondering where his protectiveness of a woman who clearly despised him had come from. When he spotted Norwich's crest on the carriage parked in front of the *Review*, he had reacted instinctively. He had been fueled by rage at the thought of Norwich exploiting Amelia Thornton's principles and worse.

"Utterly ridiculous," he muttered, turning away. Feeling protective toward a woman didn't mean he had tender feelings for her. The idea was absurd. She hated him. She was a commoner. And again, she hated him.

THE LITERARY SECRETS

T HE AIR IN Hereford's private study at his country estate hung thick with cigar smoke and laughter. The large oak doors were firmly locked, servants dismissed for the evening with strict instructions not to disturb. Two crystal decanters, one brandy, one whiskey, stood half-empty on the desk between them.

"Good God, man," Patrick Adams wiped tears of mirth from his eyes, holding up several pages of elegant script. "Listen to this passage: 'His mouth descended upon her heaving bosom like a starving man presented with a feast, his aristocratic reserve abandoned as completely as her corset.'"

Hereford snorted, nearly choking on his brandy. "Keep reading," he managed, loosening his cravat as he settled deeper into his leather chair.

"'She moaned as his noble fingers—'" Patrick broke off, overcome with laughter again. "Noble fingers! As if breeding makes one's digits particularly skilled!"

"I assure you, it does," Hereford drawled, plucking the manuscript from Patrick's hands. His eyes scanned the page, brows rising. "Well, our new authoress certainly has a vivid imagination. And an unusually comprehensive knowledge of male anatomy. She must be a mistress or at least married many times over."

The private study beneath Hereford's country manor had become the unofficial headquarters of their clandestine publishing venture, a surprisingly profitable business that had started under the leadership of the Duke of Lancaster. What had begun three years ago with a single anonymous manuscript had blossomed into a network of women writers crafting what Society would call "inappropriate literature." Stories of passion, desire, and women's pleasure that proper Society pretended didn't exist.

"Lancaster asked about our latest scandalous story yesterday," Patrick said, reaching for a leather ledger.

"Of course he did," Hereford chuckled. "He may have removed himself from our venture since marrying, but his true nature remains unchanged."

Patrick reached for a leather ledger, flipping through pages of careful accounting. "He particularly inquired after the woman who lost her livelihood after she was got with child, which symbol is she? She's used her first payment to secure lodgings away from her disapproving parents."

"Ah, Gamma. I am pleased to hear it," Hereford nodded, his playful expression sobering. "And Sigma? Has she managed to pay off her father's creditors?"

"Nearly. Another two stories should clear the debt entirely." Patrick made a notation in the margin.

As they worked in companionable silence, Hereford found himself studying his friend. Few knew that Patrick Adams—private investigator, security specialist, and publisher of scandalous literature—was not the man's birth name, but rather the anglicized version he'd adopted upon arriving in England fifteen years ago.

"You're unusually quiet tonight," Patrick observed, not looking up from his ledger. "Something troubling you?"

"Not at all," Hereford replied. "I was just thinking about how far we've come since Lancaster introduced us."

Patrick's lips quirked into a half-smile. "Who would have thought?"

"Patryk Adamski, nobleman of Warsaw, proudly peddling salacious novels," Hereford announced to an imaginary audience.

"My father would be proud. He understood survival," Patrick

said with a melancholic smile. "When Russia seized our family lands after the uprising, I learned quickly that principles without pragmatism lead to death."

Hereford nodded, respecting the man's survival instinct. Few knew the full extent of what Patrick had endured.

"Speaking of survival, the new one, the violet ink, is becoming rather popular," Patrick commented, sorting through their accounting. "Four stories in two months, each better than the last. The printer says her latest sold out within a week."

"She has a gift for the dramatic," Hereford agreed, slitting open the newest submission marked with a delicate snowflake in the corner. His eyes widened as he scanned the first page. "Well, well. Our mysterious Snowflake has outdone herself."

Patrick looked up with interest. "That good?"

"Better." Hereford passed him the first page, a slow smile spreading across his aristocratic features. "She's written something different. A widow seducing a younger man this time. A common-born businessman, no less."

"Scandalous," Patrick murmured, skimming the elegant script. "And rather politically radical, suggesting a nobleman's widow might lower herself thus."

"Indeed. Yet written with such conviction one might almost believe she'd experienced it firsthand." Hereford's fingers traced the snowflake symbol thoughtfully. "I wonder who she is."

"Anonymity is part of what makes these stories exciting," Patrick reminded him.

"And what allows them to write so freely," Hereford added.

"Speaking of secrets," Patrick said, his voice dropping slightly, "I received word from Warsaw yesterday. Three more families need passage to England."

Hereford nodded. Since taking over the Midnight Press, a significant portion of the profits had quietly funded the escape of Polish political dissidents and their families—a cause dear to Patrick's heart that both Lancaster and Hereford had come to support without reservation.

"Will the usual channels suffice?" he asked.

"Yes, though we'll need additional funds for the youngest family. They have four children, all under ten." Patrick's expression hardened with memories of his own hasty escape. "The Russian authorities are watching the borders more closely."

"Take what's needed from the Eastern Account," Hereford said without hesitation. "And add this month's profits from Snowflake's Grecian tales."

"That's generous," Patrick said, making a notation. "Her stories alone have made us a small fortune." He raised his glass in a toast. "To our causes and the most ruthlessly impractical businessmen in London."

"To business, then," Hereford conceded with a wry smile, clinking his glass against his friend's. "And to our Snowflake, who seems determined to scandalize all of London with her imagination."

"To Snowflake," Patrick agreed. "May she never discover that her scandalous literature is being published by the very aristocrats she seems to enjoy debauching on paper."

Their laughter mingled with the cigar smoke as they returned to their clandestine business.

As they sorted through the final manuscripts of the evening, Patrick commented, "Carlisle's soiree is in a week's time. No doubt his wife's friend, Thornton's sister, will be there. The one who keeps writing editorials about the moral bankruptcy of peers."

"Miss Amelia Thornton," Hereford supplied. "I suppose I should make an appearance, if only to provide her with fresh material for her next character assassination."

"She certainly seems to have formed a strong opinion of you," Patrick observed. "One might almost think she's studied you carefully."

"Yes," Hereford murmured, shuffling through another manuscript. "One might indeed."

He carefully refolded the pages, his mind already turning to their next encounter. Perhaps Miss Thornton would provide him with some fresh insight into women's secret desires, albeit unintentionally. The thought made him smile as he locked Snowflake's scandalous creation safely away until their next clandestine meeting.

➷➸

THE REFORM CLUB'S library smelled of leather and secrets. Amelia sat surrounded by stacks of reports and correspondence, her leg aching from hours of research. She'd nearly given up finding concrete evidence of systematic negligence when Lord Norwich appeared beside her table.

"Miss Thornton." His voice was quiet, mindful of the library's silence. "What a pleasant surprise."

Amelia looked up, caught off guard by his presence. "Lord Norwich. I wouldn't have expected to find you here."

"I make it a point to stay informed about social concerns." His smile held calculated charm as he gestured to the chair across from her. "May I?"

She nodded, watching as he settled into the seat. There was something compelling about his presence—a steady dignity that contrasted sharply with Hereford's restless energy.

"You're researching factory conditions." His eyes flickered over her notes. "A worthy cause."

"Do you really think so?" She studied his face. "Most men of your position seem to find such investigations… inconvenient."

"Progress requires change, Miss Thornton. And change requires brave souls willing to speak uncomfortable truths." His voice held just the right note of conviction. "Though I imagine such work can be rather exhausting."

She shifted in her chair, her wooden leg protesting the long hours. Norwich noticed immediately, moving to assist her with smooth courtesy.

"Allow me to fetch you a footstool." His hand brushed her arm as he stood. "No need to overtax yourself."

The gesture was kind, but something in his tone made her skin prickle.

"You're very solicitous, my lord."

"Not at all." He returned with the footstool, helping her arrange it. "I simply believe in supporting worthy endeavors."

Their faces were close as he adjusted the footstool. She caught the scent of expensive cologne. When their eyes met, his gaze pierced hers. The intensity she saw there gave her goose-flesh, which was not entirely pleasant.

His gloved hand covered hers where it rested on the table. The touch was possessive. "I've long advocated for reform. Among other interests we might share."

"My lord…" Her voice emerged softly.

"Robert," he corrected, leaning closer. "Please." The library's hush seemed to deepen around them. His voice dropped lower. "Miss Thornton, I find myself thinking of you far more than is proper."

The library door opened, and they both righted their postures.

"Lord Norwich." A messenger approached hurriedly. "I have with me an urgent letter, my lord."

Norwich tore open the letter and read it quietly. He then looked up at Amelia. "My apologies, Miss Thornton. I cannot tell you how much I regret this interruption. Alas, duty calls. I hope you'll ponder what I said so that we may speak of it soon."

After he'd gone, Amelia sat staring at her notes, her pulse steady at the memory of his touch, unlike the fluttering she'd felt when the marquess of Hereford's fingers had brushed hers.

Lord Norwich represented everything she should want in a husband, if she dared to dream: title, wealth, and most important-ly, a genuine commitment to reform. No scandals, no rakish behavior, no string of conquests. Just quiet competence and proper respect for her work. Even the way he'd acknowledged her injury showed perfect courtesy. No awkward avoidance or excessive concern, just practical assistance offered with dignity.

"He would be a far more suitable match," she murmured to herself. A man who shared her values, who could advance her causes through his position in Society. Not some rakish marquess who treated life as a game.

So why did her thoughts keep straying to Hereford's laughing eyes and mocking wit?

⟫⟫⟫✦⟪⟪⟪

THE DUKE OF Lancaster's London townhouse exuded quiet opulence as Hereford paced before the fireplace, his usual aristocratic languor replaced by restless energy.

"Do sit down, Lord Hereford," Elisha said. "You're making me dizzy with all that pacing."

The Duke of Lancaster glanced up from the railway proposal. "I invited you to discuss the Midland connection, yet you've scarcely looked at the maps since your arrival."

Hereford forced himself to sit, though his fingers continued to drum against the armrest. "The railway venture is, of course, of paramount importance."

"And yet," Lancaster observed, "your mind is clearly else-where. Something troubles you, old friend."

Hereford hesitated briefly. "As the duchess has witnessed, I paid a visit to the *Metropolitan Review's* offices yesterday. I found Norwich there, calling on Miss Thornton," he replied, unable to keep a sharp edge from his voice.

"Ah." Elisha exchanged a glance with her husband. "Lord Norwich has been supportive of Amelia's work on factory reform."

"How remarkably civic minded of him." Hereford's fingers stilled on the armrest.

Lancaster studied his friend with increasing interest. "You

seem unusually concerned about Norwich's involvement with Miss Thornton's newspaper."

"His business dealings have always struck me as somewhat… opaque," Hereford said, addressing Lancaster directly.

"We've heard rumors, certainly, but nothing substantial," Lancaster replied.

"I have a feeling he's scheming something with respect to Miss Thornton," Hereford continued, rising again. "I wonder if her series on child laborers has caught his attention."

"Speaking of factory safety," Elisha interjected, "Amelia has been investigating a particular factory quite intently of late."

"Which factory?" Hereford's attention sharpened.

Elisha hesitated, apparently regretting her comment. "I shouldn't say more. It's Amelia's matter to discuss if she chooses." She turned to her husband. "Edgar, I wonder if your banking connections might assist in obtaining certain financial records?"

Lancaster frowned slightly. "I must be careful. My involvement in such inquiries could be seen as ill-advised."

Hereford studied his friends, sensing undercurrents he couldn't interpret. "There's something you're not telling me."

"I would, be it my information to disclose. Alas, it is not," Elisha said. "If you truly believe Miss Thornton might be at risk, perhaps you should speak with her directly."

"Unfortunately, our conversations tend to involve more verbal sparring than productive dialogue. She would be more receptive to your warning."

"I will speak to her," the duchess remarked, "but I believe she will appreciate your concern should you discuss the matter with her."

"I'll consider it," he said finally. "Though I fear she'd sooner believe I had ulterior motives."

"And do you?" Lancaster asked, his expression unreadable.

Hereford paused at the door, a half-smile touching his lips. "That, my friend, is a question I find myself increasingly unable to answer."

As he departed, the afternoon sunlight caught a woman's emerald-green dress across the street, startlingly similar to the gown Amelia had worn the day he'd hidden behind her printing press. The memory of her unflinching candor stirred something unexpected in his chest—a complicated emotion he wasn't prepared to examine too closely.

DESPERATE FOR ATTENTION

AMELIA COULD FEEL the stares as she made her way down the portrait-lined hallway of Brooks where she entered on business. Highly irregular for a non-decorative woman to enter such an establishment, but she had gained access through the Duke of Lancaster's influence who had promised to introduce her to the members. Several wealthy members were potential advertisers for the *Review*, and she was determined to earn their patronage tonight. The *Review's* subscription numbers may be increasing but the main profit was still to be had from advertising.

The sound of familiar laughter interrupted her thoughts and drew her attention to an open door.

Inside, Lord Hereford was pressing himself against the Duchess of Rutland in what he probably imagined was a seductive instructional pose. He'd shed his coat, and his shirtsleeves were rolled up, revealing surprisingly muscular forearms. Not that she was noticing such things.

"The key, Your Grace," he was saying in a voice like warm honey, "is to imagine the foil as an extension of your arm. One must cradle it just so…" His hands slid down the duchess' arm to adjust her grip. "Like a lover's caress."

The duchess tittered, her blonde curls bouncing. "Oh, Lord Hereford, you are positively wicked. What would my late duke say?"

"That you have excellent taste in instructors, I should hope," he grinned, then caught sight of Amelia in the doorway. His expression shifted to one of exaggerated scandal as he straightened his posture. "Miss Thornton! This is hardly—"

The duchess, startled by his sudden shift in tone, whirled around with more enthusiasm than grace. Her foil, still extended, caught the fine fabric of his trousers with a telltale ripping sound. The tear started at his upper thigh and traveled upward in a way that made propriety impossible to maintain.

"Oh dear," the duchess said, pressing her free hand to her mouth in a gesture that did nothing to hide her smile. Her eyes traveled appreciatively over the exposed flesh. "How terribly clumsy of me. Though I must say, Lord Hereford, you do keep yourself in fine condition. All those fencing lessons must be quite strenuous."

Hereford's attempt to maintain his dignity while discreetly trying to hold the tear closed only succeeded in making it worse. A flash of tanned skin revealed that his lordship apparently swam or rode his horse in… Amelia started at her own imagination. She focused her attention back to the marquess' face, whose countenance revealed a rare moment of embarrassment.

Amelia decided she would enjoy his discomfort. "One imagines all that running from angry husbands provides excellent exercise." She paused deliberately. "Though perhaps more practice with defensive maneuvers would be beneficial. Your form appears somewhat… exposed."

The duchess let out an unladylike snort of laughter, while Hereford's ears turned a fascinating shade of pink. He attempted to angle himself to preserve what remained of his dignity, but the movement only caused the tear to creep higher.

"I assure you, Miss Thornton," he managed, his usual smooth charm deserting him, "this is not at all what it—" He shifted again, and there was another distinct ripping sound. "Oh, blast it all."

"Such language!" The duchess openly giggled. "Shall I fetch you a blanket, my lord? Or perhaps you'd prefer to continue the lesson? I find I'm suddenly quite motivated to improve my technique."

Hereford's eyes narrowed and voice lowered. "Deirdre, be a dear and fetch me that blanket you were kind enough to offer."

"Why, of course. And perhaps I could help you out of your torn trousers after?" With a wink and a wave, the duchess hurried out of the room.

Amelia watched the lady's expensive gown ripple as she hurried down the corridor.

"What on earth are you doing here?" Hereford barked.

"I'm here on business. I have obtained permission to be here."

He took a few steps toward her, then stopped, the effort to keep his disintegrating trousers in one piece becoming too taxing. "What could be so important that you would venture into a gentleman's club unchaperoned?"

She met his gaze steadily. "I hope you're not expecting a response, my lord, as I don't owe you an explanation."

She started when the marquess abandoned all effort to keep his bare thigh hidden and approached her slowly, his arms crossed over his chest. Her eyes widened as they swept over the gaping hole of his trousers, revealing the long sinews and powerful bulges. Hereford stopped a foot away from her, forcing her to crank her neck to look at him.

His voice growled softly when he spoke, his eyes half hooded as he gazed down at her haughtily. "This is no place for an unwed woman."

"That is an interesting opinion, my lord, considering I arrived with a dozen unwed women in scandalous clothing. Would you be more receptive to my presence had I been prepared to entertain the gentlemen?"

Amelia met his thunderous gaze without flinching, though her heart hammered against her ribs. When he spoke, his voice dropped to a whisper that dripped with condescension.

"You may be either arrogant or ignorant enough to be here,

but you do not comprehend the risk. Your brother," his gaze flickered meaningfully to her leg, "should know better than to send you unchaperoned. Leave before the evening's entertainment begins."

Amelia arched an eyebrow, deliberately casual. "Why, Lord Hereford, one might almost mistake that for concern."

"I have a responsibility to protect innocent women who stray into my domain." He adjusted his torn trousers with as much dignity as he could muster.

"Duly noted. Now I do not wish to cut into your time with pretty widows." She allowed her gaze to drift purposefully over his exposed thigh even as color flooded her cheeks.

"Why does my reputation matter so much to you, Miss Thornton?"

The question stopped her retreat. She turned around, taking in the full picture he made. Impossibly blue eyes, even more striking against his tanned skin, contrasted sharply with his stark white shirt. That perfectly tied emerald cravat accentuated his aristocratic features, while dark hair fell in artfully tousled waves. Every inch the pampered aristocrat.

"I beg your pardon?"

"Most of Society barely gives my behavior a second thought," he said, studying her with genuine curiosity. "Yet you seem to take particular interest in cataloging my failings. I wonder why."

Amelia's fingers tightened around the handle of her reticule. The unexpected perceptiveness of his question caught her off guard. Her leg throbbed suddenly, as if to remind her of the price she had paid because of men who did nothing.

"Perhaps because men like you could make so much more of a difference," she replied, her throat closing from tension. "Yes, you fund orphanages—commendable work—but you have wealth, influence, connections that could do so much more. Instead, you seem to treat your charitable ventures as side projects while spending most of your energy on frivolities."

Something flickered in his gaze—a brief shadow that might

have been hurt.

"While children toil in factories until their fingers bleed," she continued, unable to stop herself. "While families lose loved ones to unsafe conditions for mere pennies of profit. Your orphanages treat the symptoms, my lord, but what of the disease? What of the systems that create orphans in the first place?"

"You speak as if this is personal," he said quietly. "As if my supposed indifference has harmed you directly."

Amelia stiffened, conscious of how close he'd come to an uncomfortable truth. "It harms us all when those with the power to enact change remain willfully blind to suffering."

"Oh my. This is better entertainment than the theater." The Duchess of Rutland's delighted voice shattered their battle of wills. Her Grace stood in the doorway, eyes sparkling with barely suppressed mirth.

Amelia then realized more doors had opened as other members investigated the commotion. The Duke of Lancaster appeared, taking in the scene before him. Hereford with his torn trousers, the duchess clutching her foil and a pair of trousers, and Amelia's expression of arctic disdain.

"I don't want to know," he said, breaking the tension, "but I could guess. Miss Thornton was educating Hereford on the value of keeping his falls secured when the duchess chanced upon them and illustrated how best to expedite freeing the said falls."

Hereford did not turn his gaze but said with his serious expression barely flickering, "Back to your important activities, gentlemen. There's nothing to observe here. Miss Thornton here is a spy for the *Metropolitan Review*, and I was just informing her how she could find her way back."

Amelia allowed a little satisfied smile. "Gentlemen, contrary to his lordship's claim, I'm here to find men eager to see their names in print for advertisement." She gestured to Hereford. "So that you may not become this desperate for attention."

The duke laughed and other men followed suit. "And I was worried Miss Thornton would not be able to resist your boyish charms, Hereford."

"No danger there, Lancaster. The lady is positively repulsed by my charms," Hereford replied, finally taking his eyes off Amelia. "In fact, she tried most ungallantly to have me killed two weeks ago."

"Good," the duke said. "Someone should." He turned back to Amelia. "My darling wife asked me to accompany you in your endeavor tonight. Something about withdrawing her affection should any harm come to you."

"Thank you, Your Grace. The duchess is most kind."

"I believe you should retire for the night before you hurt someone, Hereford," the duke said while offering his arm to Amelia. "I believe your fencing skills are becoming rusty."

Amelia smiled slyly as she took Lancaster's arm.

The Duchess of Rutland patted Hereford's arm consolingly. "Don't fret, my dear. Not everyone can be talented at everything. You have other qualities."

Amelia heard Hereford clear his throat. She looked over her shoulder to find the Duchess of Rutland openly admiring the Duke of Lancaster's backside. Hereford met Amelia's eyes as he said, "Come now, Your Grace, we have more to review."

Amelia turned to stare straight ahead, puzzled by jealousy rising from her chest at the thought of the marquess' intimate touch on the duchess. Taking a deep breath, she reminded herself to focus her attention on the business at hand.

"Lord Symon," she heard the duke say to a portly gentleman languishing against a doorframe. "Your lovely wife shared with me about Lady Francine's impending nuptials. Wouldn't it be grand to announce it in the *Metropolitan Review*?"

HEREFORD STOOD IN the empty room alone after dismissing the duchess, his torn trousers draped over a chair. His blood still boiled. *Side projects*, she had said about the orphanages he visited religiously even in snowstorms, even the day after he had been tossed from his horse. *Frivolous*, she had said about his life. As if she had any right to judge him, wandering about London in the dark, brandishing only that sharp tongue of hers as a weapon.

He paced the length of the room, his boots striking the wooden floor with more force than necessary. The nerve of the woman. A commoner, no less, acting as though she had any right to speak to a marquess with such brazen insolence. And she didn't even try to conceal that contempt in her eyes whenever she looked at him.

He stopped short, his reflection in the wall mirror catching his attention. There was something raw in his expression that made him uncomfortable.

Of course, he cared about any lady's safety... didn't wish for anyone to be manipulated by ill-meaning scoundrels... not just Miss Thornton. Perhaps it was because he had no siblings, but the protective nature he didn't know he possessed surfaced.

"Ridiculous," he muttered, running a hand through his long dark hair. "Utterly ridiculous."

Miss Thornton had made it abundantly clear she needed no protection, least of all from him.

Her words stung more than they should have. It wasn't the first time someone had criticized his choices, but something about her disappointment... He shook his head sharply. What did it matter if some common-born spinster thought him wanting?

"A newspaper editor," he scoffed aloud. "Practically a tradesman."

And she thought him a fool.

He turned abruptly, snatching up his discarded coat. This line of thinking was dangerous. Miss Thornton was nothing to him, could be nothing to him. Her low status alone made any deeper consideration supremely inconvenient. And she had that limp which could mean Lord knows what. He needed a woman with a powerful build who could give him ten children in quick succession without blinking an eye. Love matches were the stuff of gothic novels, not real life. Well, maybe except for the Lancasters. And the Carlisles. And the Salisburys.

Damnation. He had his duties to his title, to his family name. Convenient liaisons with willing widows were one thing, but anything more…

"Utterly ridiculous," he muttered again, though whether he meant her expectations of him or his own unsettling reactions to them, he couldn't quite say.

⟫⟫⟫⟪⟪⟪

AMELIA SLIPPED INTO her chambers after one o'clock of the morning, her mind still seething with the memory of Hereford's casual intimacy with the Duchess of Rutland. She dismissed her lady's maid with a wave, claiming fatigue, but sleep was the furthest thing from her thoughts.

Once alone, she moved to her writing desk and unlocked the hidden drawer beneath her stationery compartment. From it, she withdrew several sheets of expensive cream paper and a small pot of distinctive violet ink—her private collection, separate from the supplies she used for the *Review*.

Amelia dipped her pen, watching the violet liquid cling to the nib like a drop of royal blood. She had intended to work on her *Metropolitan Review* article, but another story burned inside her, demanding release.

"Ridiculous man," she muttered, thinking of how Hereford had stood in Brooks, his shirtsleeves rolled up, revealing those muscular forearms as he pressed against the Duchess of Rutland. "The key is to imagine the foil as an extension of your arm," he had said. "Like a lover's caress."

Her pen touched paper, and words flowed with surprising intensity:

The Marquess moved with grace, his noble fingers guiding

her hand upon the polished bow stick. "Gently," he murmured, his breath warm against her neck. "An instrument responds best to a light touch."

Miss Collins trembled, acutely aware of his powerful frame behind her, the heat of him seeping through her simple muslin gown. Though she was merely a chamber maid in his grand household, he insisted on these private lessons, claiming every music student should learn how to make love to her instrument.

"My lord," she whispered, her voice catching as his hand slid from her wrist to her waist, steadying her stance. "This seems most improper."

"Propriety," he said with a wicked smile, "is merely a convention invented to keep passionate souls apart."

Amelia paused, her cheeks flushing at the direction her imagination had taken. She should stop—this was beyond scandalous. Yet her pen returned to the paper with a will of its own.

His fingers tightened at her waist, drawing her closer until her back pressed fully against his chest. The bow clattered to the floor as he turned her in his arms.

"Tell me to stop," he pleaded, his blue eyes darkening with desire. "Tell me you don't want this as much as I do."

But the chamber maid remained silent, her breath coming in short gasps as his hand slid boldly upward to cup her breast through the thin fabric...

The words poured forth, increasingly explicit, describing sensations Amelia had only imagined. She wrote of the marquess lifting his maid onto his massive desk, of papers scattering as he claimed her mouth with hungry kisses, of her legs wrapped around his waist as propriety and class distinctions melted away in the heat of their passion.

As her pen raced across the page, heat bloomed within her. She pictured Hereford—not as the insufferable aristocrat who mocked her editorials, but as the virile man she'd glimpsed at Brooks, shirtsleeves rolled up, powerful forearms exposed. In her mind's eye, those strong hands now explored a fictional woman's body with the same confidence he'd demonstrated when handling a foil. Her breath quickened as her imagination conjured the weight of him pressing down, the heat of his skin, the intensity that might burn in those blue eyes when focused on pleasure rather than mockery.

An ache formed low in her belly, insistent and demanding. Almost without conscious thought, Amelia's free hand drifted beneath the desk, gathering her skirts until her fingers found bare skin. She hesitated, propriety warring with desire. But here, alone in her chambers, who would know of her weakness? Her fictional creation certainly wouldn't judge her for seeking the same pleasure she described so boldly on paper.

Her fingers slipped higher, finding the sensitive flesh between her thighs already slick with want. A gasp escaped her lips as she circled that hidden bundle of nerves, her other hand still guiding the pen, filling the page with increasingly fevered descriptions. In her story, the maid arched beneath the marquess' skilled touch; in reality, Amelia bit her lip to stifle a moan as her own touch brought her closer to the edge.

"Charles," she whispered into the empty room, the forbidden use of his Christian name adding a thrill of transgression to her solitary pleasure. Her fingers moved faster, matching the rhythm she imagined he might set—demanding yet considerate, passionate yet precise. Heat spiraled through her body, tightening like a coil until it finally broke in waves of release that left her trembling and breathless.

When she finally set down her pen, her fingers were stained with violet ink and the candle had burned low. She read over what she had written, shocked by her own audacity. The scene was far more explicit than anything she had previously submitted, and the thought of the handsome marquess reading her words— perhaps even recognizing himself in the domineering aristocrat— sent another thrill through her spent body.

This was scandalous, yet she felt strangely liberated, as if committing these forbidden desires to paper—and indulging them in private—had somehow exorcised the uncomfortable feelings that had plagued her since seeing Hereford at the gentleman's club.

She adjusted her clothing with trembling hands, feeling a curious mixture of satisfaction and embarrassment.

Amelia folded the pages and sealed them with wax. In the corner, she carefully drew the small snowflake symbol that had become her secret mark.

"Let Hereford enjoy his duchess," she whispered, placing the pages in her dispatch box. "At least on paper, I can imagine a different story." Though even as she spoke the words, she knew the truth—the story she'd written wasn't so different after all. Only in fiction could she admit what she refused to acknowledge in reality: that beneath her disdain for Charles Bartholomew lay a dangerous attraction that threatened everything she thought she knew about herself.

THE GARDEN PARTY DISASTER

"How was the crossing from Boston?" Amelia asked, accepting a cup of tea from Charlotte in her private sitting room. "Two weeks at sea! I can hardly imagine it."

"Ghastly," Charlotte replied, settling onto the settee beside Elisha. "The *Britannia* is supposedly the finest steamship in the Cunard fleet, but I spent most days in my cabin, desperately wishing for solid ground. Though watching Andrew readjust to London Society has been endlessly entertaining. Two years in Boston's business world has quite transformed him."

"Don't tell me he's gone completely American?" Elisha asked, grinning.

"Wonderfully so," Charlotte's eyes danced with mischief. "You should have seen him at our first London dinner party. He'd forgotten all about changing for evening dress. Walked right in wearing his business attire. The faces of these stuffed-shirt aristocrats! Though I must say, watching my former dock worker husband lecture them about American shipping efficiency was worth every scandalized gasp."

"How is he finding Boston?" Amelia asked. "It must be quite a change from the London docks."

"He thrives there. No one cares that he was born common. They care that he's clever with ships and trade. When these railway investors insisted he return to London for meetings, he complained the entire voyage about having to 'play fancy lord' again."

The three women dissolved into laughter, the sound of their friendship inviting.

"Tell us about the railway meetings," Elisha said. "Edgar's been absolutely obsessed with the venture, but he only shares the dullest details."

"Lancaster's probably trying to protect you from the drama," Charlotte said, rolling her eyes. "Lord Norwich and Lord Hereford have turned every meeting into a battlefield of veiled insults and competing proposals."

"Norwich has been wonderfully helpful with my factory investigation," Amelia said. "His insights into business practices have been invaluable."

"And Hereford's been his usual insufferable self, I imagine," Charlotte said, though her tone held an odd note.

"When he bothers to notice common journalists at all." Amelia stirred her tea with more vigor than necessary. "Though he graced me by explaining my own printing press to me a while back."

"Men do love explaining things we already know," Charlotte said. "Andrew tried to tell me how to feed my own pets."

"Pets? What kind of pets?" Elisha asked.

Charlotte suddenly sat up straighter. "Wait here! I brought something back from America that you simply must see."

Her voice held barely contained excitement.

"Charlotte Carlisle, what have you done?" Amelia asked, meeting Elisha's gaze nervously.

A moment later, Charlotte's triumphant "Ta-da!" was accompanied by tiny chittering sounds and two small, masked faces in her arms.

"Are those… raccoons?" Amelia leaned forward, fascinated.

"Yes. Orphans. One is missing from the basket." Charlotte frowned as the creatures scrambled onto her shoulders. "I found them near our hotel in America. I couldn't just leave the poor things, and finding proper care while we're away proved impossible…"

"So, you smuggled them across the Atlantic?" Elisha asked, watching one kit make a determined attempt at Charlotte's earring.

"Smuggled is such an ugly word. I prefer 'diplomatically transported.'" Charlotte beamed as the raccoons investigated her elaborate hairstyle.

"And your husband agreed to this?" Amelia asked, doubting even a man as lovesick as Andrew Carlisle would tolerate such inevitable chaos.

"No, not at all. But I reasoned that they're far less trouble than the railway venture, which is why we're staying in England until they settle the main issues. If it weren't for the proposed line aiding Madame Tansley's rescue missions, I would have insisted he sell his shares. Investing in a venture across the Atlantic seems to me like an apoplexy-inducing idea."

"I believe the charitable work is what has Edgar and Lord Hereford so invested," Elisha said.

"Lord Hereford may just see it as another business opportunity."

"Don't be too quick to judge," Elisha said. "He might keep his charitable works quiet, but he's not lacking in compassion."

Amelia was distracted by Charlotte's pointed stare at her, her eyes narrowed.

"I believe you are attracted to the marquess, Amelia Thornton," Charlotte declared.

"What? That's ludicrous. You know how I object to everything he stands for." Amelia brought a hand to her cheek, feeling the heat.

"Perhaps, but it doesn't mean you cannot feel attraction. In fact," Charlotte emphasized the last word with a finger puncturing the air, "I believe you want him."

Amelia's mouth fell open. The idea was absurd.

"I was beginning to suspect that myself," Elisha joined in.

Amelia turned her head to stare at Elisha, then back at Charlotte. "And here I thought my friends knew me best! Haven't you been paying attention to my editorials?"

"That's precisely why," Elisha said, nodding her head while Charlotte rubbed her chin with exaggerated mockery.

"Remember me telling you about the son of my father's friend with whom I argued almost daily?" Charlotte addressed Elisha as if Amelia was no longer in the room. "I didn't realize until much later that I had fancied him but didn't know what to do with my feelings."

"I'm hardly a little girl who's unable to distinguish affection from annoyance," Amelia protested. "You both know how much his way of living vexes me."

"That's just it. You protest too much," Elisha pointed out. "There are men far worse whom you don't object to at all. You must believe he's just perfectly imperfect."

"Oh, blast it!" Charlotte's sudden outburst had the two women following her gaze as both raccoons launched a coordinated assault on the sugar bowl. "Perhaps we should continue this discussion in the garden before they completely destroy my sitting room."

As they hurried to rescue the tea service, Amelia found herself turning Elisha's words over in her mind. But before she could press further, the raccoons discovered Charlotte's flower arrangements, and all thoughts of a complicated man were lost in the ensuing chaos.

⇛⟫⟨⟨⟨⟨

HEREFORD ARRIVED AT the Carlisle's garden party in high spirits, trading barbs with Patrick Adams about their latest sparring at the fencing club. His laughter died in his throat, however, when he caught Miss Thornton's frigid regard from across the lawn when their eyes met. She turned away with deliberate dismissal, her gray dress stark against the colorful spring flowers.

"What have you done to earn her ire?" Patrick asked, following his gaze.

"I dared to breathe." Hereford accepted a glass of champagne from a passing footman. "That seems to be offense enough."

"There must be more to it than that." Patrick studied Miss Thornton's retreating figure. "When did this mutual animosity begin?"

"Mutual? I assure you the hostility flows entirely in one direction." Hereford took a lengthy sip. "Though I suppose I represent everything she despises, including but not limited to inherited privilege, apparent idleness, the system that keeps talented commoners in their place."

"You're hardly idle."

"Yes, well, Miss Thornton hasn't been privy to that particular information, has she?" Hereford tried for a careless shrug, though something twisted uncomfortably in his chest. He'd never cared what others thought of him before, so why did her obvious disapproval needle him so?

A commotion drew his attention back to Miss Thornton. She'd stopped to help a maid struggling with a heavy crate of china, despite the obvious strain it put on her leg. As he watched, her foot caught in her skirt, causing her to stumble.

"Damn it all," he muttered, watching her struggle to maintain her balance without dropping her end of the box. "Why must she insist on—"

Before he could finish the thought, Patrick had already run across the lawn to assist both women. Hereford remained rooted in place, feeling increasingly like a useless popinjay. He should have been the one to help. Should have moved instead of complaining...

Miss Thornton glanced in his direction again, no doubt noting his inaction. The temperature of her gaze dropped several more degrees, if such a thing were possible. Hereford realized he'd been scowling, his frustration with himself no doubt appearing as disapproval of her.

A twitter of feminine laughter drew his attention. A group of Society ladies had gathered nearby, eyeing him expectantly. Well, this he knew how to handle. Plastering on his most charming smile, he turned to them with a flourishing bow.

"Ladies, you look positively radiant today."

"Oh, my lord, we've been anticipating your arrival with bated breath!" the older one of the two said while the rosy-cheeked young lady giggled behind her fan. "I don't suppose you would regale us about the time you had to escape an angry father through the fountains?"

As they gathered closer, hanging on his every word, he caught Miss Thornton's shake of her head from the corner of his eye. The smile felt increasingly brittle on his face as he launched into the tale. Why did her opinion matter so bloody much?

"It was a warm summer evening," he began, pushing the troubling question aside, "and the fountains were looking particularly inviting—"

"Lord Hereford." Charlotte Carlisle materialized at his elbow, her smile tight. "As riveting as I'm sure this tale of debauchery is, I require your assistance with a rather urgent matter."

The ladies surrounding him made sounds of disappointment, but Charlotte was already steering him away with surprising force for such a diminutive woman. She snagged Miss Thornton as they passed, ignoring the obvious tension between her two captives.

"Lady Carlisle, what—" Hereford began.

"Not here," she hissed, glancing nervously over her shoulder. She guided them behind a towering arrangement of hydrangeas, where they wouldn't be overheard. "I need you to help me prevent a catastrophe."

"What sort of catastrophe?" Miss Thornton asked, pointedly keeping the flower arrangement between herself and Hereford.

Charlotte wrung her hands. "I don't care what it takes," she declared. "Something must be done before my baby raccoons destroy Lady Jersey's new bonnet and Andrew finds out! He was vehemently opposed to bringing the creatures, but I snuck them in."

"Baby what?" Hereford asked at the same moment Miss Thornton said, "Oh, Charlotte."

As if on cue, two masked faces peered out from beneath a refreshment table, their little hands already sticky with stolen treats. Hereford couldn't help but laugh at the absurdity of it all, earning himself a withering look from the hostess.

"Now, I must return to the party and pretend to be completely at peace while you and Lord Hereford capture the beasts."

"Me? Why me?" Miss Thornton looked around, clearly hoping to nominate someone else for the task.

"You have a soothing way about you, Amelia. The kits will believe you to be their mama and follow you. Don't worry. You won't be alone in this. Lord Hereford will gladly help. Won't you, my lord?" With a pat on Amelia's shoulder and a meaningful smile at Hereford, Charlotte disappeared to maintain the facade of a normal garden party.

Hereford watched Miss Thornton as she studied the raccoons, noting the slight furrow in her brow as she no doubt calculated the logistics of chasing after them with her injured leg. Something uncomfortable stirred in his chest again. Before he could examine the feeling too closely, he forced himself to adopt a tone of casual amusement.

"I could assist, but I admit I'm not keen on the idea." He deliberately avoided looking at her. "I find them quite entertaining and wouldn't mind a bit if they gnawed on every bonnet in this room."

The lady shot poison darts at his face.

AMELIA NOTICED HOW handsome the marquess looked with the sunlight drenching his face in a warm glow, the top of his head forming a golden halo, even while she glared at him.

"Do you believe they would end there, my lord?" she asked evenly to the man who was avoiding her gaze. "Once they've finished with bonnets, they shall come after the shiny buttons on your coat. Charlotte has entertained me with the ways the kits can wreak havoc."

"Is that so?" he said, still not looking in her direction. "That sounds like a nightmare. Where did they come from anyway?"

"Charlotte rescued the orphans in America but couldn't find anyone to look after them during their time away. So, she brought them here, but they're far cleverer than anyone had anticipated."

A shriek from the garden drew their attention. The Duchess of Rutland was standing on a chair, brandishing her parasol at a third raccoon that had apparently developed a fascination with her silk shoes.

Amelia was startled by Hereford's sudden movement, deftly stripping a nearby table of its tablecloth.

"Right then," Hereford turned to Amelia while tying the two ends of the tablecloth around his neck. "I assume you have a plan?"

"Why would you assume that?"

"Because you always have a plan, Miss Thornton, usually one involving my public humiliation."

She ignored the jab. "The raccoons are attracted to shiny objects and sweets. If we could lure them away from the guests..."

"We'd need something particularly enticing, but I don't think Lady Carlisle would appreciate me brandishing her tureen for the creatures." His gaze fell on her hair pins, glinting copper in the sunlight. "Those would do nicely."

"I'm not sacrificing my hair pins to rescue the Duchess of Rutland's shoes."

"No? What about to free the Countess of Carlisle's new Wedgwood tea service?"

They both turned to see one of the raccoons investigating the delicate china with dangerous curiosity.

"Charlotte will murder me," Amelia muttered, already reaching for her pins.

Her hair tumbled down around her shoulders as she pressed them into Hereford's hand. She was startled to see him frozen, his usual quick wit and easy smile nowhere to be seen. Instead, his blue eyes traced the cascade of her chestnut hair, following one particular curl that had fallen across her collarbone. The intensity of his gaze made her skin prickle with an awareness she'd never felt before.

"Don't lose them," she said, clearing her throat.

For a moment, he seemed to forget about the chaos around them, his attention wholly fixed on where her hair spilled over her shoulders. The look in his eyes… it wasn't the admiration he bestowed on Society beauties, or the amused condescension she was accustomed to receiving. This was something else entirely, something raw and unguarded that made her heart race.

"I wouldn't dare," he said finally, his voice rougher than a moment ago.

She ignored the heat spreading from her neck and the slight tremor in her voice. "Now, I'll create a distraction so you can attempt to coax our furry friends to a more appropriate venue."

"What sort of distraction?" he asked.

"Something scandalous, I should think."

Hereford stared at her once again with his lips parted slightly. "Do I, um, perhaps you could give me a sample of this distraction you speak of."

"My lord! Please go before the wild beasts destroy all the china!"

As color crept up his face, Hereford mumbled an apology and was gone. Amelia watched him weaving through the crowd with her pins glinting in his hands. She took a deep breath, conscious of her loose hair.

"Lord Carlisle!" she called out, pitching her voice to carry. "Is it true that in America, ladies and gentlemen dance together without gloves?"

A collective gasp rose from the assembled guests. Charlotte's husband, clearly confused but good-natured, smiled. "Among other things, Miss Thornton. Would you care for a demonstration?"

As all eyes turned to watch this potential scandal unfold with Carlisle reaching for his wife. Amelia caught glimpses of Hereford darting between the hedges, her hairpins creating tempting flashes of light while the tablecloth flapped from his neck in the breeze. One by one, the raccoons abandoned their prizes to follow the new attraction.

Amelia watched the marquess disappear around a hedge. The raccoons were following him but not closely enough to catch.

"Silly man," she muttered, gathering her skirts and moving as quickly as her leg would allow. She could already feel the ache in her leg building. She cut across the lawn, taking the shortcut to intercept Hereford's path.

She emerged from behind a flowering shrub just as he passed, reaching out to catch his arm. "Wait," she said, slightly breathless. Before he could protest, she'd stepped close, perhaps closer than propriety allowed, and untied the tablecloth from his neck. She ignored the feeling of humiliation when he drew back and stiffened upon her gloved fingers brushing his throat. Apparently, he found even her touch unpleasant.

No doubt he had noticed the impact his proximity had on her just like every other woman in Society. It is likely the man had never had a commoner touch his bare skin… *Wake up, Amelia. Of course, he must have bedded the servants and Lord knows who else.*

"A better plan, Miss Thornton?" His voice was low and strained, presumably from discomfort.

"Always." She slapped the loose tablecloth against his chest and snatched her pins from his hands.

"I shall lure them to me. You grab two. I'll try to grab the last one and hand it to you."

She then plopped down on the ground, holding out one of her pins. The smallest raccoon crept forward, whiskers twitching with interest.

"Be ready," she whispered to Hereford.

He moved behind her, cloth held ready, as two more baby raccoons ventured closer.

"Now!"

Hereford swooped down with the tablecloth as Amelia not so much rolled as she had planned but tipped to the side, her movement less graceful than she'd have liked. The maneuver was effective nonetheless. Hereford somehow managed to capture all three small bundles of fur, who then found themselves neatly wrapped in fine linen, their surprised squeaks muffled by the fabric.

Amelia fixed her dress and hair without seeing herself and hesitated when Hereford extended a gloved hand, holding the bundle like a purse in his other hand. She didn't want his help but had no choice given the significant pain she was in. As she gripped his hand, the strength of his body became obvious with how solid his arm felt as he easily pulled her up.

"Are you well? You seem to be in discomfort," he observed.

"I'm perfectly well, my lord," she said with a lift of her chin, noticing how the wind was playing with a strand of his loose hair.

"Allow me to assist." He presented his shoulder to lean on while he carried the bundle of moving linen.

"Thank you, but I'll manage," she said before disappearing behind the hedges onto the shortcut.

Once alone, Amelia took the weight off her injured leg with a wince. More difficult than fighting the pain was her treacherous thought that Lord Hereford was far more dangerous when he was being helpful than when he was being scandalous.

HEREFORD TRACED HIS steps back through the garden maze, ostensibly searching for his missing cufflink, though he couldn't quite explain why such a trivial trinket suddenly seemed so urgent. The late afternoon sun cast long shadows through the hedges, and that's when he saw her.

Miss Thornton stood partially concealed behind a flowering shrub, her guard finally lowered now that she thought herself alone. The sight made him pause. Her chestnut hair caught the sunlight, turning the loose strands into burnished copper, and for a moment he forgot to breathe. She was attempting to fix the mess he'd inadvertently caused, her fingers working deftly.

But it was the pain in her expression that made his chest tighten unexpectedly. She shifted her weight, a wince crossing her features. The mask of competence and sharp wit she usually wore had slipped, revealing something raw and vulnerable underneath. The realization that she'd rather suffer in silence than accept help—especially his help—stirred something in him.

"Stubborn woman," he muttered under his breath, though the words held none of their usual mockery. Instead, he found himself admiring the steel in her spine, the way she squared her shoulders even when no one was watching. She was... magnificent, really.

He watched as she gathered herself, piece by piece, reconstructing her armor of wit and propriety. The transformation was fascinating. The way she schooled her features, adjusted her posture, tucked away any sign of discomfort. Yet now that he'd seen beneath the surface, he couldn't unsee it.

Hereford backed away silently, the cufflink forgotten, before she could notice his presence. He had witnessed something that made it impossible to maintain his carefully cultivated indifference toward Miss Thornton.

Hereford made his way back to the party, his thoughts still uncomfortably tangled around the image of Miss Thornton's vulnerability. The gathering had grown more boisterous in his absence. Charlotte had arranged for music, and couples were beginning to dance on the lawn. He accepted a fresh glass of champagne, hoping it might dull the nagging sensation in his chest.

"There you are!" The Duchess of Rutland appeared at his elbow, fanning herself vigorously. "I've been looking everywhere. You promised to demonstrate that Italian thrust you learned in Florence."

He forced himself to focus on her radiant smile, on the familiar dance of flirtation. This was safe territory. "Did I? How careless of me to keep a lady waiting."

"Indeed." She placed her hand on his arm. "I've been practicing what you showed me last week, though I fear I still haven't quite mastered the proper form."

As he followed her toward the cleared space where several guests had expressed interest in a fencing demonstration, he caught sight of Miss Thornton again. She'd managed to repair her hair and was in conversation with the Duke of Lancaster, no doubt discussing something dreadfully serious. But he noticed how her eyes occasionally flicked toward the impromptu fencing area with poorly concealed interest.

"Your Grace," he said, pitching his voice low. "Why don't we wait until we're at the Swordsman's Society? This is hardly the right place for serious instruction."

"Oh, nonsense, Hereford. This is the perfect place. The lighting, music, audience…" the duchess said with a wink.

He gripped the cane a gentleman handed him with reluctance, aware of Miss Thornton's attention even as he focused on the duchess. The Italian style had always been his favorite when impressing females who feigned interest in fencing when all they really wanted was to admire his backside. The Italian was all flourish and dramatic gestures, perfect for seduction. Except he wasn't feeling too seductive at the moment.

"Now," he said, sounding as official as possible while moving behind the duchess stiffly to adjust her stance, "the key is in the positioning…"

He didn't need to look to know Miss Thornton was watching. He could feel her disapproval from here.

"Come, Hereford. Why have you turned so stiff all of a sudden?" the duchess chided. "This lesson is a lot less interesting and instructive than I recall from Brooks."

"My apologies, Your Grace. I rather feel uncomfortable about performing in front of an audience at the moment."

The Duchess of Rutland whirled around in his arms, standing with her front flush with his. Hereford took a step backward. She narrowed her gaze.

"Have you taken another lover, Hereford?" she whispered so only he could hear.

"No."

"Then it's me you're tired of."

Hereford made the grave mistake of hesitating. Her eyes gaping wide open, the duchess shoved hard at his chest. "How dare you!"

"What? I said nothing!"

"That's precisely the problem!" she shouted as she stomped away from him.

He wasn't sure how long he'd been standing there, staring after the duchess, when he heard a soft, silky voice. "Looks like your skills seem to be waning, Lord Hereford." Her voice cut through the noise in his head, sharp as any blade. It came from near his ear, Miss Thornton having stood on her toes to reach it. He felt the tiny tremors run through his body as her warm breath touched his skin.

He felt her withdraw quickly and he knew she had misunderstood his shudder as something undesirable. Nothing could have been further from the truth, but he wasn't about to admit her proximity had aroused him.

He turned to face her hurt countenance and found her standing beyond his arm's length.

"On the contrary," he said in a lighthearted tone to cover up both of their embarrassment. "That was precisely the effect I had wished for." He stood erect and folded his hands behind his back. "One does begin to wish for a variety in female company, if you understand my meaning."

A scowl replaced her hurt expression. "Unfortunately, I do."

Hereford straightened his shoulders in false confidence. "Is there something I can help you with, Miss?"

"Teach me."

He went still. "Teach you? You don't mean... Teach you what?"

"Teach me to fence." She lifted her chin. "You're clearly qualified although I'd prefer the straightforward method, not the one you have reserved for your... mistresses."

"This is absurd." He rubbed the back of his neck, trying to ignore the flush at her décolletage. "Ladies don't fence."

"Yet you teach the duchess."

"That's different. She's... She's..."

"Your lover?" she whispered as she stepped toward him. Her tone became teasing and seductive, making the hair on his neck tingle. "Willing to let you press against her while adjusting her grip?" Hereford closed his eyes briefly, letting her voice wash over his sensitized skin.

He opened his eyes, then let his gaze drift down to her mouth. "A friend, Miss Thornton. And careful. One might think you were jealous."

"One might think you were afraid to teach me." She took a step closer, close enough that he could smell her soap. "What are you afraid of?"

He studied her for a long moment—the way she refused to let her injury define her limitations. It was admirable, damn it all. And dangerous.

"No," he said finally, his voice firmer than he felt. "Find another hobby. Watercolors, perhaps."

"Watercolors," she gritted out. "How delightfully conventional of you."

He exhaled, frustration evident in its tone. "Miss Thornton, while your enthusiasm is admirable, fencing requires certain physical demands."

"Tell me, my lord, are all women incapable of meeting the physical demands or specifically the crippled ones?" Her voice was sharp enough to wound, and her lips pressed into a thin line.

"If you get hurt, I may lose credibility. Not only that, you will not do other women any favors."

Her eyes flashed emerald with fury as she stepped closer, voice trembling with barely contained rage. "Do not pretend to care about women's aspirations. You have no intention of teaching us anything beyond the path to your bedchamber. That's where you prefer us, isn't it? Silent and submissive?"

The muscle in his jaw ticked. "I take offense at your insinuation, Miss Thornton." His lips curved into a smile. "I rather enjoy when women are vocal in my bed."

Amelia recoiled, her mouth opening and closing soundlessly before she found her voice. "How perfectly characteristic."

"You don't know me at all," he said softly, crowding her space until she had to tilt her head back to maintain eye contact. His voice dropped to a dangerous whisper. "Not even slightly."

"Wonderful." She lifted her chin, refusing to step back despite his looming presence. "Let us remain thus, shall we?"

"Let's think practically for a moment." He stepped back and walked in a small circle, regaining his composure before stopping to face her again. "How do you propose to lunge with a lethal weapon when you can barely maintain your balance on level ground?"

"I do not struggle with balance!" Her hands balled into fists at her sides. "Only on uneven terrain might I occasionally, but I always catch myself!"

"That is precisely my point! I won't teach someone who presents a danger to herself and others during lessons."

"We'll be wearing protective gear!"

"Which may fail if you fall. The fact is, you need absolute control, but you're at a constant disadvantage. Any misstep could—"

"I do not misstep!" She stamped her foot, immediately proving his point as she had to shift to maintain her balance. "I have not fallen, and I never shall!"

"Think with logic rather than pride, woman!" His voice rose with exasperation. "Fencing requires agility—bouncing, skipping, lunging, quick sidesteps—"

"I shall adapt! I always have. Just teach me the basics, and I'll master the rest myself."

"Why? Why are you so desperate to learn?"

She paused, schooling her features to one of vapid interest. "It's exercise, which I need. It's practical. It's beautiful—like a dance with weapons. When I watch it, I feel… connected."

His expression softened for a fraction of a second before hardening again. "And it's forbidden to women. Isn't that the real appeal? Or is this some publicity stunt for your newspaper?"

One would have thought he had slapped her by the way ice replaced the fire in her eyes. Amelia straightened her spine before speaking calmly. "Do explain to your student, the Duchess of Rutland, why some women are worthy of instruction while others are not." She turned away, each word precise and cutting.

He watched her walk away, her gait measured despite her obvious fury. Guilt and self-loathing warred in his chest.

"Confound it," he muttered, rubbing the stubble beginning to appear on his chin. The woman was impossible, an infuriating, illegitimate commoner. And completely wrong for him.

He was going to be glad to have refused her. He just didn't know why yet.

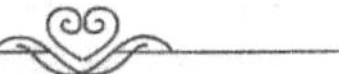

THE MOST INCONVENIENT PROPOSAL

HEREFORD WAS HAVING a rather delicious dream involving Amelia Thornton's chestnut hair spilling across his pillows when thunderous pounding dragged him from sleep. In the hazy space between dreams and waking, he could still feel the phantom sensation of her curves pressed against him, taste the sweetness of her mouth…

"This better be about a beautiful lady caller waiting for me, Cooper," he growled as his butler opened the door, looking distinctly ruffled.

"My lord, the Duke of Lancaster, the Earl of Carlisle, Mr. Thornton, and Viscount Norwich are here. They insist it's urgent."

"Are they foxed?"

"Not in an obvious way, my lord."

Hereford released a long groan, trying to banish the lingering images of Miss Thornton's lips parted in pleasure. What the devil was wrong with him, dreaming of that sharp-tongued termagant? True, she had magnificent eyes that turned forest green when she was angry, and that limp of hers made her hips sway in a rather hypnotic fashion…

He shook his head sharply. Clearly, he needed to find a new mistress if he was having erotic dreams about a woman who'd compared his intelligence to that of livestock.

"ARE YOU COMING DOWN OR SHALL WE DRAG YOU OUT OF BED?" Carlisle's voice boomed from below.

Cursing, Hereford grabbed his banyan and headed downstairs. Whatever had brought four powerful men to his home at this ungodly hour, it couldn't be good news.

But as he descended the stairs, his treacherous mind kept returning to how Miss Thornton's hair had felt sliding through his fingers in that dream…

He found the four men in his study, helping themselves to his best brandy. Lancaster paced before the fireplace while Carlisle slouched in a chair, looking grim. Steven Thornton stood ramrod straight by the window, his expression unreadable. Norwich appeared to be the only one relaxed enough to enjoy the brandy. They all seemed to have been dragged out of bed.

"This had better be good," Hereford growled, running a hand through his disheveled hair. "Do you know what time it is?"

"We wouldn't have interrupted you if it wasn't important. We know how much you treasure your beauty sleep," Carlisle said.

"We have a problem," Lancaster said. "The railway investment we're involved in. Apparently, there's an old law still on the books—all major investors must be from noble families."

Hereford dropped into a chair. "And this couldn't wait until morning?"

"Our solicitor just confirmed it," Carlisle said, his usual good humor absent from his face. "If we don't resolve this within a few days, we could lose everything we've invested. The whole project could collapse."

"And you've come to a solution, I take it?" Hereford reached for the brandy, noting the peculiar tension in the room.

"Yes," Steven said quietly. "You could solve our predicament."

Hereford's glass froze halfway to his lips. "How?"

Three of the four men exchanged loaded glances while Norwich fixed Hereford with a steady, almost challenging stare.

Lancaster cleared his throat before speaking. "By marrying Miss Thornton."

Brandy burned Hereford's throat as he choked. "I beg your pardon?"

"If Amelia becomes a marchioness," Steven explained, his voice steady despite the audacity of the suggestion, "I would be connected to nobility through marriage. The law's requirements would be satisfied."

"You're mad. All of you." Hereford stood, pacing the length of his study. "I will not marry under duress, especially to a woman who makes her contempt for me abundantly clear." He turned to Steven. "My apologies, Thornton, but my mother would have an apoplexy. I'd rather lose my investment than test her health."

"More than just money hangs in the balance," Carlisle said softly, running a hand over his stubbled jaw. His eyes held something that made Hereford pause.

"I told you he'd refuse," Norwich said, his cultured voice carrying a hint of satisfaction. "The Hereford line is too precarious for such a hasty match. No doubt the marchioness has a carefully curated list of suitable debutantes awaiting her son's attention."

Though the words were true enough, Hereford felt his jaw tighten at Norwich's casual reference to his family's generations of difficulty producing heirs. Being the third generation of only children was not something he cared to have bandied about.

"I assure you my sister is quite capable," Steven said, his quiet tone carrying an edge of steel.

"With that leg of hers?" Hereford's laugh held more discomfort than humor. "Come now, Thornton. I need someone sturdy, someone who can withstand multiple pregnancies. And she's hardly the type to inspire…" he hesitated, reluctant to finish the thought, "marital enthusiasm."

The temperature in the room plummeted. Steven's expression turned dangerous, his fingers whitening around his glass.

"You've known her for years. Even with her injury," Steven said with careful control, "she works longer hours than anyone at her publishing house. She hasn't taken a sick day since her recovery. You've seen her capability firsthand."

"The stakes here go beyond marriage," Lancaster cut in, leaning forward intently. "This railway could revolutionize everything, how we pass messages, how we protect Madame Tansley's women. This is larger than any of our personal legacies, Hereford."

Hereford ran a hand over his face, exhaustion warring with growing unease. "Surely there must be a more suitable bachelor, one your sister doesn't actively despise."

"She doesn't hate you," Steven said dryly. "She's merely irritated by you. A state I imagine many share."

"What of her literary circles?" Hereford pressed. "Surely she has admirers there."

"None of noble birth," Steven replied. "And no current suitors of note."

Hereford shook his head, trying to ignore how that last detail pleased him. "Miss Thornton has made her opinion of me abundantly clear. And she's been on the shelf for years. I couldn't be certain of her ability to provide an heir."

"Pity. We rather thought you'd be preferable to Norwich," Carlisle said casually.

"Norwich?" Hereford's head snapped toward the viscount, who wasn't quite managing to hide his smile. "You'd consider him for your sister, Thornton? The man's a snake."

"Watch yourself!" Norwich surged to his feet, his face coloring.

"Settle down, both of you," Lancaster thundered, his voice cutting through the tension. He turned to Hereford, his expression severe. "It's not your decision to make unless you agree to marry Miss Thornton. Norwich has already expressed his willingness, and right now, Thornton considers him our next best option."

"Indeed," Norwich said, smoothing his waistcoat as he retook his seat. A smile played at his lips that made Hereford's fists clench. "As his lordship is declining the match, we needn't waste more of his time. I shall obtain a special license within days. Miss Thornton and I have spent considerable time together this past week, and we've found ourselves quite compatible."

Hereford's vision blurred at the edges as an unfamiliar rage swept through him. The thought of Amelia—when had she become Amelia in his mind?—with Norwich made his blood run cold, then hot. He could picture it all too clearly. Norwich's charm, his careful cultivation of her trust, those calculating eyes watching her every move. The same eyes that had watched his own wife waste away years ago, if the rumors were true.

The brandy glass creaked ominously in his grip as he imagined Norwich's hands on her, that serpentine smile as he led her through Society's machinations. The sudden, visceral need to prevent this match startled him with its intensity. It was one thing to decline the marriage himself, quite another to hand her over to a man who treated wives like sacrificial lambs.

He found himself standing without conscious decision, his body thrumming with an emotion he wasn't ready to name.

"I'll do it." The words burst from Hereford before he could stop them, rough with an urgency he didn't want to examine too closely.

"You will?" Thornton's voice balanced precariously between hope and doubt. "You'll actually marry my sister?"

"Consider carefully, Thornton," Norwich cut in, his cultured voice taking on an edge of desperation. "Would you truly condemn your sister to a life of endless scandals? We all know Hereford's reputation with women of questionable virtue. Miss Thornton deserves better than spending her nights wondering which widow's bed her husband warms."

"As if your own reputation sparkles like diamonds," Thornton said coldly. "At least Hereford's indiscretions are honest ones."

"I've been as chaste as morning dew since my wife's passing," Norwich bristled.

All four men scoffed simultaneously. "Only in appearances because you dally with the innocents who dare not speak out. Your maids, for instance," Hereford said with disgust.

"And your suspicious business practice," Thornton said icily. "If you have nothing to hide, then tell me the names of your factories and other holdings." Several seconds ticked by painfully slowly while Norwich avoided Thornton's stare.

"Yes, I will marry her," Hereford broke the silence, his voice carrying a finality that eased the tension. Norwich whirled away with a muttered curse while the others smiled and congratulated him on his betrothal.

He tried to ignore how satisfying it felt to thwart Norwich's obvious designs on Amelia. This was about protecting her from a snake, nothing more, even if she detested him. It had nothing to do with how his blood boiled at the thought of her in another man's arms.

Nothing at all.

Despite himself, Hereford's mind flooded with unbidden images of Amelia at the last garden party, sunlight setting her hair ablaze with copper highlights, that maddening combination of competence and fire that simultaneously drew and unsettled him. The way her eyes sparked emerald when she was truly angry. The thought of watching that fire slowly die, of seeing her wilt under the weight of a loveless marriage... He couldn't bear it. Better to give her freedom after the railway venture established itself than watch her spirit break.

"She'll never agree," he said quietly, more to himself than the others.

"Leave Amelia to me," Thornton replied. "Do we have an agreement?"

Hereford stared into the amber depths of his brandy, seeing another future crystallize. "One year."

The silence that followed was deafening.

"You cannot simply abandon her after a year," Thornton's voice turned sharp. "It would destroy any future prospects."

"It may be your sister who wishes to leave," Hereford countered, though the words tasted bitter. "She's devoted to her newspaper. She may prefer freedom… to be with someone more suitable." He forced himself to meet Steven's gaze. "There needs to be an escape clause. One year. That's my condition."

The three men exchanged loaded glances. "You may separate only with her agreement at the one year mark," Thornton said.

Hereford nodded. "Very well."

"Welcome to the family, Hereford."

After they shook hands, save one man who stormed out, his unexpected visitors departed.

Hereford stood alone in his study, watching the fire die to embers. He'd just agreed to marry, within days, a woman who thought him barely more worthwhile than the ink smudge on her fingers, all for the sake of business. Or at least that's what he was trying to tell himself.

"Well done, old boy," he muttered, reaching again for the brandy. "This can't possibly go wrong."

But as he raised the glass to his lips, his treacherous mind wandered to how Amelia might look in the morning light, her chestnut hair spilled across his pillows, her sharp tongue softened by sleep.

⟫⟪

"HAVE YOU LOST your mind?" Amelia exclaimed, watching Steven sip his tea with infuriating calm in her tiny parlor. "What of Lord Norwich? He's shown interest in my work, supports reform, and actually respects women's intelligence."

Steven set down his cup with unusual force. "Absolutely not. I've heard concerning things about his conduct with women."

"Rumors and gossip," Amelia dismissed. "He's been nothing

but kind and supportive of my endeavors."

"That's what worries me." Steven's face hardened. "His support feels calculated, Amelia. Too perfect, too convenient. I don't trust a man who never shows his flaws."

"Unlike Lord Hereford, who shows his contempt quite openly?" Her laugh held no humor. "At least Lord Norwich values my work, understands the importance of reform."

"And yet he's never been transparent about his business holdings." Steven leaned forward intently. "Think, Amelia. Have you ever seen him take action beyond pleasant words?"

"I haven't known him long enough to answer that. Please, Steven. You're sacrificing me to a marriage devoid of love and respect for greater wealth." She stood, pacing the small room. "You already have too much and no one to spend it on. Abandon the railway, let others proceed with the plan."

"It's too late." Steven's voice held genuine regret. "My signature is on every document. Starting over would jeopardize all the carefully negotiated terms. And it's not just about money. They need my contacts in India, my expertise in foreign investment."

"But, Steven," her voice softened with hurt, "you're asking me to sacrifice my happiness, my independence."

"Not necessarily. Hereford is a good man beneath his facade. He'll make you a proper husband."

"A good man?" She scoffed. "All he cares about is his bodily comfort and pleasure. He'll forget his wife amid his mistresses. He's supremely arrogant, impossibly condescending, and he's repulsed by my injury."

"I doubt that very much." Steven's eyes held something she couldn't quite read. "You two are fond of each other but are too busy fighting to notice. Even if you were right, who better than you to prove him wrong? Show him who you truly are."

"Fond? You are delusional. I'll become his property upon marriage! The *Metropolitan Review* will belong to him. He could turn it into one of his erotic publications, undo everything Elisha and I have built."

"We'll protect your interests in the marriage contract."

Amelia buried her face in her lap, her mind whirling with conflicting emotions. The railway project could help so many women escape desperate situations. She'd seen firsthand how vital quick, discreet transportation could be for Madame Tansley's rescues. And if she was being honest, she had fantasized about his impressive physique, but this was not the same as living with the man.

She pictured Hereford's mocking smile, the way his eyes would slide past her at social gatherings as if she were merely part of the furniture. He would no doubt parade sturdier women about at their shared home, if the marquess' housekeeper could be believed. Her fingers unconsciously traced the outline of her wooden leg through her skirts.

"I'd be more than willing to marry Viscount Norwich, Steven. Why—"

"Absolutely not, and you won't change my mind about him. There's something about the man I don't trust," Steven said firmly, then softened his voice. "Consider this. As Hereford's wife, you'd have access to resources, connections that could further our reform efforts. Your voice would carry the weight of a marchioness."

A marchioness with a limp and common blood. She could already hear the whispers, see the pitying glances. And Lord Hereford... would he parade her through Society like some curiosity? Or worse, hide her away in that grand house of his, ashamed of his mismatched bride?

But if she refused and the railway project collapsed, how many women would suffer? How many children would remain trapped in dangerous factories because she'd put her pride above their needs?

"I hate this," she whispered, lifting her head. Steel entered her voice as she continued, "But I shall do what's required. Just ensure my assets are protected, that I maintain ownership of the publishing house."

Steven placed a hand on her shoulder. "Thank you. It shall be done."

"How did you convince the marquess to agree to this? I'm certain he is just as averse to this as I am, if not more," she said, looking up at her brother.

Steven hesitated before responding, "He's asked to stipulate that you separate after one year."

The words washed over her like ice water. Humiliation burned through her veins. "You mean to say you agreed to have me disgraced after a year? Abandoned by my husband?"

"Only upon your agreement. Should you choose to separate, you shall be a very wealthy woman," Steven said.

"Regardless. He's counting on me to be a temporary inconvenience." A year of enduring his indifference. Her throat tightened at the thought. She couldn't quite say why his rejection stung so sharply.

"Best case scenario, you realize you're perfect for each other. Worst case scenario, you elevate your social status, gain wealth and freedom," Steven said gently. "It needn't be humiliating."

"And what of children?" Her voice caught. "If I have them? If I don't? What becomes of me then?"

Steven knelt before her, taking her cold hands in his. "If I didn't believe Hereford could make you happy, I would never suggest this match. There's more to him than you realize."

"You're a man. You can't understand what it means to lie awake at night, wondering which woman's bed your husband warms while you're alone."

"That is the fate of most wives of wealthy or handsome men. Hereford is both." Steven's matter-of-fact tone made her flinch. "Given his reputation, you should prepare yourself for—"

"Never!" The word burst from her. "The marriage contract must stipulate that any infidelity within the first year requires him to pay me five thousand pounds. Our union may lack love, but I will not be made a fool of."

Steven nodded with a slight curve in the corner of his mouth.

"I'll see it done. Now, I must speak with the solicitor." He squeezed her hands once before rising. "Pack your things. The wedding will be within days."

Amelia stood on shaking legs, then collapsed back onto the divan as her strength deserted her. She could already imagine Hereford's barely concealed disgust as she limped down the aisle, his sighs of resignation as he resigned himself to a year with an invalid bride. The wooden leg that had never felt particularly heavy before suddenly seemed to weigh as much as all her fears combined.

SLEEPLESS BEFORE THE WEDDING

THE SILK WHISPERED against Amelia's skin as the dressmaker fussed with the hem. She stared at her reflection, hardly recognizing the woman in the elegant ivory gown.

"You'll need to stand straighter, my lady," the dressmaker muttered around a mouthful of pins. "The line of the dress requires—"

"I stand as straight as I'm able, Madame Beaumont." Amelia's fingers twisted in the delicate fabric. "Perhaps we should consider a different style."

"Nonsense," Elisha said from her perch near the window. "The dress is perfect. I'm sure our esteemed madame will create something magnificent with the measurements she has if you need to rest. You look like you're attending your own funeral rather than your wedding."

"Aren't I?" Amelia caught her friend's eye in the mirror. "In three days, I'll be Lady Hereford, bound to a man who finds me barely more tolerable than a head cold."

"Hold still, my lady," Madame Beaumont commanded, tugging at the skirt. The movement caused Amelia to shift her weight, her wooden leg protesting after standing so long.

"I need a moment," she said, stepping carefully off the fitting platform. "Some tea, perhaps."

Once the dressmaker had bustled away, Amelia sank onto the

divan next to her friend, her composure cracking. "How am I to do this, Elisha? The dress, the ceremony, the… wedding night. My leg—"

"Stop." Elisha gripped her hands. "Your leg has never defined you. Don't let it start now."

"It will when I'm sharing a home with a man known for his appreciation of physical perfection." Amelia's laugh held no humor. "Have you seen the women he favors? I'm hardly in their league even with two good legs."

"You're not seeing what I see." Elisha's voice softened. "The way he watches you when he thinks no one's looking."

"With horror, no doubt."

"With fascination." Elisha squeezed her hands. "As if you're a puzzle he can't quite solve."

"Fascination," Amelia repeated softly, unsure how to feel about this observation.

In three days, she would become this man's wife. The thought terrified her, but why did it make her nervous with anticipation as well?

⤜⤜⤜✦⤛⤛⤛

"I ASSUME THE dowager marchioness had opinions about your choice of bride?" Lancaster's voice held careful neutrality.

"Mother threatened to disinherit me," Hereford said, leaning against White's leather-padded window seat with forced casualness. "Then she remembered she can't."

Patrick Adams choked on his brandy while Lancaster tried to hide his smile behind his glass. The three men had retreated to their usual corner of the club, seeking refuge from the torrent of gossip Hereford's hasty engagement had unleashed.

"'Have you lost your mind?'" Hereford mimicked his mother's shrill tone. "'A newspaper editor? A cripple? Charles, darling, what of the succession?'" He drained his glass. "She's written to every eligible debutante's mother in Hampshire, apologizing for my temporary insanity."

"And yet you're going through with it," Patrick observed.

Hereford's fingers tightened on his empty glass. "Better me than Norwich."

"Is that the only reason?" Lancaster's shrewd eyes studied his friend. "You've been rather distracted lately. Especially when a certain lady editor is mentioned."

"Nonsense." But Hereford's gaze drifted to the window, where a glimpse of a woman with chestnut hair passing on the street had caught his attention. Not Amelia. She would be at the *Review's* offices at this hour, but the similarity made his pulse race inexplicably. "She's made her opinion of me quite clear. I'm merely saving her from a worse fate."

"And yet you've read every edition of her newspaper for the past few months," Patrick said. "Including that rather pointed editorial comparing your behavior to that of a lazy housecat."

"Know thy enemy." The words felt hollow even to his own ears.

"Enemy?" Lancaster's smile widened. "Is that what we're calling it now?"

"I must be mad," Hereford muttered, turning back to his friends. "Marrying a woman who can barely stand the sight of me, all because Norwich..." He broke off, the memory of Norwich's words about Amelia warming his bed still rankling.

"Because Norwich what?" Patrick pressed.

"Nothing." Hereford signaled for another brandy. "It's purely a business arrangement."

"Of course," Lancaster said mildly. "Though you might want to inform your face of that. You've been staring into space with longing."

"Don't be ridiculous." But Hereford couldn't quite stop his mind from wandering to thoughts of Amelia, wondering what she was doing at this moment. Writing another scathing editorial about him, perhaps? "I simply want to ensure she's prepared for her new position."

"Naturally." Patrick's voice dripped skepticism. "And I'm sure your sudden interest in newspaper circulation numbers is purely professional as well?"

Hereford didn't bother responding. He was too busy wondering why the mere thought of Amelia made his chest feel tight.

Three days. In three days, she would be his wife. The thought should have filled him with dread. But it felt instead like standing on the edge of something both terrifying and thrilling.

⊱⋙⋘⊰

THE SHARP RAP at her door startled Amelia from her work. She glanced at the clock—past midnight. Steven wouldn't call this late, and Elisha was dining with the Carlisles. She looked through the peephole which Steven had insisted on.

Surprised, she opened the door to find Lord Hereford on her doorstep, his evening clothes immaculate despite the late hour. His eyes swept past her to take in the empty parlor behind.

"You're alone?" His voice held barely contained outrage. "At this hour? Where is your servant?"

"Mrs. Pierce retires early." Amelia closed the door and returned to her desk, determined not to reveal how much his unexpected presence frazzled her. "Did you need something, my lord?"

He followed her inside, his tall frame making her modest parlor feel suddenly cramped. "This is completely inappropriate. Any man could call on you. There's not even a footman—"

"Men like you, you mean?" She shuffled papers with deliberate casualness. "Other than my brother and now you, no one else calls on me. Pray tell. Was there a purpose to your visit, or did you simply come to criticize my living arrangements?"

"Your brother allows this?"

"My brother doesn't 'allow' anything. I'm of age to make my

own decisions." She finally looked up, meeting his thunderous expression. "Just as I'm not yet yours, my lord. Until our wedding, my arrangements are none of your concern."

"They become my concern when my future wife puts herself at risk." He paced the small room, his agitation evident in every movement. "What if some drunk decided to call? Or a thief? How would you defend yourself?"

"The same way I've defended myself for the past five years." She gestured to the door. "By not opening it. Though I doubt you came here at this hour to discuss my security measures. What do you want, Lord Hereford?"

He stopped pacing, running a hand through his hair in frustration. "I came to discuss the marriage contract. Certain provisions regarding your newspaper—"

"Which could have waited until tomorrow." She studied him carefully. "Why are you really here?"

"Because I couldn't sleep!" The words burst from him with force. "Because I keep thinking about this madness we're about to embark upon, about how you'll be legally bound to a man you clearly despise—"

"I don't despise you," she said quietly.

"No?" His laugh held no humor. "You merely think me an idle aristocrat who contributes nothing of value to Society. Who treats life as a game and women as playthings. Have I missed any of your published opinions about my character?"

"You've read my editorials?"

"Every damn one." He moved closer, looming over her desk. "Tell me, do you truly believe everything you've written about me? Or do you simply enjoy proving your cleverness at my expense?"

Amelia stood, refusing to be intimidated by his proximity. "I believe what I observe. A man who spends his days in pleasure while others suffer. Who uses his privilege as a shield rather than a tool for change."

"You see what you wish to see," he said, his voice dropping

dangerously low. "Just as you've already decided what kind of husband I'll be."

"Haven't you done the same?" She lifted her chin. "Already determined I'll be an unsuitable marchioness? A poor breeder for your precious line? Not to mention being uninspiring."

Color touched his cheekbones. "How did you hear that?"

"Servants. They hear everything." She softened her tone, seeing real discomfort in his expression. "I don't blame you. You spoke honestly, just as I do in my editorials. I respect that, at least." She moved around the desk, needing distance from his unsettling presence. "Now, if you'll excuse me, I have work to finish."

"Of course." His voice turned to ice. "Far be it from me to interrupt your important task of cataloging my many faults. Though surely a writer of your talent could find worthier subjects?"

"I wasn't writing about you specifically," she said. "Rather the broader ignorance of aristocrats to the plight of common folk."

"And I happen to be your favorite example?" His smile held no warmth. "The worst of the breed, am I?"

"I can't say." She met his gaze steadily. "Though you do seem to feature rather prominently in the scandal sheets."

"There's little I can do about attracting attention." Frustration and something deeper flashed in his eyes. "Remember, Miss Thornton, you've seen only one side of the page. Good night."

He was gone before she could respond, leaving behind only the lingering scent of his cologne and the uncomfortable feeling that they'd both missed something important in their clash of wills.

Amelia sank back into her chair, staring at the door he'd slammed with rather more force than necessary. In three days, she would be bound to that impossible man for a year.

God help them both.

THE WEDDING EVE

T HE NIGHT BEFORE the wedding found Amelia in her modest parlor, surrounded by stacks of crated belongings ready to be transported to the Hereford townhouse. Elisha had arrived with a bottle of fine champagne—"Edgar's best," she'd announced—while Charlotte carried a leather folio that looked suspiciously official for what was meant to be a social call.

"I can't believe this is my last night here," Amelia said, running her fingers along the familiar worn arm of her reading chair. "Five years I've built a life in this home, and tomorrow it all changes."

"Not everything," Elisha said, deftly removing the cork from the champagne bottle with a muted pop. "You'll still have the *Review*, your writing, and us."

"And quite possibly your independence," Charlotte added, "Although such documents are only as binding as your husband is willing to honor them."

"Steven assured me the settlement protects my assets," Amelia said, accepting a glass of champagne from Elisha.

"That it does, as thoroughly as possible given the current laws," Charlotte replied with a smug smile. "I insisted on reviewing every clause, much to the solicitor's visible discomfort at having a woman present. However," she continued, lowering her voice conspiratorially, "should you wish to gently persuade him to do your bidding, you can always leave his bed cold. Even legal documents cannot compel certain marital obligations."

Elisha raised an eyebrow. "Are you suggesting Amelia refuse Hereford's conjugal rights?"

"I'm merely presenting options," Charlotte said, though her slight smile suggested otherwise. "Andrew and I delayed consummation for four days after our wedding."

"Four days?" Amelia's eyes widened. "That isn't even close to a year. Are men capable of not bedding their wives for one whole year? Especially a man like Hereford?"

"Men will agree to many things when sufficient anticipation is created," Charlotte replied, her smile turning distinctly wicked. "Though I must admit, by the fourth night I was rather anticipating it myself."

Elisha laughed, refilling their glasses. "The countess speaks truth. I felt the same way. Besides, there's a reason so many widows pursue Hereford, and it's not merely for his title."

"Please," Amelia groaned, covering her face. "I'm trying to determine how to avoid his bed, not occupy it."

"But why avoid it entirely?" Elisha asked, her tone gentler. "Even if this marriage isn't consummated, there are other ways to enjoy his charms and expertise."

Amelia stared into her champagne, watching the bubbles rise and burst. "It's not just our strained acquaintance or his reputation that would have me avoiding his bed," she confessed, her voice dropping to barely above a whisper.

"Is it your injury, Amelia?" Elisha asked, her tone gentle.

Amelia nodded, her eyes suddenly glistening with unshed tears. "No one has seen my leg, and he never will. It's hideous." Her voice cracked on the last word, the vulnerability she rarely showed breaking through her composure.

Charlotte and Elisha exchanged a glance before both moved to her side. They enveloped her in their arms, their shared warmth offering comfort where words fell short. Amelia stiffened momentarily before surrendering to their embrace, allowing herself this rare moment of weakness.

"He's marrying you despite the unfavorable terms," Charlotte noted gently. "Despite his mother's objections. Despite Society's expectations. That suggests something more complex than a simple marriage of convenience, railway investments or not."

Amelia swiped quickly at her eyes, embarrassed by her momentary lapse. "Perhaps he simply doesn't understand the reality of it," she murmured. "The scarring, the awkwardness of intimacy."

"Or perhaps he sees beyond it," Elisha suggested, squeezing Amelia's hand.

Charlotte nodded in agreement, her practical nature reasserting itself. "You have options," she said, smoothly transitioning to business matters. She reached for her folio, extracting several pages marked with legal seals. "Now, there's language specifying that non-consummation for a period of up to three months cannot be used as grounds for breach. This gives you time to evaluate your options."

"I wouldn't be so certain about the non-consummation." Elisha's lips curved into a knowing smile as she pinned a last orange blossom into place. "You underestimate men's willingness to do almost anything for amorous encounters, as well as your own appeal. In addition, it can be rather thrilling to blindfold him—"

"Elisha Lancaster!" Amelia pressed a scandalized hand to her chest. "Is that really you speaking? What happened to the woman who once declared all men to be 'useless creatures guided by their baser instincts'?"

Elisha dabbed at her eyes with a delicate handkerchief, trying to hide her knowing smile. "It turns out a generous husband's baser instincts can be quite… enlightening. Wouldn't you agree, Charlotte?"

Charlotte's usually composed face flushed pink. "I never would have believed it myself, but yes. The marriage bed can be…" She bit her lip, color deepening. "Rather heavenly."

The three women dissolved into shocked giggles, the sound

echoing off the dressing room walls like they were young girls again, sharing secrets at a finishing school, instead of respected married ladies (and one very nervous bride).

"Well," Amelia managed once she caught her breath, "your endorsements are intriguing, though not quite enough to overcome my reluctance to bare myself before anyone, husband or not." Her hand drifted unconsciously to her leg.

"I think what you need is knowledge," Charlotte said, her voice gentle but firm. She reached into her folio and extracted a small book bound in discreet brown leather. "This might prove educational regarding certain marital activities, should you choose to explore them."

Amelia took the book with curiosity, then gasped as she flipped it open to find remarkably detailed illustrations of intimate acts between men and women. "Charlotte Carlisle! Where did you get such a thing?"

"Boston has a robust underground publishing industry," Charlotte replied with unrepentant delight. "Page forty-seven is particularly enlightening regarding positions that favor a woman with limited mobility in one leg."

Elisha leaned over to peek at the indicated page, her eyes widening. "Good heavens! Is that anatomically possible?"

"Quite," Charlotte confirmed, sipping her champagne as if they were discussing the weather. "Andrew was initially skeptical but became an enthusiastic convert."

Amelia closed the book with burning cheeks, but not before noting the page number for later reference. "This is hardly proper conversation for…"

"Knowledge is power, Amelia," Elisha stated firmly. "Especially in the bedchamber."

"Besides," Charlotte added, "if Hereford is half as experienced as rumor suggests, wouldn't you prefer to meet him on somewhat equal footing?"

"I doubt Lord Hereford expects any marital relations," Amelia protested, though the book remained clutched in her hand.

"Darling," Elisha said, refilling Amelia's glass, "a man doesn't look at a woman the way Hereford looks at you if he's not thinking of marital relations. Even Lancaster has noticed it."

"How does he look at me?" Amelia asked somewhat eagerly before she could stop herself.

Elisha thought for a moment before replying, "Like you captivate and frustrate him in equal measure."

"Like he's torn between wanting to argue with you and wanting to kiss you senseless," Charlotte added.

Amelia fell silent, remembering the intensity in Hereford's eyes during their verbal sparring, the way his gaze sometimes lingered on her mouth when she challenged him.

"It doesn't matter," she said finally. "Even if there were… inclinations… on either side, this marriage has an expiration date. Becoming physically entangled would only complicate matters."

"Life is complicated," Charlotte said simply. "The question is whether the complication brings more pleasure than pain."

Elisha raised her glass. "To Amelia—may your marriage, however temporary, bring unexpected pleasures."

"And may the contract ensure you maintain complete control over which pleasures you choose to accept," Charlotte added, clinking her glass against Elisha's.

Amelia joined the toast with reluctant amusement, the weight of tomorrow's ceremony momentarily lightened by her friends' practical support. The book of illustrations sat beside her on the settee, its presence both scandalous and reassuring. A reminder that whatever happened, she had options.

Options, and friends who would help her navigate them.

"Now," Elisha said, setting down her empty glass, "let's discuss what you're wearing beneath that wedding gown. I've brought the most scandalous French silk chemise…"

Amelia's laughter echoed through the small parlor as the night deepened, the champagne flowed, and three women fortified one of their own for the battlefield of marriage with the most powerful weapons they possessed: knowledge, strategy, and friendship.

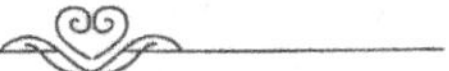

MARRIAGE OF INCONVENIENCE

AMELIA'S FINGERS TWISTED in the silk of her wedding gown as Elisha and Charlotte fussed with her veil. Her heart hammered so violently she feared they might see it through the delicate fabric. In the mirror, her reflection looked like a stranger—pale and wide-eyed beneath the cloud of white tulle.

"You really are stunning," Elisha whispered, her voice thick with emotion as she adjusted a stray curl. Their eyes met in the mirror, and Amelia watched tears well in her friend's eyes.

"Don't you dare cry, Elisha Lancaster." Amelia reached back to squeeze her hand. "If you start, I'll start, and I refuse to walk down the aisle looking like a painted cat caught in the rain."

"Your groom will assume they're tears of joy." Charlotte smoothed an invisible wrinkle from the train, her practical tone belied by the tremor in her voice. "How could he think otherwise with the marriage contract you've signed? You'll have more protections than the Crown Jewels," she jested through her tears.

A sharp rap at the door silenced them. Steven entered, cutting a striking figure in his black suit. For a moment, Amelia saw their father in his proud stance—the little she had glimpsed of him in her childhood. Her throat tightened.

"You look beautiful," he said softly after greeting Charlotte and Elisha. His eyes shone with unshed tears as he extended his arm. "Shall we?"

Amelia drew in a shaky breath, suddenly overwhelmed by the

weight of what was about to happen. In a few minutes, she would no longer be Miss Thornton, respected newspaper editor and independent woman. She would be Lady Hereford, wife and property to a marquess who had barely looked at her during their countless encounters at literary events.

Steven patted her trembling hand where it rested on his arm. "Come, sister," he whispered. "Let us begin your future now."

The words hung in the air like a prayer or perhaps a prophecy. Amelia straightened her spine and lifted her chin, determined to face whatever came next with dignity. Even if her heart felt like a trapped bird in her chest.

⇶⬥⫷

HEREFORD STOOD AT the altar, forcing himself to maintain the serene expression expected of a bridegroom despite the growing knot in his stomach. When the organ music began and the church doors opened, he turned, following tradition, and felt a knot form in his chest.

Amelia was crying.

Not the delicate tears of joy he'd seen at other weddings, but continuous weeping she seemed unable to control. Though she held her head high, her shoulders trembled. Steven patted her hand repeatedly as they walked, his own expression grave.

"Steady now," Hereford heard him whisper as he handed her over.

Her fingers were ice-cold when they touched his. Up close, he could see how she struggled to master herself, each shuddering breath threatening to break into a sob. The sight made something in his chest constrict painfully.

Was the thought of marrying him truly so devastating?

As the vicar began the ceremony, Hereford found himself studying her profile, noting how she bit her lower lip when particularly strong waves of emotion hit her. He'd seen her angry, disdainful, even triumphant, but never like this. Never broken.

Perhaps there was someone else. Some man of letters or fellow journalist who couldn't offer her marriage but had won her heart nonetheless? Or could it be Norwich she yearned for? The thought shouldn't have bothered him, but it did.

"I, Charles Eldem Bartholomew…" he repeated mechanically, wondering if her mysterious lover was in the church right now, watching her marry another man.

When it came time for her vows, her voice was barely audible, choked with tears. Hereford had to resist the urge to pull her close, to offer some comfort. But of course, that would only make things worse. She'd made her feelings about him perfectly clear.

One year, he reminded himself as he slipped the ring onto her finger. Just one year of civil coexistence, then they could both go their separate ways. Though the thought of twelve months without feminine companionship made him groan internally. He had no illusions about sharing her bed. She could barely stand to touch his hand during the ceremony.

"You may kiss the bride," the vicar announced.

Hereford leaned in carefully, catching the scent of orange blossoms in her hair, the way her tears had caught in her lashes, making them spike into dark stars. Something twisted in his chest again.

His lips brushed hers, featherlight, and he felt her lips tremble.

"I'll do my utmost," he whispered, so quietly only she could hear. "I know this isn't what you wanted."

Fresh tears spilled down her cheeks as she nodded once, quickly. Hereford offered her his arm, plastering on his most convincing smile as they turned to face their guests. One year. He could do this. Even if her tears felt like accusations against his conscience.

He just wished they didn't affect him quite so much.

THE WEDDING BREAKFAST had been mercifully brief, with only close family and friends in attendance. Now, as Amelia stood in Hereford's drawing room—her new home—she felt distinctly out of place among the luxurious furniture and crystal decanters. Her wedding gown seemed to mock her with its pristine whiteness, a symbol of tradition that held no meaning in this nuptial.

Hereford poured two glasses of brandy without asking if she wanted one. "I assume you'd like to discuss arrangements," he said, handing her a glass. His cravat was slightly loosened, the only sign that the day had affected him at all.

"Yes." Amelia accepted the brandy but didn't drink. "I believe we should establish clear boundaries."

"Very well." He leaned against his desk, studying her with those impossibly blue eyes. "Though I must admit, your brother and Lady Carlisle's demands were quite thorough. What more could you possibly require?"

"To begin with, I expect complete discretion regarding my… physical limitation." She lifted her chin. "I won't have you discussing it with anyone of your… acquaintances."

His expression hardened. "You think rather poorly of me, don't you?"

"I think exactly what you've shown me to think, my lord. So let us be clear. I have no intention of sharing your bed, neither for heirs nor pleasure. You may not seek your entertainment elsewhere either. I won't have my reputation tarnished by association with your scandals."

Hereford set down his glass with care. "And what of your own impropriety? Do you plan to continue running about London unchaperoned, visiting gentlemen's clubs?"

"I plan to continue running my newspaper, yes." Her voice turned sharp. "That was explicitly covered in the marriage contract."

"The contract doesn't specify your behavior." He straightened, using his height to loom over her. "As your husband, I have certain rights—"

"You have no rights over me beyond what was negotiated. I expect you to honor our marriage contract. This is a business arrangement, nothing more."

Something flickered in his eyes, but his voice remained controlled. "And you believe you can simply dictate the terms of our marriage bed without consideration for my wishes?"

"You've agreed to the terms. Let us not lock the stable door after the horse has bolted."

Hereford ran a hand through his hair, disturbing its careful styling. "This is precisely why I insisted on the one-year clause. We're clearly incompatible."

"On that, at least, we agree." Amelia finally took a sip of brandy, welcoming its burn.

He was quiet for a long moment, swirling the amber liquid in his glass. "I know you would have preferred Norwich."

She cleared her throat and set down her glass. "You needn't worry about my association with the viscount. I shall maintain my professionalism and interact with him only as business dictates."

His eyes peered into hers. "Tell me. Did you develop affections for Norwich?"

Amelia stared back, searching her heart for the answer. "I found him pleasant, and I respect his stance on equality. I hadn't known him long enough to develop any feelings."

Hereford turned away and poured himself another glass of brandy. When he spoke, his voice had dropped lower, taking on an edge she couldn't quite interpret. "And you believe that we can simply ignore each other's existence while living under the same roof?"

"I don't see why not. The house is certainly large enough."

He stepped closer, near enough that she could smell his cologne—that familiar scent of leather and spice that had haunted her dreams more often than she cared to admit. "And what if I don't wish to ignore you?"

Amelia's heart thundered against her ribs, but she held her ground. "Then that is your misfortune, my lord. I've made my position clear."

"Have you?" His eyes searched her face. "Because I'm beginning to wonder if you protest too much, Miss Thornton. I beg your pardon. I should say, Lady Hereford."

The new title sent an unexpected shiver down her spine. "Don't."

"Don't what?" He was closer still, though she couldn't remember him moving. "Don't remind you that you're my wife now? That despite all your conditions and protests, we're bound together?"

"Only for a year," she whispered, hating how breathless she sounded.

"A year can be a long time." His hand rose as if to touch her face, then dropped. "But have it your way, my lady. We'll maintain our separate lives, ignore the tension between us, and pretend this is nothing more than a marriage of necessity. Though I wonder…"

"What?"

"I wonder which of us you're trying harder to convince." He stepped back abruptly, retrieving his glass. "I'll have Cooper show you to your rooms. I trust you'll find them satisfactory."

Amelia gathered her skirts, desperate to escape before he could see how his proximity had affected her. "Perfect. Good afternoon, my lord."

"Good afternoon… wife."

She fled before he could see her shiver again at his use of the word wife. But as she followed the butler through the grand house that was now her home, she couldn't shake the memory of Hereford's intense gaze, or the way his voice had caressed that final word. One year suddenly seemed like both an eternity and not nearly long enough.

THEIR FIRST DINNER as husband and wife was served in the formal dining room, though "formal" seemed an inadequate word for the vast space with its gleaming mahogany table that could seat thirty. Tonight, only two places were set, one at each end of the polished expanse.

Amelia wore a gray silk for dinner, the most muted color she had in her wardrobe, her hair carefully arranged. She found Hereford already seated, looking annoyingly at ease in his evening attire—his cravat loosened just enough to reveal the strong column of his throat, his dark hair slightly mussed as if he'd run his fingers through it. The distance between them made conversation optional, which was presumably his intent.

"This is ridiculous," she said, her voice echoing slightly in the cavernous room. "I can hardly see you through the centerpiece."

He glanced up from his soup, one eyebrow raised, and she felt the full force of his attention like a physical touch. "Would you prefer closer quarters, my lady?" His voice was low, intimate despite the space between them, and carried implications that made her pulse quicken.

"I would prefer not to shout across half of London to request the salt."

A predatory smile curved his lips. "Cooper," he called to the butler, never taking his eyes off her. "Please reset Lady Hereford's place to my right."

Amelia regretted her complaint the moment servants began efficiently relocating her settings. Now she would be close enough to catch his scent, to feel the heat radiating from his body, to notice every subtle expression that crossed his devastatingly handsome face.

When she settled into her new seat, the reality was worse than she'd feared. His cologne—sandalwood and something darker, more masculine—filled her senses. At one point, his leg brushed against her skirts.

"Better?" he asked, and there was something wicked in his tone that suggested he was perfectly aware of her discomfort.

They ate in tense silence, but Amelia found herself stealing glances at his hands—elegant yet undeniably strong as they handled his silverware—the way his throat moved when he swallowed wine. Heat pooled low in her belly.

"I trust you've found your chambers satisfactory?" he asked finally, his voice a low rumble that seemed to vibrate through her bones.

"Quite." She focused determinedly on her soup, trying to ignore how he was watching her mouth as she spoke. "Though I noticed the connecting door to our rooms doesn't close properly."

It was a mistake to look up then as his eyes had darkened with unmistakable hunger. "Yes. It's been that way for as long as I can remember." He leaned slightly closer, his voice dropping to a whisper that made her skin prickle. "I assure you I did not tamper with the door, though I confess I'm grateful for the… proximity it provides."

She swallowed and blurted hastily, "What does your mother say about our arrangement?"

"My mother," he said—his wide mouth curving into a smile that had her staring at it, wondering—"has expressed her opinions quite thoroughly. She'll be dining with us tomorrow evening, by the way." His hand moved to rest on the table dangerously close to hers. "I couldn't refuse any further without causing her bodily harm."

"Of course." She tore her gaze away from his mouth and reached for her wine glass, suddenly parched. Her fingers brushed his knuckles, and the contact made her tingle. "Well, I'm sure it will be a delightful evening," she managed.

"You're nervous," he observed, his voice soft. "Your breathing is shallow." His eyes dropped to her chest, and the attention made her chest rise and fall more dramatically.

"I'm not—" she began, but he was already leaning closer.

"I can see it," he murmured, so close now that his breath stirred the loose tendrils of hair at her temple. "Your breathing…" His finger hovered just above her chest, not quite touching but close enough that she could feel the heat of his skin. "Quite… distracting."

She couldn't breathe. Couldn't think. Could only stare at his mouth, now mere inches from hers, and wonder what would happen if she closed the distance between them.

The arrival of the fish course broke the spell, forcing him to lean back. But she noticed how his eyes had darkened, the barely audible groan as he made space for the server. A barely perceptible movement of his eyes had the servants vacating the room all at once.

She was struggling with a particularly difficult cut when he took over. "Allow me," he said.

"I can manage," she whispered.

"I know you can." His voice was a low rasp that sent shivers down her spine. "But I find myself… eager to assist my wife in any way possible."

His hands cut the fish with ease, but instead of returning his attention to his own plate, he lifted a perfectly cut piece on the fork, bringing it toward her lips.

"Open," he commanded softly, his voice rough with something that made her stomach flutter.

"Charles, this is… you are…"

He raised a brow, one corner of his lips curving up. "I am?"

"You are trying to seduce me… I think," she blurted, feeling heat rise from her chest to her face.

"Not at all. What purpose would I have to seduce you?" He put down the fork and leaned back in his chair, giving her a much-needed reprieve from the magnetic force.

"Perhaps you wish to negotiate better terms." To her chagrin, her voice was still breathless.

Hereford stood slowly, startling her. "If I wished to seduce my wife, I would have stood behind her," he said as he positioned himself thus and bent over her, his hands reaching for her fork and holding the morsel of fish near her lips.

Not knowing what to do, she opened her mouth and took the bite.

"Delicious?" he finished, his breath warm against her ear as she chewed carefully. "I've been meaning to ask about the library."

His free hand came to rest on the back of her chair, his knuckles lightly brushing the exposed skin at the nape of her neck. She shivered involuntarily.

"Will you require any modifications?" he continued conversationally, as if feeding his wife from behind while whispering in her ear was perfectly normal. He cut another piece, holding it to her lips. "A more comfortable chair, perhaps?"

She accepted the bite, exceedingly aware of his warm breath against her neck.

"Softer lighting for evening work?" Another piece appeared at her lips. When she hesitated, he traced the fork gently along her lower lip. "I want you comfortable when you pour all your... passion into your writing."

The low rumble of his voice sent a shiver down her spine. She took the offered bite, her lips parting. Was his breath becoming shallower?

"Perhaps a comfortable settee," he continued, his voice growing rougher, "for when I join you... Purely for intellectual pursuits, of course."

His hand moved from the chair to stroke the strand of hair near her ear. She could feel the heat radiating from his hand.

"I could have the room redecorated entirely to your specifications," he murmured, while the hand, devastatingly, came to rest on her bare shoulder. His thumb traced a small circle against her skin. "New furnishings, whatever books you desire... I find myself quite invested in ensuring my wife has everything she needs."

She could barely focus on his words, overwhelmed by his touch, his scent, the way his voice seemed to vibrate through her entire body. When he offered her another bite, she turned slightly to accept it and found herself looking directly into his darkened eyes.

"You're trying to confuse me," she accused breathlessly, though she made no move to escape his ministrations. "Using proximity and… and seduction to gain some advantage."

His low chuckle rumbled against her cheek as he set down the fork, his hand lightly massaging her shoulder. "Is it working?" When she didn't answer, he leaned closer, his lips nearly brushing her ear. "Because I must confess, wife, if anyone is being seduced here, it's decidedly not you."

"You're insufferable," she managed, but her voice lacked any real conviction.

"And you," he murmured, both hands resting on the table, caging her in, "are driving me to distraction. Do you have any idea what you do to me?"

The temptation to lean back against him, to discover what his mouth would feel like on hers, was becoming unbearable. Before she could do something foolish—like surrender to the desire coursing through her—she stood abruptly, her chair scraping against the floor as he stepped back with impressive agility.

"I should retire," she said, not daring to look at him, her voice unsteady. "It's been a long day."

When she finally risked a glance, his eyes were dark with desire.

"Of course," he said, his voice carefully controlled though she could hear the strain beneath it. "Sleep well, wife."

As she fled toward the door on unsteady legs, she heard him add softly, almost to himself, "Though I suspect neither of us will manage much sleep tonight."

A SURPRISING HUSBAND

AMELIA HAD SPECIFICALLY requested to take breakfast in the private parlor connecting the master and mistress suites. The small, sun-drenched room would provide the solitude she desperately needed after last night's dinner—after the way he'd fed her with his own hands, his thumb drawing circles on her skin, the dangerous hunger in his voice as he'd whispered. She needed space to think, to rebuild the defenses he'd so effortlessly dismantled with nothing more than proximity and that devastating smile.

The small, sun-drenched room would provide the solitude she craved before facing her day at the *Review's* offices. Mrs. Hudson, the Hereford housekeeper, had informed her that his lordship invariably took his morning meal in the main breakfast room.

But as she stepped through the doorway precisely at seven o'clock, she found her careful planning thwarted. Her new husband sat lounging in a comfortable chair by the window, his long legs stretched before him, shirtsleeves rolled to the elbows, and the top buttons of his fine linen shirt casually undone. His dark hair was appealingly tousled from sleep, the pillow's impression still visible on his temple. Seeing the marquess in this state was surprising enough, but most shocking of all was the fact that a pair of spectacles perched on his aristocratic nose as he read what appeared to be—

"Is that my newspaper?" she asked, losing her train of thought.

Hereford glanced up, removing his spectacles languidly. "Good morning, wife. And yes, it is." His lips quirked into a half-smile, blue eyes dancing with amusement. "I find your editorial on educational reform quite stimulating, though your conjugation of 'amo' is erroneous."

Amelia moved to the table, determined not to show how his unexpected presence had disconcerted her. "I hadn't expected you to be an early riser."

"Disappointed to have your solitude disrupted? I'd already wagered with Cooper that you'd arrive at seven. Though he insisted you'd choose six-thirty to avoid me entirely."

"How unfortunate for Cooper," she replied dryly, settling into her chair with as much dignity as she could muster. She winced slightly as her leg felt especially stiff in the morning—a discomfort she'd never admit to anyone.

A servant appeared with a fresh pot of coffee and a plate of toast already prepared with orange marmalade, precisely how she preferred it. The attention to such a small detail caught her off guard.

"You requested information about my preferences?" she asked, unable to keep the surprise from her voice. "Or was this arrangement merely coincidental?"

"From your brother," Hereford confirmed, folding the newspaper and setting it aside. "Entirely intentional, I assure you. I find that attending to small comforts makes difficult situations more bearable." He gestured to the silver pot. "The marmalade is imported from Seville. Apparently the best."

Something warm and unfamiliar flickered in Amelia's chest. She tamped it down immediately. "That was… thoughtful," she managed, busying herself with her toast to avoid meeting his eyes.

"I'm occasionally capable of consideration," he replied, his tone light but with an undercurrent she couldn't quite identify.

"Shocking, I know."

Amelia smoothed her napkin across her lap, buying time to clear her head. "I appreciate the gesture, Lord Hereford. Though it does make me wonder what other aspects of my life you've investigated."

"Lord Hereford?" he asked with a cocking of his brow but said nothing further. "How terribly formal of you, wife. I hope to progress beyond such frigid civilities soon." Despite his pleasant expression, there was something heavy in his tone. "As for your investigation, only the most critical matters of state. Your preference in literary journals, your opinion on Wagner's operas, and your inexplicable attachment to those hideously uncomfortable wooden chairs at the *Review*."

Despite herself, Amelia felt her lips twitch. "They're not uncomfortable. They promote proper posture."

"They promote spinal torture," he corrected, buttering a piece of toast. "Even the medieval rack offered more comfort."

She would not laugh. She absolutely would not laugh at his ridiculous exaggeration.

His tone was gentle when he continued, "Would you permit me to commission a more comfortable chair for your office at the *Review*? Those wooden monstrosities you insist on using must be terribly hard on your back."

"I manage quite well, thank you," she said, even as her spine was stiffening. The wooden leg suddenly felt heavier, more conspicuous, though she knew it was hidden beneath her skirts. "I don't need special accommodations."

Hereford studied her for a long moment, his expression softening. "Not special, Amelia. Simply comfortable. There's no weakness in that."

The use of her given name, coupled with the gentle understanding in his tone, disarmed her more effectively than any argument could have. Amelia swallowed past the sudden tightness in her throat.

"I'll consider it," she said, her voice soft. Giving herself a mental shake, she stood taller, determined not to be affected by this surprising man. "Perhaps we should discuss our arrangement. I've prepared some notes regarding household affairs."

"As have I," he replied, producing a folded document from underneath the breakfast tray with a flourish. "Though I suspect our approaches may differ somewhat."

Amelia extracted her own list from her reticule—three pages of neatly written points covering everything from meal schedules to staff management to the use of common areas. She placed it on the table between them like a declaration of war.

Hereford glanced at her pages, then at his single sheet, and a slow smile spread across his face. "I see you've been thorough."

"I believe in clarity," she replied primly.

"Evidently," he said, his eyes crinkling with amusement, then cleared his throat dramatically. "May I begin?"

"Please," she replied, steeling herself not to laugh.

"'Item the first,'" he read with mock gravity. "I would appreciate being informed of your general whereabouts when you venture out. Not as your keeper," he added as she opened her mouth to protest, "but as someone concerned for your safety."

"My schedule at the *Review* makes that impractical," she explained. "Sometimes investigations require discretion and flexibility."

He studied her for a moment, then nodded. "Very well. Though perhaps you might consider using the Hereford carriage when venturing into less savory areas? London can be dangerous after dark."

Amelia's fingers unconsciously gripped her napkin tighter. The thought of being helped in and out of his ostentatious carriage, the Hereford crest announcing her presence to all of London, made her stomach twist. How many curious eyes would watch, wondering about the crippled woman who had somehow snared the notorious marquess? How many would whisper about her ungainly movements as she struggled with the carriage steps?

"Your carriage is rather... conspicuous. It would draw attention that might compromise my work."

Hereford stroked his chin thoughtfully. "Then allow me to provide an unmarked carriage. Something discreet but safer than hackney cabs."

The consideration in his offer made it difficult to refuse. "Thank you. I'd appreciate that."

"Excellent." He made a small notation on his paper. "Now, regarding the library—"

"I require full access," she interrupted, then winced at her own defensiveness.

To her relief, he simply nodded. "I was going to suggest you take the east and north walls, which receive the best light for reading. I'll use the south and west, which are primarily filled with my grandfather's tedious treatises on crop rotation."

"Oh," she said, finding herself wrong-footed again. "That's sensible."

"I'm occasionally that as well," he replied, his eyes crinkling at the corners. "Continuing on, I'd like to request that we share at least three dinners weekly. I promise to be only moderately insufferable."

Despite herself, Amelia felt her lips curve into a smile. "Only moderately?"

"I contain multitudes, my lady," he said with a dramatic sigh. "Some more bearable than others. Tuesdays, Fridays, and Sundays perhaps? Cook's beefsteak pudding on Fridays is particularly fortifying."

"I will try, but if I have investigative work, I will join you another evening."

His eyes lit with unexpected triumph, as if he'd won a significant concession. "Splendid. Now, one more matter—the pianoforte."

"The pianoforte?"

"Yes. I should warn you that I play it rather abominably after midnight." His expression turned sheepish. "It's a habit I've never managed to break. I find it soothing when sleep eludes me."

The image of the notorious Marquess of Hereford playing piano in the darkened hours was yet another fact incongruous with his reputation. "I assume you're not requesting permission?"

"Merely providing fair warning," he clarified.

Amelia nodded. "I appreciate that."

Something passed between them then—a moment of connection that neither had anticipated. It shimmered in the morning light, fragile and unexpected.

The spell was broken by Cooper's discreet entrance, announcing the arrival of Amelia's hackney carriage. She rose, gathering her notes with a newfound awareness of her husband— still insufferable in many ways, but perhaps not entirely as she'd expected.

"We'll continue our negotiations this evening?" she asked, suddenly uncertain.

"I look forward to it," he replied, rising as well. His eyes dropped to her hands, where she clutched her lists. "Though perhaps we might set aside the formal documentation and simply… converse?"

Amelia hesitated, then gave him a small nod. "Perhaps."

As she turned to leave, he called after her: "Oh, and, my lady? The word you wanted in your editorial was 'docui,' not 'docueram.' If you're going to mock our educational system, best to be grammatically impeccable."

She paused at the doorway, glancing back over her shoulder. Her emerald eyes met his blue ones across the sunlit room. "Thank you for the correction, my lord. Though I maintain that teaching Latin to sheep would be more productive than the current system at Eton."

His surprised laugh followed her into the corridor, warm and genuine in a way she hadn't heard before. As she made her way to her waiting carriage, Amelia found herself contemplating the stranger who was her husband. The Marquess of Hereford wore reading glasses, played the pianoforte badly at midnight, and was more considerate than she could have imagined. None of these details aligned with the rake she'd thought him to be.

Perhaps, she thought as she settled into her carriage, this marriage of convenience might prove more interesting than expected—though suddenly more complicated.

➤➤➤✦◄◄◄

HEREFORD WAITED UNTIL he heard the door close behind his new wife before he allowed himself to slump in his chair. He hadn't expected her presence to affect him so. He'd known she'd join him. He had interrogated the housekeeper for that purpose. Yet when she strode into the parlor with her luminous skin glowing in the morning light, with her rosy cheeks and rosier lips... Seeing her in the morning in his private quarters...

"Bloody hell," he muttered, reaching for the brandy before remembering the hour.

"Rather early for that, my lord."

Hereford didn't need to look up to recognize Barker's voice.

"I wasn't actually going to pour any, Barker."

"Of course not, my lord." Barker's tone suggested he believed otherwise. He began tidying the meal trays. "I trust breakfast was informative?"

Hereford shot him a sharp look. "To what, pray, are you alluding?"

"Merely that it's the first time in recent memory you've been awake to see the sunrise. And to arrange such specific breakfast preparations..." Barker picked up a discarded copy of the *Review*, his expression carefully neutral. "Most unusual."

"I was simply ensuring the household runs smoothly."

"Indeed." Barker's tone could have dried the Thames. "Just as you were 'simply ensuring efficiency' when you had Cooper station William at the front steps specifically to assist Her Ladyship?"

"Basic courtesy," Hereford muttered.

"Ah yes. The same courtesy that prompted you to have the library lamp replaced? And to import marmalade from Seville? And to save every edition of the *Review* containing her editorials?"

"Barker." Hereford's warning tone would have silenced most servants.

"I've known you since you were in leading strings, my lord," Barker continued undaunted. "I served your father for thirty years before you. Which is why I feel compelled to point out—you're either developing genuine feelings for Her Ladyship, in which case these little gestures, while charming, are insufficient, or you're attempting to manipulate her, in which case…" He shook his head as he gazed heavenward. "Well, she strikes me as rather too clever to be managed that way."

"I'm not developing feelings," Hereford mumbled.

"Of course not, my lord." Barker adjusted the newspapers with maddening precision. "Though I can't help but notice you've been reading Her Ladyship's editorial upon waking and before retiring each day."

Hereford tossed the *Review* aside as if it had offended him and opened the *Times*. "I was merely looking after my business interests."

"Naturally." Barker paused in his tidying. "Your father used to say that intelligence in a woman was like fire—fascinating to observe but dangerous to handle carelessly."

"What's your point, Barker?"

"Simply that Lady Hereford strikes me as particularly… incendiary." He picked up the brandy decanter Hereford had been eyeing. "Especially where matters of social reform are concerned. The factory commission report, for instance—"

Hereford's head snapped up. "What about it?"

"Her ladyship seems quite interested in investigating ownership records based on what Mrs. Hudson tells me." Barker's gaze was pointed. "Records that might prove… revealing."

The muscle in Hereford's jaw ticked. "Those investments are perfectly legal."

"Legal, yes. But perhaps not something a wife dedicated to workers' rights would appreciate discovering about her husband?"

Before Hereford could respond, Cooper appeared in the doorway. "My lord? The dowager marchioness' secretary just called. She's requesting to move dinner to eight. Apparently, she requires extra time to gather her thoughts about Lady Hereford's most recent editorial."

Hereford groaned. *Perfect. Just perfect.*

"Oh, and my lord?" Cooper hesitated. "Mrs. Pierce mentioned that Her Ladyship sometimes forgets to eat when working. Should I have a tray sent to the *Review* office?"

Hereford was tempted to wave him away, irritated by his own concern. It wasn't his responsibility to ensure she ate properly. She'd made it quite clear she wanted no interference.

And yet…

"Indeed," he said to the butler. "Have them include those little almond cakes she liked at breakfast this morning." He paused. "And tell her they're from Mrs. Pierce."

"Of course, my lord." Cooper and Barker exchanged a look.

"That will be all," Hereford said pointedly. "Both of you."

Alone again, he stared at the brandy decanter Barker had deliberately placed just out of reach, trying to ignore the growing complexity of his situation. One year. He just had to maintain this delicate balance for one year.

The thought filled him with dread.

FRIEND OR FOE?

THE DOWAGER MARCHIONESS of Hereford swept into the dining room at precisely eight o'clock, her silver-streaked dark hair arranged in an elegant coiffure that made Amelia conscious of her own simpler style.

"Charles, darling," she said, kissing the air near her son's cheek before taking her seat. Her eyes swept over Amelia with the kind of practiced dismissal that only decades in Society could perfect.

"Mother." Hereford signaled for the first course. "I trust you had a pleasant journey from Hampshire?"

"As pleasant as one can expect when traveling alone." The dowager's smile turned pointed. "Usually, a son would escort his mother, but I understand you had more pressing matters to attend to."

"My heartfelt apologies. I was utterly captivated by my wife's intellect and beauty," Hereford replied with a warmth that seemed to surprise even his mother. "My heart could not wait for your return. I feared if I escorted you to Hampshire, another suitor might steal her affections in my absence."

"Ah yes, love's urgent demands." The dowager turned her attention to Amelia, skepticism evident in her arched brow. "I understand that's what precipitated this... extraordinarily hasty arrangement. Though I must say, my dear, you've caused quite a stir with your latest publication and now this whirlwind marriage to my son. Your views on women's property rights were particularly revolutionary."

Amelia felt heat rise in her cheeks. Of course, the dowager had read her editorial arguing that married women should maintain control of their own assets. "I merely suggested that economic independence needn't threaten the sanctity of marriage."

"Indeed?" The dowager's smile didn't waver as her eyes flickered briefly to Amelia's waistline. "And how fortunate that you're now in a position to observe such matters firsthand. Though I wonder, does your newspaper intend to continue operating now that you have more appropriate duties to attend to? I imagine you'll soon have other pressing concerns that require your attention."

Before Amelia could respond, Hereford spoke. "The *Review's* circulation has doubled this quarter. It would be poor business sense to interrupt such success."

Amelia nearly dropped her spoon. How did he know the *Review's* circulation numbers?

"Business sense?" The dowager's laugh tinkled like breaking glass. "My dear boy, a marchioness has no need for business sense. She needs to focus on more important matters. The Hampshire estate requires significant attention, and of course, there's the matter of securing the succession…"

"The soup is particularly good tonight," Hereford interrupted, his voice pleasant. "Cooper, please ensure Mother has a fresh glass of wine."

Amelia noticed how he'd smoothly redirected the conversation before it could venture into more dangerous waters. She'd seen him deploy similar tactics at social gatherings but never realized how skillfully he wielded such small deflections.

"I was thinking," the dowager continued undeterred, "of hosting a small gathering next month. Just family, of course. It would give dear Amelia a chance to learn our traditions before the Season begins."

"Unfortunately," Hereford said, "we'll be quite occupied with the railway expansion. The investors' meeting alone will require significant preparation."

"The investors' meeting?" The dowager's eyebrows rose. "Surely you don't intend to involve your wife in business matters?"

"Why not? Her networking prowess is precisely what the venture needs." He gave his mother a lazy smile. "Besides, isn't that what you always taught me? To recognize valuable assets?"

Amelia nearly choked on her soup. Had Hereford just defended her capabilities? He had certainly saved her from tiresome lectures from the dowager.

"Charles." The dowager's voice held a warning. "You know how I feel about women involving themselves in men's affairs. It's not natural. And with her condition—"

"I find nothing unnatural about intelligence," Hereford said mildly, though Amelia saw him signal for the next course, cutting his mother's comment short. "Though speaking of natural talents, I hear cousin Beatrice's daughter is making her debut this Season. Perhaps we should discuss her prospects?"

The dowager brightened at this more appropriate topic, launching into a detailed analysis of eligible bachelors. Amelia realized with reluctant gratitude and admiration what Hereford had done—redirected his mother's attention to safer waters while simultaneously preventing any further discussion of Amelia's "condition."

The rest of dinner proceeded in similar fashion. Whenever the dowager approached a potentially cutting remark about Amelia's background or capabilities, Hereford would smoothly interject with a new topic or casual observation. He did it so naturally that Amelia might not have noticed if she hadn't been watching for it.

It wasn't until the final course that the dowager managed to land a direct hit. "I do hope, my dear," she said to Amelia, "that you'll consider redecorating the family drawing room. It's been quite some time since a woman's touch graced these halls. Though perhaps something subtle would be best. Given your background."

"Actually," Hereford drawled before Amelia could respond, "I've given the drawing room considerable thought. It needs a complete overhaul—something bold and modern. The *Review's* offices are particularly well designed. Perhaps you could offer some suggestions, my darling wife?"

Amelia looked at him sharply, but his expression revealed nothing beyond mild interest. The dowager, however, looked as though she'd swallowed something sour.

"Bold?" she repeated faintly. "But the drawing room has been the same since your grandmother's time…"

"Exactly." Hereford smiled. "Time for a change, wouldn't you say? Though we can discuss the details another evening. You must be tired from your journey, Mother."

The dismissal was gentle but clear. As servants appeared to escort the dowager to her carriage, Amelia found herself studying her husband with new eyes and reluctant appreciation. Every barb had been deflected, every potential insult redirected, yet he'd done it so skillfully that his mother likely hadn't even realized she'd been managed.

"Something on your mind, my lady?" he asked, catching her scrutiny.

"No," she said slowly. "Though I do wonder—was there some reason you felt compelled to mention the *Review's* circulation numbers?"

His lips curved slightly. "Merely establishing your credentials. Mother respects success, even if she disapproves of how it's achieved." He stood, adjusting his cuffs. "Though I should mention, your Latin may have been incorrect, but your point about classical education was rather well-argued."

He left her there, staring after him in confusion. Had that been a compliment buried beneath the criticism? And why did she suddenly feel as though she'd underestimated him rather severely?

AMELIA STOOD IN her night rail before the connecting door between their chambers, her fingers hovering over the smooth wood. From the other side came the muffled sounds of movement—the soft thud of boots being removed, the rustle of fabric, the quiet splash of water in a basin. Such ordinary sounds, yet they painted vivid pictures in her mind: Hereford loosening his cravat, those elegant fingers unbuttoning his shirt, water trailing down his throat…

"This is madness," she whispered to herself, drawing back. And yet she remained, caught between proper behavior and improper curiosity.

As she leaned closer, she recalled that the door didn't properly close, leaving a sliver of space through which candlelight from his chamber spilled into her darkened room. Through this narrow gap, she caught glimpses of him and his valet moving about: the broad expanse of his back as he removed his coat, the flex of muscle as he stretched his arms above his head.

He'd surprised her at dinner. The way he'd handled his mother, all subtle maneuvering beneath that indolent facade. She'd glimpsed something of the real man tonight—clever, strategic, unexpectedly… capable. It made her remember other glimpses she'd caught: the flex of muscle beneath his coat when he'd vaulted over her printing press, the grace of his movements during fencing practice, the intensity in his eyes even as he teased her.

A quiet curse from his chamber drew her attention back to the door. She saw him now, struggling with his cufflinks, the gold buttons of his waistcoat partially undone. A pair of hands appeared to lend assistance followed by Hereford's low baritone murmuring something she couldn't hear. Another male voice chuckled faintly.

The memory of his morning disarray rose unbidden: dark

hair tousled from sleep, shirt wrinkled, that single undone button at his throat. She'd noticed, God help her. Just as she'd noticed the breadth of his shoulders beneath his evening coat tonight, the strength in his hands as he'd gripped his wine glass, the way candlelight caught the angular planes of his face.

"Stop this," she commanded herself. But her mind wandered treacherously to that day at Brooks, when the Duchess of Rutland's foil had torn his trousers. She'd seen more than was proper then. The powerful muscles of his thigh, the tanned skin conjuring up images of him riding without…

Something crashed in his chamber, followed by more cursing. Amelia jumped back from the door, heart racing. What was she doing, standing here like some lovesick girl, pining after her fake… no, pretend? No, temporary husband.

And yet the way he'd defended her tonight… The way he'd known her breakfast preferences, remembered her editorials. The contradictions of him were maddening.

Amelia retreated to her bed, lay across it, her body tense with a longing she'd experienced no matter how much she had tried to deny it. Almost of their own volition, her hands began to wander, one sliding up to cup her breast through the thin fabric of her nightgown, the other drifting lower, beneath the hem.

Her fingers found the sensitive flesh between her thighs already slick with desire. She gasped softly at the contact, then bit her lip to stifle the sound. What was she doing? This was improper… unwise—touching herself while thinking of a man who would be gone in a year.

Yet she couldn't stop. Her fingers moved in gentle circles, each touch sending waves of pleasure through her trembling body. In her mind, it was Charles touching her, Charles whispering her name, Charles claiming her as more than just a temporary arrangement.

A soft laugh drifted through the door. He must be reading something amusing. The sound sent an unexpected shiver down her spine, remembering how that same laugh had wrapped around the word "wife" this morning.

When she finally found release, it was his name that nearly escaped her lips—a confession swallowed back just in time as pleasure shuddered through her. She lay there afterward, breathing heavily, shame and satisfaction warring within her.

Amelia reminded herself she would not spend her nights yearning after a man who saw her as an unfit wife and mother even if he lusted after her—possible only because he didn't know the full extent of her injury.

Even if that man was currently separated from her by nothing more than a wooden door and her own stubbornness.

"One year," she whispered into her pillow. "Just one year."

But in the darkness, with the faint sounds of him moving about his chamber, that year stretched before her like both a promise and a threat. How was she supposed to maintain her emotional distance when every interaction left her more intrigued? When even his most infuriating qualities—that aristocratic arrogance, that carefully cultivated indolence—were beginning to fascinate rather than repel?

Sleep was a long time coming, and when it did, her dreams were full of undone buttons and candlelight on bare skin, of elegant fingers and knowing smiles, of doors that remained stubbornly, maddeningly closed.

CHARLES LOOSENED HIS cravat with a weary sigh, the weight of the evening finally settling on his shoulders. The dinner with his mother had been a success by any measure—Amelia had been remarkable, holding her own against the dowager's thinly veiled barbs with grace and wit. He couldn't help but admire her refusal to be intimidated by his mother's formidable presence.

As he worked the gold buttons of his waistcoat, a flicker of movement caught his eye—a moving shadow darkening the narrow gap where the connecting door stood slightly ajar. He paused, fingers stilling on the third button. Amelia must be moving about in her chambers, perhaps unable to sleep after the tension of the evening.

The thought sent a thrill through him.

He continued undressing, removing his waistcoat before tackling his cufflinks. These proved particularly troublesome tonight—or perhaps his distraction made them seem so.

"Damn these infernal things," he muttered, struggling with the intricate fastening.

Barker appeared silently at his elbow, as was his custom. "Allow me, my lord," he said, handing him a glass of brandy and taking over the cufflink duty. "A difficult evening with the dowager marchioness requires fortification."

Charles accepted the drink gratefully, lifting the glass to his lips as his valet made quick work of the cufflinks. His attention drifted back to the connecting door and paused amid taking a sip of the brandy. Someone was standing by the crack of the door. The shadow was close and unmoving which suggested deliberate observation.

The realization that Amelia was indeed watching him—studying him in this private moment—sent a jolt of awareness through his body. His hand jerked involuntarily, the brandy glass slipping from his fingers and shattering against the hardwood floor.

"My lord," Barker observed with a long-suffering sigh, eyeing the amber liquid pooling among the crystal shards, "at this rate, we shall need to outfit your chambers entirely in unbreakable materials. Perhaps cork floors and pewter glasses, as one might provide a particularly clumsy child."

Despite his distraction, Charles couldn't help but laugh.

"Your concern for my dignity is touching as always, Barker," he said absently as his valet cleaned the floor, his attention returning to the door and its hidden observer. "That will be all for tonight."

Barker bowed slightly as he quit the room. "Good night, my lord."

Once alone, Charles moved toward the connecting door, wondering if Amelia had wanted something from him. Perhaps she wished to discuss the evening, to debrief after his mother's visit. The shadow had disappeared, but he allowed himself to open the door a fraction wider, just enough to peer through—and froze at the sight that greeted him.

Amelia lay on her bed, her nightgown hiked up to reveal the smooth expanse of her thighs. From his angle, he couldn't see below her knees or above her chest, but what he could see was enough to send desire coursing through him like wildfire. One of her hands moved beneath the bunched fabric between her thighs while the other kneaded her breast and massaged her peak. The sounds of stifled moans and pants had his blood shooting straight to his cock.

He should close the door. He should withdraw, grant her the privacy she deserved. Yet he found himself transfixed, unable to look away as she arched her back, her hand moving in regular rhythm.

This was his Amelia—his wife. She was not the composed or prudish woman he thought she would be, but a woman of passion and liberal mind. A woman pleasuring herself, perhaps thinking of...

A soft gasp escaped her lips, and Charles felt answering heat pool in his groin. His own breath quickened as he watched her movements grow more urgent, her hips rising to meet her fingers. There was something unbearably arousing about witnessing her like this—unguarded against pleasure.

When she reached her climax, her body tensing and then shuddering in release, Charles could barely restrain a groan. He backed away from the door, pressing himself against the wall of his chamber, his arousal painful in its intensity.

Almost without conscious thought, his hand moved to his falls, freeing his straining member. With Amelia's image still vivid in his mind—her hand between her thighs, her breast in her hand—he found his own release in quick, urgent strokes.

As the waves of pleasure subsided, Charles slid down the wall until he sat on the floor, his breathing ragged, his mind reeling with the implications of what had just transpired. Whatever arrangement they had agreed upon, whatever distance they had tried to maintain, was clearly crumbling. There was something building between them—something that transcended their practical agreement.

And God help him, he found himself unable to regret it.

With a sigh, Charles rose and moved to his bed, knowing sleep would prove elusive tonight. The image of Amelia in the throes of passion would haunt his dreams, a tantalizing glimpse of what might be possible if they both gave in to their base desires.

DIFFERENT STROKES

"REMIND ME AGAIN why we're attending your cousin's wedding anniversary?" Amelia asked as their carriage rolled toward the Hollingshead estate. She smoothed her emerald silk gown, a creation far more elaborate than her usual practical attire. "Surely our own recent nuptials excuse us from social obligations for at least a month."

Hereford, resplendent in black evening wear that emphasized the breadth of his shoulders, looked up from adjusting his cufflinks. "Because Cousin Sophia is the dowager marchioness' favorite niece, and defying both of them would be tantamount to declaring war on the entire eastern branch of the family." His lips quirked upward. "Besides, I thought you might enjoy the spectacle of aristocrats engaging in their natural habitat—excessive consumption paired with vicious gossip."

Amelia hid a smile. "You make your own class sound like exotic wildlife."

"More dangerous, I assure you. Tigers are predictable by comparison." He studied her for a moment, his expression softening. "You look lovely. The color suits you."

The unexpected compliment caught her off guard. "Thank you," she managed, fighting the heat rising in her cheeks. "Though I still think we should have prepared more thoroughly for the evening."

"It's a dinner, not a diplomatic mission."

"It might as well be. Your mother has no doubt informed everyone about the penniless bluestocking who dared to set her cap at a marquess."

Hereford's expression turned wry. "Perhaps. Which is why we should convince them of our affection for each other."

"Affection?"

Hereford gazed into her eyes with a soulful entreaty that had her almost believe in his sincerity. "The guests shall see the depth of my feelings for you by the way I regard you. They'll be convinced that the notorious Marquess of Hereford was smitten by the brilliant Miss Thornton and simply couldn't wait another moment to make her his marchioness," he said with exaggerated flourish. "Society abhors a marriage of convenience almost as much as it loves a love match."

Amelia raised an eyebrow. "And you think they'll believe the infamous rake reformed overnight? Your mother certainly doesn't."

"People believe what they wish to believe." He leaned forward, his eyes dancing with mischief. "I suggest we tell them I was captivated by your scathing editorial comparing aristocratic men's moral fortitude to weathervanes."

"You read that?" she asked, surprised.

"I read all your work," he replied with unexpected seriousness before his customary smirk returned. "Your metaphors about the House of Lords were particularly creative."

Before Amelia could respond, the carriage slowed as they approached Hollingshead House, a grand Georgian mansion blazing with lights. Footmen in elaborate livery stood ready to assist arriving guests, and strains of chamber music drifted through the open windows.

Hereford's hand covered hers briefly. "Ready, Wife?"

The casual endearment sent an unexpected warmth through her. "As I'll ever be."

As they entered the grand ballroom, Amelia was acutely aware of the attention they attracted. Conversations paused, fans fluttered more rapidly, and heads bent together in whispered observations. Hereford, perfectly at ease in this environment, placed his hand at the small of her back, guiding her forward with a protective assurance that she found both irritating and oddly comforting.

"Charles, darling!" The dowager marchioness materialized before them, resplendent in purple silk and ancestral diamonds. "And Amelia," she added, as if the name tasted peculiar. "How… well you look."

"Mother," Hereford bent to kiss her cheek. "You've outdone yourself with the diamonds tonight. Planning to blind the competition?"

"Don't be ridiculous," she said, though she preened visibly under her son's attention. "Lady Rutherford's new necklace is positively vulgar. One must maintain standards." Her gaze swept over Amelia with clinical assessment. "That shade of green is surprisingly flattering with your coloring, my dear. Though perhaps a higher neckline would be more appropriate for a woman of your… figure."

"Thank you for your concern, my lady," Amelia replied smoothly. "But Charles seems to appreciate the current design."

Hereford's arm slipped around her waist, drawing her closer against his side. "Immensely," he agreed, his voice dropping to a register that made Amelia's skin tingle.

The dowager's eyes narrowed fractionally. "Yes, well. Everyone is most eager to meet the woman who captured my son's heart so… precipitously. Lady Bancroft was particularly devastated by the news, you know. She had such hopes for her daughter this Season."

"How fortunate I didn't keep her waiting," Hereford replied blandly. "Shall we pay our respects to Cousin Sophia?"

As they moved away, Amelia felt tension coiling between her shoulder blades. "This will be a very long evening," she muttered.

"Indeed. Though you handled my mother admirably."

"Years of dealing with hostile interview subjects," she replied with forced lightness. "Though none quite so formidable."

Hereford chuckled. "Wait until you meet Aunt Gertrude. Mother is the beacon of diplomacy by comparison."

The next hour passed in a blur of introductions and carefully navigated conversations. Amelia found herself repeating the story Hereford had constructed—that he was captivated by her criticism of aristocratic men's moral fortitude and had to make her acquaintance.

"And when precisely did you realize you were in love?" demanded Lady Bancroft, whose disappointed daughter sulked nearby. "It must have been quite the epiphany to prompt such a hasty ceremony."

Amelia opened her mouth to recite their agreed-upon answer about a moment of clarity during a charity event, but Hereford spoke first.

"It was when she compared me to a peacock with more feathers than sense in the *Metropolitan Review*," he said, his expression softening with what appeared to be genuine fondness. "Most women simper and flatter. Amelia told me exactly what she thought of my 'frivolous existence' and 'wasteful privileges.' I found it refreshingly honest."

Lady Bancroft looked scandalized. "And that attracted you?"

"Immensely," Hereford replied, his gaze fixed on Amelia with warmth. "Intelligence is the most compelling quality a woman can possess."

Amelia felt heat rising in her cheeks. This wasn't part of their agreed narrative.

"How unconventional," Lady Bancroft sniffed. "Though I suppose some men enjoy being challenged. My late husband preferred a more traditional arrangement."

"Different strokes," Hereford murmured, his hand finding Amelia's waist again as he guided her away. Once they were out of earshot, he leaned close to whisper, "Sorry about the deviation from our script. I couldn't resist."

"You're enjoying this far too much," she accused, though

without real heat.

"Immensely," he repeated with a wink. "Though I meant what I said about your intelligence."

Before she could formulate a response, a voice called out to Hereford. "Charles! Come settle a debate about that horse you purchased at Tattersalls."

"Duty calls," he said with a dramatic sigh. "Will you be all right for a moment?"

"I'm not a child at her first dance," Amelia replied. "Go discuss your horses. I'll survive."

She watched him move across the room, noting how different groups seemed to brighten as he joined them. For all his rakish reputation, Charles possessed an undeniable charm that drew people to him. She found herself wondering how much of it was genuine and how much was calculated performance.

"Well, well. The mysterious new Lady Hereford."

Amelia turned to find an elderly woman regarding her through a gold-rimmed quizzing glass. The infamous Aunt Gertrude, she presumed, recognizing the family resemblance to her niece, the dowager.

"Lady Beecham," Amelia curtseyed. "A pleasure to make your acquaintance."

"Hmph." The old woman circled her like a military inspector. "You're not what I expected. Charles usually favors more ornamental women."

"Perhaps he decided substance was a welcome change."

Aunt Gertrude cackled. "Oh, you've got spine! Good. You may call me Aunt Gertrude since you don't look like you'd collapse under the weight of the Hereford name." She lowered her voice conspiratorially. "The last three generations of Hereford marriages were disasters. Beautiful, empty-headed girls who couldn't manage more than producing the requisite heir before retreating to their country estates with various nervous ailments."

"I assure you, my lady, I don't suffer from nerves."

"Evidently not. Though I hear you suffer from other physical challenges." Her gaze dropped pointedly to Amelia's left leg.

Amelia felt her spine stiffen. "I manage quite well, thank you."

"Yes, I can see that." The old woman's eyes were sharp with intelligence. "Though I wonder if you'll manage the more intimate aspects of marriage equally well? The Hereford men have always been rather... vigorous in their appetites."

Heat flooded Amelia's face. "I don't believe that's an appropriate—"

"Aunt Gertrude," the dowager marchioness interrupted, materializing beside them. "I see you've met my new daughter-in-law."

"Indeed." The old woman's expression remained calculating. "I was just inquiring about her fitness for her new role. Particularly given her age and impediment."

To Amelia's astonishment, the dowager's expression hardened. "Amelia's leg is hardly relevant to her capabilities as a marchioness. Her background is concerning enough without drawing attention to physical matters."

"Yet one must consider the succession," Aunt Gertrude persisted. "Can she bear healthy children with such a condition?"

"My condition affects only my mobility, not my reproductive capabilities," Amelia cut in, her voice cool despite the humiliation burning in her chest. "Though I fail to see how my personal medical details are appropriate for a discussion."

"Well said, my dear." The dowager's voice carried surprising approval. "Really, Aunt Gertrude, such questions are both vulgar and unnecessary. Besides, Charles seems quite enamored. I doubt he's given a moment's thought to such practical considerations."

Aunt Gertrude sniffed. "In my day, practical considerations were paramount in marriage. Not like these modern love matches."

"Indeed. Times change," the dowager replied with finality. "Now, I believe dinner is about to be announced."

As the old woman moved away, the dowager turned to Amelia with an expression that hovered between resignation and grudging respect. "You handled that remarkably well. Aunt Gertrude has terrorized this family for decades."

"Thank you for your intervention," Amelia said, still stunned by the sudden alliance.

The dowager's lips thinned. "While I may have reservations about your suitability, you are now a Hereford. The Hereford family matters are not for our kinsmen to dissect." Her voice softened marginally. "Besides, Charles would be furious if he heard anyone questioning your capabilities in such a manner."

While Amelia was pondering the dowager's statement, the dinner announcement rang out. As couples began to form the procession into the dining room, she found herself momentarily adrift. Hereford was nowhere in sight, and she hesitated, uncertain of the proper protocol.

"My lady." His voice came from behind her, warm and reassuring. "May I escort you?"

She turned to find him offering his arm, his expression softer than she'd seen it before. "Thank you," she said quietly, grateful for his timely appearance.

As they took their places in the procession, he bent his head to murmur, "I saw Aunt Gertrude cornering you. Are you all right?"

"Yes, though your mother came to my rescue, strangely enough."

Surprise flickered across his features. "Did she? Wonders never cease." His hand covered hers where it rested on his arm. "What did Aunt Gertrude say that required rescue?"

Amelia hesitated. "She questioned whether my... leg... would affect my ability to bear children."

Hereford's expression darkened dangerously. "That interfering old—"

"No matter," she interrupted quickly. "Your mother put her in her place quite effectively."

His jaw remained tight. "I should have been there."

"You can't protect me from every unpleasant conversation, Charles."

"I can certainly try," he muttered, then seemed to catch himself. "Though I imagine you're perfectly capable of handling most situations."

"Most," she agreed with a small smile. "Though I appreciate the sentiment."

Their eyes met, and something shifted in the air between them—a moment of genuine connection amid the performance they'd been maintaining for the evening.

The moment shattered as they were ushered to their seats at the long dining table. Amelia found herself between an elderly duke who seemed half-asleep and a young viscount who spent the first course staring openly at her décolletage.

"So, Lady Hereford," the viscount finally managed, dragging his gaze to her face with visible effort. "Everyone's dying to know how you managed to tame the notorious marquess."

"Tame?" Amelia echoed, taking a sip of wine. "I wasn't aware my husband required taming."

"Oh, come now," the young man chuckled. "Hereford's reputation is legendary."

"I find gossip tedious," Amelia interrupted, her tone frosty. "Perhaps we could discuss something of substance? Do you perchance have interests in railway development?"

The viscount looked taken aback. "Railways? Good God, no. Leave that to the merchants." He lowered his voice to a confidential whisper. "Though between us, was it his prowess—"

"Lord Dorset," Hereford's voice cut through the conversation from across the table, his tone pleasant but his eyes dangerously cold. "I believe you're discussing matters inappropriate for mixed company."

The viscount flushed. "Just making conversation with your charming bride, Lord Hereford."

"Find another topic," Hereford said sharply, his smile not

reaching his eyes. "My wife's scholarly work, perhaps. Her latest editorial on parliamentary reform was particularly incisive."

"Parliamentary reform?" Dorset looked as if Hereford had suggested discussing sheep farming. "I hadn't realized Lady Hereford was politically inclined."

"Among her many talents," Hereford replied, his gaze softening as it met Amelia's. "Though her most remarkable quality is her ability to see through pretense. It's quite uncanny."

Dorset shifted uncomfortably. "Indeed? How… unusual."

The rest of dinner passed more pleasantly as conversation turned to safer topics. Amelia found herself watching Hereford when he wasn't looking—the easy grace with which he navigated social waters, the genuine interest he showed in others' conversations, the way his laugh transformed his face from merely handsome to truly striking.

After dinner, as the men prepared to retire for port while the ladies withdrew to the drawing room, Hereford caught her elbow.

"I'll join the gentlemen briefly, then make our excuses," he murmured. "Unless you're enjoying yourself?"

"I've endured worse evenings," she replied, no longer surprised by the consideration. "Though I wouldn't object to an early departure."

His smile was conspiratorial. "Give me half an hour."

True to his word, Hereford appeared in the drawing room shortly after, smoothly inserting himself into the conversation around Amelia.

"I apologize, ladies, but I must steal my wife away," he announced with practiced charm. "We have an early engagement tomorrow."

As they made their farewells, the dowager marchioness drew Amelia aside. "You conducted yourself well tonight," she said, her tone reluctantly approving. "Though that gown really is too daring for a woman of your position."

"Thank you for your concern," Amelia replied evenly. "And

for your intervention with Lady Beecham earlier."

"Yes, well. Family matters should remain private." The older woman hesitated, then added more quietly, "Charles seems different with you."

"Different how?"

"More focused. Less frivolous," the dowager said after consideration. "More like his father in his better days." Her expression softened fractionally. "It suits him."

Before Amelia could respond to this revelation, Hereford appeared at her side. "Mother, we really must be going. I'm sure we'll see you soon."

The dowager reached up to straighten his cravat, the gesture maternal. "Mind you take care of your wife, Charles. She handled Gertrude admirably, but these gatherings can be exhausting for those unaccustomed to them."

Despite the look of surprise, Hereford said nothing and only kissed his mother farewell.

In the carriage ride home, a comfortable silence settled between them—unexpected after the tension of the evening.

"Thank you," Amelia said finally. "For extracting us at a reasonable hour."

"My pleasure." Hereford leaned back against the cushions, looking more relaxed than she'd seen him all evening. "You were magnificent, you know. Even Aunt Gertrude seemed impressed, and she once reduced a visiting ambassador to tears over dinner."

Amelia smiled despite herself. "Your family is formidable."

"They're dragons, the lot of them," he corrected with a chuckle. "Though Mother seemed almost approving of you by the end."

"I'm still bewildered by your mother defending me against Lady Beecham."

Hereford's expression softened. "Despite her many faults, Mother understands dignity. She wouldn't tolerate anyone questioning a Hereford publicly—even one she hasn't fully accepted yet."

"Is that what I am now? A Hereford?" The question slipped out before she could stop it.

In the dim light of the carriage lanterns, his gaze met hers with surprising intensity. "Yes," he said simply. "Whether either of us planned it or not."

Something warm unfurled in Amelia's chest at the quiet certainty in his voice. This evening had revealed aspects of Charles she hadn't anticipated—his protectiveness, his attentiveness, the careful way he'd shielded her from the worst of Society's scrutiny.

As the carriage rolled toward home, she found herself wondering how many other facets of the marquess remained to be discovered beneath his carefully cultivated facade. And more disturbingly, why the prospect of discovering them suddenly seemed so appealing.

STEADY ON, OLD BOY

HEREFORD WAS REVIEWING his notes before the railway investors' meeting when a burst of masculine laughter drew his attention to the entrance. He looked up to find his wife—his *wife*—surrounded by a cluster of journalists, all hanging on her every word as if she were delivering the gospel itself.

He hadn't expected her here. She'd made it abundantly clear their professional lives were to remain separate, yet there she stood, perfectly at ease among London's leading newspapermen. Her hair was coming loose from its pins—she must have walked rather than taken the carriage—and her cheeks were flushed with animation as she debated something with James Mitchell from the *Times*.

Mitchell was standing entirely too close.

"The railway commission's report clearly indicates—" Amelia was saying, gesturing with her notebook in a way that made Mitchell lean in unnecessarily.

"Brilliant analysis as always, Miss Th—" Mitchell caught himself. "Lady Hereford."

The correction drew Hereford's attention to how the other men had adjusted to her new status. Some seemed unsure whether to treat her as a peer or a marchioness. Others—like Mitchell—appeared determined to maintain their previous familiarity. One fellow had actually placed his hand on her elbow to draw her attention to something in his notes.

The crystal goblet in Hereford's hand creaked ominously.

"Steady on, old boy," Lancaster murmured beside him. "Your wife's reputation among the press is beyond reproach."

"I'm not concerned about her reputation," Hereford said coolly, though he couldn't quite drag his gaze away from where Dowson—wasn't the man married?—was now showing Amelia something in his portfolio, standing close enough that she had to tilt her head back to meet his eyes.

She'd never looked at *him* with such open interest.

"The factory safety regulations—" Blake was saying, and Hereford felt his stomach tighten. But Amelia was already turning away, her attention caught by another colleague.

She moved through the crowd of men with surprising grace despite the limp, her natural authority evident in how they deferred to her opinions, included her in their professional discourse. This was a side of his wife he'd never seen—confident, respected, completely in her element.

It was damnably attractive.

"Lady Hereford seems to have quite the following," observed Carlisle, materializing at Hereford's elbow. "One might almost forget she's a woman at all."

Hereford's fingers tightened on his glass. "I assure you, Carlisle, no one who looks at my wife could forget she's a woman."

Carlisle's eyebrows rose at his tone, shifting his attention when the meeting was called to order. Hereford watched as the journalists settled into their designated area, noting how Mitchell and Blake both maneuvered to sit near Amelia. She pulled out her notebook, all business now, but he caught the small smile she gave Mitchell when he passed her a spare pencil.

Had she smiled at *him* like that? He couldn't recall.

The meeting proceeded, but Hereford found his attention divided between the railway proposals and the press section. He noticed how Amelia paused writing to massage her fingers— something he'd observed during their marriage negotiations but hadn't thought significant at the time. Without seeming to think about it, Mitchell steadied her inkwell before it could spill. The casual intimacy of the gesture made something hot and unfamiliar curl in Hereford's chest.

These men knew his wife's habits, her methods, her small struggles. They anticipated her needs with the ease of long familiarity while he, her own husband, was still learning how she took her tea.

When Blake leaned over to whisper something that made Amelia press her lips together to suppress a smile, Hereford nearly stood up. Only years of social training kept him in his seat, maintained his expression of aristocratic boredom. But beneath that careful facade, something primitive growled at the sight of another man making his wife smile.

Not your wife, he reminded himself harshly. *Not really.*

Yet as the meeting drew to a close, he found himself moving toward her before he could stop himself. She was gathering her things, still deep in discussion with Mitchell about some point of railway policy.

"My lady," he said smoothly, noting how the other journalists straightened at his approach. "I trust you found the proceedings illuminating?"

She looked up, surprise flickering across her features before her professional mask slipped into place. "Quite, my lord. Though I have some questions about the proposed safety measures—"

"Perhaps we could discuss them over dinner tonight?" The invitation escaped before he could consider their prearranged schedule.

Now she was definitely staring at him. "I... have a deadline to meet."

"Of course." He kept his tone casual, though something in him bristled at her refusal. "Another time, perhaps."

Mitchell was watching this exchange with entirely too much interest. Hereford felt a perverse need to demonstrate... something. Without allowing himself to examine his motives too closely, he reached out and tucked a loose strand of hair behind her ear.

The gesture was proprietary, intimate, completely unlike their careful interactions thus far. He felt her sharp intake of breath, saw the color rise in her cheeks. Around them, the journalists suddenly found other places to be.

"Your hair was coming loose," he said softly, letting his fingers brush her cheek as he withdrew his hand.

For a moment, they stared at each other. Something sparked in the air between them—awareness, possibility, danger.

Then she stepped back, clutching her notebook like a shield. "Good day, my lord."

He watched her leave with her colleagues, noting how they maintained a more respectful distance now. The satisfaction he felt at this was ludicrous.

"Merely a business arrangement, eh?" Lancaster's amused voice broke into his thoughts.

Hereford didn't bother responding. He was too busy watching his wife disappear into a hackney with James Mitchell, discussing God knows what about railway safety regulations.

He was going to need a large brandy.

IN THE HACKNEY, Amelia's hands trembled slightly as she folded them on her lap, though whether from anger or something else entirely, she couldn't quite say. The memory of Hereford's fingers brushing her cheek lingered like a brand, his touch far more intimate than their careful arrangement warranted. She could still feel the weight of every journalist's stare, the sudden shift in their demeanor after that calculated display of possession.

"Insufferable man," she muttered, nearly dropping her inkwell. James Mitchell caught it before it could spill, his familiar efficiency now tinged with an awkwardness that hadn't existed before Hereford's intervention.

Mitchell attempted to resume their discussion about the railway safety regulations, but the easy flow of their usual debates was gone. Every time she leaned forward to make a point, she caught him glancing at where Hereford had touched her hair, as if expecting her husband to materialize and stake his claim again.

"James." She sighed, forcing herself to meet his eyes. "I'm still the same person who argued with you about printer's ink last week. The title doesn't change that."

But it had changed something. She could see it in how her colleague carefully maintained his distance now, how their easy camaraderie had been replaced by careful deference. One touch, one possessive gesture from her husband, and years of professional respect had been overshadowed by her new social position.

"This is precisely why I wanted to keep our lives separate," she said suddenly, cutting through Mitchell's careful analysis of the proposed safety measures.

"My lady?"

"Nothing." She turned to stare out the window, her reflection wavering in the glass. The loose strand of hair that had prompted Hereford's display still refused to stay in place. She resisted the urge to touch it, to trace the path his fingers had taken.

What game was he playing? She was a means to an end. Yet the way he'd touched her, the casual intimacy of the gesture... it had felt like a display of possession. For a moment, she'd caught something in his eyes that looked almost like—

"No," she whispered to herself. She would not read meaning into simple actions. Hereford was protecting his investment. Making it clear to Society that despite their unusual arrangement, she was still his wife. Still his property.

The thought should have angered her. Instead, she found herself remembering the warmth of his fingers against her skin, the subtle spice of his cologne as he'd leaned close. How his eyes looked almost molten as he'd staked his claim before all of London's press.

"The *Review* offices, my lady?" Mitchell's question startled her from her thoughts.

"Yes, of course." She straightened her spine, forcing her mind back to work. She had an article to write, deadlines to meet. She would not waste time analyzing her husband's contradictions.

Even if he was apparently reading her editorials "religiously." Even if he'd defended her work while simultaneously mocking it. Even if the memory of his touch made her skin prickle with awareness hours later.

THE TRIGGER FOR ACTION

AMELIA SAT AT her desk in the *Review's* offices, poring over the railway commission's safety reports. The investors' meeting had unsettled her more than she cared to admit—not just Hereford's unexpected possessiveness, but the undercurrent of tension whenever factory regulations were mentioned.

The report before her detailed a recent factory collapse in Manchester. Fifteen dead, dozens maimed. All because corners had been cut on basic structural requirements.

"Miss… Forgive me. Lady Hereford?" A hesitant voice broke her concentration.

She looked up to find Freddy, one of their errand boys, shifting nervously in her doorway. "Yes, Freddy?"

"There's someone asking to see you. Says it's urgent." He lowered his voice. "Looks like a factory girl, ma'am. Her hand's all bandaged up."

Amelia felt something cold settle in her stomach. "Send her in, please."

The girl couldn't have been more than twelve. Thin face, work-worn hands, one wrapped in dirty bandages that couldn't quite hide the dark stains beneath. She clutched her injured hand to her chest, tears streaming down her face as she fought to hold herself together.

"They said you might help," the girl said, her voice breaking. "At the factory. Said you write about people like us."

"Which factory?" Amelia asked, though a sick certainty was already forming.

"Crown Street Textiles," the girl whimpered.

The location stunned Amelia into silence. Thirteen years had passed since she'd set foot in that place. Her leg began to throb with memory.

"What happened to your hand?" Amelia asked, forcing her voice to remain steady.

"Got caught in the new looms," the girl explained between ragged breaths. "Foreman said it was my fault for not being careful. Doctor wants to take three fingers, says they're beyond saving. But if he does, I can't work, and my family…"

She couldn't finish as pain overwhelmed her again.

"What's your name?" Amelia asked softly.

"Mary Collins."

"Mary." Amelia rose immediately, reaching for her cloak. "We're going to see a proper doctor right now."

"But Miss, I can't afford—"

"I will take care of everything." Amelia guided the girl toward the door. "Thompson, cancel my appointments. I'll return when I can."

An hour later, with Mary's hand properly treated by a competent surgeon who believed all three fingers could be saved, Amelia helped the exhausted girl back into the hackney. She pressed several banknotes into Mary's uninjured hand along with a notecard bearing another address.

"This is where you can find temporary work while you heal. Tell the Duchess of Lancaster I sent you."

After returning to her office, Amelia sat motionless, staring at the factory report without seeing it. Her wooden leg seemed to weigh heavier than usual, a physical reminder of what she'd lost. What had been taken from her.

After all these years, nothing had changed. The same dangerous conditions, the same callous disregard for lives treated as mere currency. She'd channeled her pain into advocating for reform, believing her words might eventually make a difference. But seeing Mary—a mirror of her younger self—made her realize the futility of mere words against men willing to sacrifice lives for coins.

With sudden clarity, Amelia knew what she needed to do. She needed to face the demon that had haunted her nightmares for a decade.

Standing with deliberate purpose, she gathered her notes and called for a hackney. It was time to revisit the past. Not as a victim, but as someone with the power to ensure there would be no more Mary Collinses.

THE FACTORY LOOMED against the graying sky, its brick walls stained black from years of soot. Amelia sat in the hired hackney across the street, her wooden leg propped carefully on the opposite seat. She hadn't returned since that day, had deliberately taken alternate routes to avoid even glimpsing the building that had altered the course of her life.

"Sure you wouldn't rather go home, m'lady?" the driver asked, clearly uncomfortable with keeping a lady waiting in this part of London.

"Wait," she said softly, her eyes fixed on the factory door.

Workers trickled out as the sun set—women with worn shawls and tired eyes, children who looked far older than their years. A young girl limped past the hackney, favoring her left leg. How many others had been maimed here? How many lives had been casually altered by some man's arithmetic of human worth?

Hours passed. Finally, a private carriage pulled up to the factory's side entrance. Peter Moore emerged from the building, looking official in a suit. Years of journalistic experience had taught her not to dismiss any opportunities.

"Follow that carriage," she ordered. "Discreetly."

They wound through London's darkening streets until the carriage stopped before a small townhouse. Amelia watched Moore disappear inside without a backward glance, unaware of the eyes that followed him.

"Where to now, m'lady?" the driver asked quietly.

"Home," she said finally, the word tasting bitter on her tongue. "The Hereford townhouse."

As the hackney turned toward home, she asked herself what she'd hoped to accomplish tonight. Perhaps she'd simply needed to give her demons a name, a shape.

In her chambers, she sat before her mirror and slowly unpinned her hair. The face that looked back at her was neither the girl who'd once worked in that factory nor the hardened newspaper editor she'd become. A woman with shadows in her eyes and steel in her spine, who now knew exactly where to find her demons.

Hereford barely registered the soft knock before Barker entered, carrying a pressed shirt and tomorrow's selected waistcoat. The valet moved efficiently about the chamber, hanging garments and collecting discarded items without comment.

"My lord," Barker said mildly as he retrieved a carelessly dropped cufflink from beneath the escritoire, "might I observe that you've worn quite a groove in the carpet this evening?"

Hereford paused mid-stride. "I was merely… thinking."

"Indeed." Barker moved to the washstand, replacing used towels with fresh ones. "Though your thinking appears to have increased considerably since Her Ladyship began these evening excursions." He glanced meaningfully at the connecting door. "One might almost mistake it for concern."

"Don't be ridiculous," Hereford muttered, resuming his restless movement.

Barker said nothing as he laid out tomorrow's small clothes, though he did pause to straighten a picture frame that had been jarred askew during one of Hereford's more vigorous turns.

"Barker," Hereford said suddenly, "in your experience, how does one… that is, what would you recommend when…"

"When one has developed inconvenient feelings for one's temporary wife?" Barker supplied helpfully, not looking up from brushing lint from a coat sleeve.

"I haven't—" Hereford began hotly.

"Of course not, my lord." Barker moved toward the door with an armload of laundry, then paused at the threshold. "If I may be so bold, my lord—the sooner a gentleman acknowledges what's perfectly obvious to his household staff, the sooner he might actually enjoy his marriage. Rather than wearing holes in expensive carpeting."

With that, Barker disappeared into the corridor, leaving Hereford staring after him.

The sound of Amelia's chamber door opening made Hereford's head snap toward the connecting door. Relief flooded through him so powerfully it left him momentarily lightheaded, only to be immediately replaced by a surge of anger.

His hand rose to the door handle for the tenth time that hour. He had every right to demand answers. He was her husband, damn it all. Even if she had no respect for him. Even if their marriage was a sham. She couldn't just disappear into London's dangerous streets doing… No, he couldn't entertain the idea. It would drive him mad with worry.

Before he could lose his nerve, he rapped sharply on the connecting door.

"Enter," came her voice.

He found her at her dressing table, still fully clothed in her day dress, removing pins from her hair. In the lamplight, she looked pale and tired. The sight of her, safe and whole, made his chest tighten with an emotion he wasn't prepared to examine.

"You're quite late," he said without preamble, his voice more severe than intended.

"I wasn't aware I needed to report my schedule to you." She didn't meet his eyes in the mirror, and that evasion sent irritation spiking through him.

"A simple message would have sufficed. I was concerned." The word felt inadequate for the bone-deep fear that had gripped him, the images of her hurt or worse that had tortured him for hours.

She turned to face him, her expression cool, and he felt the familiar frustration at her ability to mask her emotions so completely. "Concerned or simply practicing for your next public display of ownership?"

Heat flooded his face with anger.

"That little performance at the investors' meeting. Touching my hair, marking your territory like some rutting stag." Her voice was sharp with accusation, and the unrefined comparison added to his temperature. "Did you enjoy the way every man there suddenly remembered I was property?"

"It's my right as your husband." He stepped closer, his hands clenching at his sides as frustration built like steam in a kettle. "Especially when other men seem unaware of it."

"They're not 'other men'," she said bitterly. "They're my colleagues with whom I've worked hard to gain respect for my work."

"Those men." His voice dropped dangerously low, jealousy burning through him like acid. The memory of Mitchell's hand on her arm, Blake's proximity as he whispered in her ear, made his vision tinge red. "Mitchell with his hands constantly on your arm. Blake standing close enough to breathe down your neck. They don't just respect your work, Amelia."

"Don't be ridiculous."

"Ridiculous?" He moved closer still, backing her against the dressing table, his body thrumming with the need to touch her, to claim her, to erase every other man's touch from her memory.

"I've seen how they look at you. How they find excuses to touch you, to lean close, to whisper in your ear."

The heat of her body so close to his was intoxicating, her scent filling his senses and making his head swim with want.

"They're friends. Colleagues."

"They're men." His hands braced on either side of her, trapping her between his arms, and he could feel the rapid rise and fall of her chest, could see her pupils dilating despite her protests. "And they want what's mine."

"I'm not yours," she whispered, but her breathing had quickened, and he saw the way arousal began to bloom beneath her defiance.

"Aren't you?" His voice was rough with possession, with the fear that had clawed at him all evening. The thought of losing her, of her choosing another, made something desperate and wild unfurl in his chest. "Then where were you tonight, Wife? Who were you with that you couldn't send word?"

"I was working—"

"Liar." He was close enough now to feel the heat radiating from her skin. The need to touch her, to prove she was real and safe and here, overwhelmed every rational thought. "You left the office hours ago."

Her lips parted, but before she could speak, his mouth crashed down on hers. The kiss was hungry, desperate, born of hours of worry and jealousy and need so acute it felt like starvation finally being fed. She stiffened for a moment—one terrible heartbeat where he thought she might push him away—then melted against him with a soft moan that shot arousal straight to his groin.

The taste of her exploded across his senses—wine and something sweet, something uniquely Amelia that he knew he'd crave for the rest of his life. His hands tangled in her hair, scattering the remaining pins with a chime as they hit the floor, the silky strands sliding through his fingers like liquid copper.

"Where were you?" he murmured against her lips, his voice

hoarse with need and fear and desire.

"Charles…" Her hands fisted in his shirt, pulling him closer even as she tried to speak, and the gesture sent heat spiraling through him.

"Tell me." His mouth moved to her throat, finding that sensitive spot just below her ear that made her gasp and arch against him. She trembled against his lips, her pulse matching the rhythm of his own racing heart. "Tell me you weren't with another man."

"I wasn't—" The words died as his hand slid down her body, gathering her skirts with desperation, the need to touch her, to feel her respond to him, overriding every other thought.

His fingers found the heat between her thighs through her drawers, and the discovery that the thin fabric was soaked made him groan against her neck. "So wet already," he growled, his voice rough with wonder and possession. "Is this for me, or for whoever kept you out so late?"

"You," she gasped, her head falling back as he stroked her, her body taut against his like a bowstring ready to snap. "Only you."

The words sent triumph surging through him, primal and fierce. "Prove it." His fingers found the opening in her drawers, sliding against her slick flesh, and the feel of her—hot and wet and wanting—nearly brought him to his knees. "Come for me, Amelia. Let me feel you fall apart in my hands."

She bit her lip to stifle her moans as he worked her with skilled fingers, and the sight of her trying to maintain control even as pleasure overtook her was the most erotic thing he'd ever witnessed. Her inner walls clenched around his fingers as he slipped them inside her, tight and perfect, while his thumb circled that sensitive bundle of nerves until she was shaking against him like a leaf in a storm.

The feel of her responding to his touch, the way her body opened for him, welcomed him, made something fierce and alive roar to life in his chest. This was his wife, his Amelia, clinging to him, and the knowledge was more intoxicating than any wine.

"That's it," he whispered, his thumb pressing against her

most sensitive spot while his fingers worked inside her, feeling every flutter, every clench, every sign of her approaching climax. "Let go for me, Wife."

She shattered with a cry she couldn't quite muffle, her body convulsing around his fingers as waves of pleasure crashed over her. The feel of her release, the way she pulsed around him, the broken sound of his name on her lips, sent such a surge of satisfaction through him that his own body ached with need. He held her through it, his mouth claiming hers again to swallow her gasps, tasting her pleasure on her lips.

When the tremors finally subsided, she slumped back against the dressing table, her face flushed, her breathing uneven, looking thoroughly debauched and utterly beautiful. He withdrew his hand slowly, bringing his fingers to his lips to taste her essence, and the flavor—sweet and musky—made him want to fall to his knees and worship her properly.

"Mine," he said quietly, his eyes burning into hers, the word torn from somewhere deep in his chest. "Whatever game you're playing, wherever you've been—remember that you're mine."

He left her there, trembling and undone, the taste of her still on his lips and the knowledge that he was lost to her completely burning in his chest like a brand. The careful distance he'd maintained, the rational approach to their arrangement—all of it had crumbled the moment he'd felt her respond to his touch. She was under his skin now, in his blood, and he had no idea how he was supposed to let her go.

No One Needs to Know

"Good morning," Hereford said over his coffee the next morning when Amelia joined him, not quite meeting his gaze. "I trust you slept well?"

Amelia sat across from him and immediately picked up a toast. "Yes, thank you. And you?"

He carefully buttered his own toast. "I did not, thanks to your late-night activities. London can be dangerous after dark. I was busy pondering providing you with a protection officer. Someone discreet."

"No thank you to the protection officer. I spent enough time being afraid after my accident. Jumping at shadows, flinching at every loud noise. I refuse to live that way again."

"This isn't about fear," he said, leaning back. "You're a wealthy woman now. There are practical considerations."

"Teach me to fence."

The words hung between them. Hereford slowed his chewing. "We've already discussed this."

Amelia studied his face as he tried to tamp his frustration. "I'm asking you again. You're supposedly one of the finest swordsmen in London. Why won't you even try to teach me?"

"I've told you before. No." He picked up his coffee cup. "I can provide you with any protection you require—"

"I don't want your protection. I want the skills to protect myself."

He put down his cup with more force than necessary. "It's impractical for your injury. Should you be involved in a confrontation, you'll lose. Men are stronger, faster, and have likely been wielding the sword since childhood. Your false confidence after a few lessons will be more dangerous than not knowing anything at all."

"You underestimate me as everyone does. Teach me unless you're too busy with the Duchess of Rutland."

His jaw tightened as he stood.

"Why do you persist in thinking the worst of me? Have I given you any reason, any at all, to doubt my fidelity since our marriage?"

"Your reputation—"

"Damn my reputation!" His hands flew up as he paced the length of the table. "You know nothing about me beyond Society gossip and your own prejudices. You've decided I'm some sort of rakehell who cares nothing for honor or duty, and no evidence to the contrary seems to sway your opinion."

"My lord—"

"Perhaps I should live up to your expectations," he cut in, his voice dangerously soft. "Since you're determined to believe the worst, I might as well enjoy the benefits of such a reputation."

"That would only prove my point," she said, lifting her chin.

"Would it?" He whirled to face her. "Or would it simply make it easier for you to run to Norwich? Or one of your fellow journalists."

For a moment, they stared at each other, the air between them crackling with something that wasn't quite anger. Then Hereford straightened abruptly.

"Perhaps," he said, his voice dropping lower, "we should discuss the real issue. Why maintain this pretense of propriety when we could simply consummate our marriage? No one needs to know if you still wish to leave after the year."

Amelia's hands trembled slightly as she placed her cup in its saucer. "If I recall correctly, my lord, you were the one who insisted on ending this marriage after a year."

"That was before I knew you'd think the worst of me. If I'm bedding you, at least you won't wonder if I'm bedding someone else."

"And what happens when I'm with child and you've found a new widow to warm your sheets?"

"Confound it, Amelia! You're my wife! I'd take care of you!"

"Beyond the one year?"

His expression hardened. "The one-year stipulation was for both of our sakes as you've made your opinion of my character quite clear. I don't want to watch you suffer unnecessarily. However, it's not a requirement."

"All I want from you is fencing lessons."

Something dangerous lurked in his chest. He bit out, "Seven tonight at Swordsman's Society. This is for a trial, to determine whether you can learn to fence without jeopardizing your safety. Or mine. Don't be late."

He strode from the room without a backward glance, leaving Amelia to stare after him.

Hereford stalked into his bedchamber but almost retreated upon seeing his valet. He didn't fancy receiving Barker's tongue lashing in that dry way of his. He stood his ground, however. What kind of master would he be if he feared his servants?

"My lord," Barker moved with his usual unflappable calm despite the obvious tension radiating from his employer. "You seem rather... animated after your discussion with her ladyship."

"Animated," Hereford repeated flatly. "Yes, that's one word for it."

"Indeed." Barker disappeared into the dressing room and emerged with a fresh shirt. "I confess, I was somewhat startled by the volume of your... agreement to her ladyship's request."

Hereford shot him a dark look. "I suppose you heard everything."

"Merely the general theme, my lord. Something about fencing lessons and jeopardized safety." Barker spread the shirt perfectly on the bed. "I shall have your fencing attire prepared. The white kit, I assume? Or perhaps the black would better suit your current disposition."

"This is madness, Barker. She could be seriously injured."

"Quite possibly, my lord." Barker straightened his back. "Though I suspect the greater danger lies in underestimating her determination. In my experience, such ladies tend to find alternative methods regardless, often more perilous than the original proposal."

Hereford paused in his pacing. "Meaning?"

"Merely that her ladyship might seek… less qualified instruction elsewhere." Barker's tone remained mild. "I believe there are several establishments in Whitechapel that offer such services. Considerably less reputable than the Swordsman's Society, naturally."

The thought of Amelia in some back-alley fencing den made Hereford's blood run cold. "Point taken."

"I thought you might see the wisdom in it, my lord." Barker moved toward the dressing room, then paused. "If I may suggest—perhaps approach this as you would training a spirited horse? Firm guidance, patience, and the occasional reward for good behavior."

"Did you just compare my wife to a horse?"

"A particularly fine one, my lord. Superior intelligence, tenacity, and an unfortunate tendency toward independence." Barker's expression remained perfectly serious. "The sort that requires a skilled hand rather than a heavy one."

THE SMALL PRACTICE room at the Swordsman's Society felt even more confined as Hereford handed her the practice clothes. "It's not equipped for female students," he explained, positioning himself before the door. "You'll have to change here."

Amelia stared at the men's trousers with sudden apprehension. She hadn't considered this part—the close-fitting garment would make her prosthetic obvious. "Turn around," she commanded, though anxiety made her voice sharper than intended.

He obeyed, facing the door, and she quickly changed, keeping her thick stockings on beneath the trousers. The fabric pulled oddly around her wooden leg, but perhaps in the dim light...

"The protective gear goes on over your clothes," he said, his voice carefully neutral. "Let me know when you're decent."

"I'm ready." She tugged self-consciously at the trousers, trying to arrange them to disguise the unnatural line of her leg.

His eyes flickered briefly to her left leg when he turned, but his expression remained impassive as he helped her into the padded jacket. His fingers were gentle as he adjusted the straps, his proximity making her heart race for reasons that had nothing to do with anxiety.

The real challenge began with the basic stance. The *en garde* position required both knees to bend slightly, both ankles to flex. Her wooden prosthetic refused to cooperate, remaining rigid and unyielding.

"Like this?" she asked, struggling to maintain her balance as she attempted to mirror his stance.

She saw the moment he truly noticed, saw his eyes narrow as he observed her left leg's complete inability to bend at the ankle.

"You're favoring your right side," he said carefully, moving to support her elbow. "Try to distribute your weight more evenly."

She gritted her teeth and tried to shift her weight, but the prosthetic fought against every movement. She wobbled, and his hand shot out to steady her waist, the touch far more intimate than she'd anticipated.

"Perhaps we should modify the traditional stance," he suggested, his voice gentler than she'd ever heard it. "Find what works best for your particular..."

"I can do it," she interrupted, heat flooding her cheeks. She didn't want his pity, didn't want him to treat her as fragile.

"My lady." His hand remained at her waist, warm and steady. "There's no shame in adapting technique. Every swordsman must work with their own physical realities."

She met his eyes, searching for mockery or pity, but found only professional assessment. "You're not going to ask?"

"About the extent of your injury?" His thumb moved slightly against her waist, an unconscious gesture that sent shivers down her spine. "No. You'll tell me what I need to know to teach you effectively."

Relief warred with something else. Something that felt dangerously like attraction. This wasn't the rakish lord who flirted with duchesses. This was someone else entirely—patient, observant, astonishingly kind.

"The ankle doesn't bend," she admitted finally. "It's... rigid."

He nodded, processing this information. "Then we adjust. Here..." He shifted his grip to her hands, repositioning her. "Weight more on your right foot, left leg slightly back. Don't fight against the rigidity—work with it."

They spent the next hour finding adaptations that worked with her body rather than against it. Each adjustment required his touch, his proximity. By the end, Amelia wasn't sure what made her more breathless—the physical exertion or the gentle authority in his hands as he guided her through modified forms.

"Enough for today," he said finally, his voice rougher than usual. His hands lingered at her waist as he steadied her one last time. "You've done well."

She looked up at him, suddenly aware of how close they stood, how his eyes had darkened as he watched her move through the sequences he'd created just for her.

"Same time tomorrow?" she asked, cursing the breathlessness in her voice.

He hesitated. "Are you sure this is wise?"

"No," she admitted. "But I'm going to continue anyway."

Something like admiration flickered across his features. Then his eyes dropped to her left leg, and his expression turned serious. "We'll need to make some modifications to your practice clothes. The current cut of the trousers isn't..." He cleared his throat. "I'll have something more suitable made."

She stiffened, pride warring with practicality. "I don't need—"

"Proper equipment is essential," he cut in smoothly. "For any student."

They stared at each other for a long moment, the air between them charged with everything unsaid. Finally, she nodded. "Thank you."

He stepped back, creating distance between them. "I have a prior engagement this evening. Perhaps I will see you at breakfast. Otherwise, seven tomorrow." He paused at the door. "And leave your corset at home. You need to be able to breathe and move freely."

He was gone before she could respond, leaving her to wonder how this man, this startling version of her husband, could unsettle her so thoroughly with just a few kind words and careful touches.

She wasn't sure which was more dangerous. His previous rakish charm or this new, gentle competence.

THE REVEAL

"A GAIN," HEREFORD COMMANDED the next day, pacing around her with growing frustration. She had not seen him following their lesson or at breakfast. Had he spent the night elsewhere? She was distracted by her husband's whereabouts and why she couldn't stop wondering.

"The lunge must be fluid. You're hesitating before the forward movement."

Sweat trickled down Amelia's back as she resumed the *en garde* position for what felt like the hundredth time. Her flesh ached where it met the wooden leg, protesting the repeated movements.

"I said again," he snapped when she didn't immediately move. "How do you expect to defend yourself if you can't manage a basic lunge?"

"I'm trying," she gritted out, teeth clenched against both pain and anger.

"Try harder. Your enemies won't wait for you to find your balance."

She bit back a retort and attempted the lunge again. This time something shifted wrong in her prosthetic—the straps loosened by repeated movement, the wood worn smooth with sweat. Her forward momentum carried her past the point of recovery.

She hit the floor hard, but that wasn't what made her blood run cold. The distinctive clatter of wood against wood echoed through the practice room, followed by a shocked silence.

Her prosthetic foot, still in its shoe and stocking, had skittered across the floor to rest at Hereford's feet.

"Dear God," he breathed, staring at it. Then his eyes snapped to her, taking in her incomplete form on the floor, understanding dawning in his expression.

Amelia pushed herself up, face burning, unable to meet his gaze. "Don't…"

But he was already moving, bending to retrieve her prosthetic with careful hands. When she finally forced herself to look at him, she found no disgust in his face. No pity either. Just a kind of wondering comprehension.

"So this is why your balance is so unstable," he said softly. He crossed back to her, kneeling beside her with her prosthetic cradled almost reverently in his hands. "May I help you reattach it?"

She stared at him, thrown by his matter-of-fact response. "I… no. Please turn around. I can manage."

He nodded and turned his back, but his voice remained gentle. "The straps must have worked loose with the repeated movements. We'll need to account for that in future lessons." A pause. "How does it usually attach?"

Amelia's fingers trembled as she worked with the familiar straps and buckles. "Leather straps around my knee. It's… the wood can grow slick with sweat."

"We could line the contact points with felt," he said thoughtfully. "Absorb some of the moisture. And perhaps add a secondary strap above the knee for stability?"

She secured the last buckle, oddly touched by his practical response. "You're not… disturbed?"

He turned back to face her, offering his hand to help her up. "By what? Your determination to learn despite what must be considerable discomfort? Your ability to move so well that I didn't even realize the extent of your injury?" His lips quirked slightly. "Or the fact that you've been hiding a wooden leg in those trousers for two lessons without my noticing?"

A startled laugh escaped her. "When you put it that way…"

"Tell me about the mechanics," he said, still holding her hand. "How much flexibility does it allow? What movements are most difficult? We'll adapt the techniques accordingly."

She studied his face, looking for any sign of the revulsion she'd feared, but found only professional interest and something warmer, almost like admiration.

"Why aren't you angry?" she asked suddenly. "That I kept this from you?"

His expression softened. "My lady, you owe me no explanations about your private matters." He squeezed her hand once before releasing it. "Though as your fencing instructor, I do need to understand your physical capabilities. So, shall we discuss modifications to your equipment?"

Amelia felt something shift between them—some wall crumbling, some trust beginning to build. She nodded slowly. "The ankle is fixed, obviously. And the knee joint…" She gestured to her leg. "Would you like to see how it works?"

"Please." He pulled a bench closer. "Show me everything. We'll design our lessons around your strengths rather than fighting against the prosthetic's limitations."

As she demonstrated the prosthetic's mechanisms, she kept waiting for his professional demeanor to crack, for disgust or pity to show through. But he remained engaged and analytical, asking intelligent questions about pressure points and weight distribution.

"Right then," he said finally, standing. "Shall we try that lunge again? This time with proper adjustments for your equipment?"

She looked up at him, this man who had somehow transformed from a rakish aristocrat into someone else entirely—someone who saw her limitations not as weaknesses to be pitied but as challenges to be solved.

"Yes," she said softly. "Though perhaps with an extra strap

this time?"

His answering smile was warm enough to make her forget, just for a moment, that she was supposed to dislike him.

She was beginning to suspect that nothing about Charles Bartholomew Hereford was quite what it seemed.

HEREFORD SAT IN his study, a glass of brandy untouched before him, turning Amelia's wooden prosthetic over and over in his mind. The moment of its discovery kept replaying. The hollow sound it made hitting the floor, the look of mortification on her face, the way she'd waited for him to recoil in horror.

What kind of life had she led to expect such a reaction? How many times had she seen disgust or pity in others' eyes?

He picked up the brandy, then set it down again without drinking. His initial frustration with her seeming reluctance now filled him with shame. She'd been pushing herself far harder than he'd realized, working against limitations he hadn't even understood.

And yet she'd never complained. Never made excuses. Never asked for special treatment.

"Bloody hell," he muttered, rubbing fatigue from his face. All those Society events where she'd stood for hours. All those times he'd watched her navigate crowded ballrooms and uneven garden paths. He'd known she had some sort of injury, yes, but this...

The memory of her demonstration rose unbidden. Her matter-of-fact explanation of straps and joints, her clever modifications to compensate for the prosthetic's limitations. She'd turned catastrophic injury into an engineering problem to be solved.

He found himself desperately curious about the accident itself. A factory injury, he knew that much. But the details? She guarded them as carefully as she'd guarded the extent of her disability.

His eyes drifted to his desk where several sketches lay half-finished—ideas for improving the straps, for adding stability without sacrificing what little flexibility she had. He'd started envisioning them while she explained the prosthetic's mechanics, his mind already racing ahead to solutions.

"Focus on the practical," he told himself firmly. This wasn't about his growing admiration for her determination, or the strange ache he'd felt watching her brace for his rejection. This was about ensuring his student had proper equipment.

But he couldn't quite forget how her face had transformed when he'd treated her prosthetic as a technical challenge rather than a source of shame. For just a moment, her guard had dropped, revealing something vulnerable and wondering in her expression.

He'd seen Amelia angry, disdainful, coldly professional. He'd seen her match wits with journalists and trade barbs with Society's elite. But he'd never seen her look quite so vulnerable. As if no one had ever simply accepted her exactly as she was.

The thought made something protective stir in his chest. Which was ridiculous, of course. She'd made it abundantly clear she neither wanted nor needed his protection. And this was still just a marriage of convenience with an expiration date.

Even if he was beginning to wonder what else he might have misunderstood about his wife.

"Right," he said aloud, standing abruptly. "Seven tomorrow." He had modifications to design, equipment to procure. He needed to focus on the practical aspects of teaching her to fence, not on the way her rare, genuine smile had made his chest tighten.

But as he moved to his desk to refine his sketches for improved straps, he couldn't quite suppress a different kind of wondering. What else was Amelia hiding beneath that carefully maintained facade of independence? What other surprises lay behind those walls she'd built so high?

For the first time since their marriage, he found himself genuinely looking forward to finding out.

PREY OR PREDATOR?

THE DRUMMONDS' FAMILY dining room glowed with candle-light as servants moved silently around the table, replacing empty plates with the next course. Despite Lady Drummond's assurance of an "informal" dinner, the gathering had somehow grown to include twelve of Society's most notorious gossips.

"And how are you finding married life, Lady Hereford?" Lady Jersey's question cut through the general conversation like a knife. "Such a whirlwind courtship. One hardly had time to prepare for the announcement."

Amelia felt every eye at the table turn to her. "Quite satisfactory, thank you." She took a deliberate sip of wine. "Though I confess, I've been rather focused on the *Metropolitan Review*."

"The *Review*?" Lady Jersey's perfectly plucked brows rose. "Surely you don't mean to continue with that endeavor now that you're a marchioness?"

Before Amelia could respond, Hereford's voice drawled from her left. "And deprive London of its most incisive commentary? That would be tragic indeed." His tone was impossible to read. Mockery or genuine praise? "Though I must say, my dear, your latest editorial on the decline of working conditions in factories was rather pointed."

Amelia stiffened. "Do you disagree?"

"Of course not." He smiled at Lady Jersey. "My wife has quite the sharp wit, doesn't she? Though I do wish she'd stop using me as her primary example of aristocratic idiocy."

Nervous titters circled the table. Amelia fought to keep her expression neutral as she noticed something odd. Hereford had positioned himself between her and the most critical gazes, effectively shielding her from the worst of the scrutiny. It seemed unconscious on his part, but the effect was noticeable.

"Speaking of wit," the Duchess of Rutland spoke up from Hereford's other side, "I heard the most fascinating rumor about your fencing lessons, Charles." Her smile turned predatory. "Such dedication to physical… instruction."

Amelia's fingers tightened on her fork as the duchess leaned closer to Hereford, her décolletage practically brushing his arm. But instead of his usual flirtatious response, he shifted slightly away.

"Ah, you must have heard about my lessons with my wife, Your Grace. Lady Hereford is a natural, and she's highly committed, which I can't say for most female students who request lessons from me." His voice remained pleasant but held a new distance.

"Lord Hereford," Lady Jersey's voice cut in again, "surely you'll be relocating to your country estate soon? The London Season is nearly over, and I imagine Lady Hereford would benefit from quieter surroundings."

Amelia tensed, knowing what the woman was implying. That a marchioness with a limp should be hidden away in the country rather than embarrassing her husband in London Society.

"Actually," Hereford said while cutting into his fish, "we'll remain in London through autumn. My wife's business requires her presence, and I find myself rather enjoying city life at present." He glanced at Amelia, something unreadable flickering in his eyes. "Besides, the *Review's* readership has doubled since last quarter and approximately half of them are the younger generation, our future. It would be poor business sense to interrupt such success."

The rest of dinner passed in a blur of subtle power plays and veiled implications. Through it all, Hereford maintained his carefully casual air, never quite defending her but somehow making it clear that criticizing his wife would not be tolerated.

Later, as their carriage rolled through London's darkened streets, Amelia finally spoke. "You've been studying my company."

"Yes," he replied, his eyes meeting hers in the dim light of the carriage lantern.

"How long?" she asked, surprised by his candor.

"Since before our marriage," he admitted. "Your circulation figures, your editorial positions. It's quite impressive how you've built the *Review* from nothing."

Amelia felt oddly unsettled by this revelation. "Why would you take such interest?"

"Perhaps I simply admire competence, whatever its source," he suggested with a hint of his usual mockery, though his eyes remained serious.

Amelia turned to stare out the window, unwilling to examine her surprisingly diligent husband. But she couldn't quite suppress a shiver when his voice dropped lower.

"You did well tonight, my lady. Though I must caution you about your investigation into factory conditions." His tone turned serious. "These owners are not men to be trifled with. They employ local thugs to protect their interests, and they care little for proper channels of justice."

Amelia kept her gaze fixed on the darkened streets outside. "I'm merely reporting facts, my lord. Surely you don't suggest I ignore clear violations of safety regulations?"

"I suggest you value your safety above your principles." His voice held an edge of frustration. "These men have ways of silencing those who probe too deeply into their affairs."

Despite herself, Amelia felt her lips curve into a bitter smile. "Oh, I'm quite aware of their methods, my lord. More aware than you know."

A heavy silence filled the carriage. When Hereford spoke

again, his voice was quieter, almost gentle. "Then you understand why I ask you to be careful. Promise me you'll exercise caution in your investigations."

But Amelia had already retreated behind her usual wall of cool professionalism, leaving his request unanswered as London's shadows flickered past.

A RHYTHMIC THUD dragged Hereford from sleep. Not loud enough to wake the household, but persistent enough to catch his attention. He lay still for a moment, trying to place the sound. It wasn't the usual settling of the old house or servants moving about. This was something deliberate. Focused.

Thud. Scrape. Thud. Scrape.

He pulled on his banyan and moved silently through the darkened halls, following the sound to the small library they'd converted for fencing practice. Moonlight spilled through tall windows, catching on a familiar figure as she lunged again and again.

Amelia hadn't changed from her evening clothes. Her dinner gown was hiked up awkwardly, one hand gripping the skirts while the other thrust forward with the practice foil. Her hair had come completely loose, falling in dark waves down her back as she drove forward relentlessly.

Thud—the wooden foot landing. Scrape—as she pulled back to position.

She wasn't practicing the defensive moves he'd shown her. This was pure attack—aggressive, almost desperate. Her breathing came in harsh gasps as she repeated the same punishing sequence: lunge, withdraw, lunge again. Even in the dim light, he could see the tremors in her arms, the way she favored her good leg.

"Your form is suffering," he said quietly from the doorway.

She whirled, the foil coming up instinctively before she recognized him. For a moment, something wild and unfamiliar blazed in her eyes. Something that made him wonder what demons drove her to practice in the dark.

"Couldn't sleep," she said finally, lowering the blade.

"Evidently." He moved into the room, noting how she shifted to maintain distance between them. "Though most people read when insomnia strikes. They don't practice killing blows at midnight."

Her fingers tightened on the foil. "I need to master this sequence."

"Why?" He circled slowly, taking in her disheveled state. A drop of sweat traced down her temple despite the cool night air. "What's so urgent it can't wait for our regular lessons?"

"I…" Her shoulders tensed as she turned away from him. In the moonlight, her profile was etched with something that went beyond mere determination. "Nothing. I simply want to improve."

But the tremor in her voice betrayed her. This wasn't about improvement. This was about survival. He recognized that raw edge of desperation, had seen it in soldiers preparing for battle, in men with everything to lose. He thought of her fierce focus during their lessons, how her eyes flashed whenever he demonstrated a killing strike, how she pushed relentlessly for more aggressive techniques despite his emphasis on defensive basics.

"The lunge you're practicing," he said carefully, watching her knuckles whiten around the hilt, "it's meant to disable, not defend."

When she didn't respond, he stepped closer, his voice dropping lower. "Who are you planning to fight, my lady?"

"No one." The word came too quickly, too sharply. She exhaled, her shoulders sagging slightly. "I simply want to… feel less vulnerable. More in control of my body, my fate." The last word hung between them, heavy with unspoken meaning.

He moved toward her then, drawn by something in her voice

that resonated with his own hidden scars. Close enough now to see the sheen of perspiration on her skin, the slight tremor in her hands that spoke of hours of relentless practice. The fierce, wounded dignity in her stance stirred his need to defend her at all costs.

He reached out slowly, giving her time to pull away, and wrapped his hand gently over hers on the foil. "Your technique suffers when you're tired." His voice was soft. "Here…"

His hands found her waist, steadying her stance with a touch that was half instruction, half comfort. "You're letting your left shoulder drop. It announces your intent."

She remained rigid under his touch, a current of tension running through her that had nothing to do with their usual antagonism. But she didn't pull away. Instead, she leaned almost imperceptibly into his guidance, allowing him this momentary intimacy.

He guided her through the proper form, his body moving in concert with hers, noting how she absorbed each correction with a desperate intensity that troubled him. This wasn't ambition or even stubbornness. This was something darker, something born of necessity.

"Better," he said finally, reluctantly stepping back, instantly missing the warmth of her. "Though perhaps we should continue this in the morning when you're properly rested."

"I'm fine." The words were firm, but her voice betrayed her, a slight quaver undermining her resolve.

"Of course you are." He moved to the door, then paused, turning back to her silhouette illuminated by moonlight. "Just remember, my lady. A blade cuts both ways. Wounds need time to heal."

His eyes held hers across the shadowed room. "Whatever battle you're preparing for… make sure the victory is worth the cost."

He felt her gaze follow him as he left, burning into his back with unspoken emotions. He'd barely reached the corridor when the sound of her practice resumed. Thud, scrape, thud, scrape. Each strike resonated with a strange mixture of desperation and relief. As if each lunge purged something painful from her soul.

Sleep was long in coming as he lay awake, her words echoing in his mind: *More in control of my body, my fate.* What demons haunted a woman like Amelia, who faced the world with such fierce intelligence and pride? What battle was she preparing to fight with such single-minded devotion?

The rhythmic sound of her practice continued deep into the night, floating through the quiet house like a ghost's footsteps. Each thrust of the blade carried the weight of secrets he couldn't yet fathom. Whatever burden she carried, he had a sinking feeling she'd find no peace until she confronted the beast that haunted her.

And God help anyone who stood in her way when that moment came.

Proper Height for Sewing Tables

The Parliamentary Select Committee on Industrial Standards met quarterly in the imposing chambers of Westminster Palace. Amelia adjusted her position on the hard wooden bench in the ladies' gallery, separated from the main proceedings by an ornate grille. The restrictive viewing space—designed, it seemed, to remind women of their place as observers rather than participants—had forced her to arrive two hours early to secure a seat with a clear view.

Below, male journalists from every major London newspaper sat in the press gallery, pens poised over notebooks, while the committee members and witnesses occupied the main floor. Charles sat with perfect posture at the witness table, his aristocratic bearing unmistakable even from Amelia's distance.

Lord Montgomery, the committee chairman, gestured toward the witness table. "Lord Hereford, as a significant investor in manufacturing interests, what is your assessment of the proposed requirements for safety guards on textile machinery?"

From her elevated position behind the grille, Amelia watched Charles clear his throat, his expression carefully neutral.

"Safety innovations must be considered thoroughly before implementation," he began. "While worker welfare is naturally a concern, hasty regulations could place undue financial strain on operations already functioning on narrow margins."

Amelia's pen stilled mid-sentence. A wash of disappointment swept over her like a chill winter draft, causing her to gaze down at her husband without making marks upon her page. Through small apertures in his carefully maintained facade, she had glimpsed kindnesses that had kindled a hope—that beneath his aristocratic veneer beat a heart sympathetic to the plight of the laboring classes.

How foolish she had been to allow such sentiments to take root! For his testimony continued in precisely the vein one might expect of a man of his station—offering perfunctory acknowledgment of concerns while ultimately espousing the virtues of gradualism and that most toothless of remedies, "voluntary compliance." The words hung in the chamber like smoke, insubstantial yet suffocating to one who had witnessed firsthand the human cost of such equivocation.

When the committee opened for questions, Lord Montgomery called upon journalists from the press gallery. Amelia, segregated behind the ladies' grille, had no chance of being recognized. She watched in growing frustration as a reporter from the *Times* was called upon, then one from the *Chronicle*, each asking cautious questions that failed to challenge the committee's assumptions.

After the fifth male journalist was recognized—a young man who appeared to be dozing through much of the testimony—Amelia had reached her limit. With a deliberate motion, she raised her wooden leg and brought it down hard against the iron grille. The sharp crack echoed through the chamber, causing heads to turn upward in startled unison.

"I believe someone in the ladies' gallery wishes to make their presence known," Lord Montgomery said flatly. "Though I must remind our observers that this is not a public forum."

Amelia rose to her feet, making herself visible through the decorative ironwork. "The *Metropolitan Review* has a question, my lord," she called clearly, her voice carrying despite the architectural barriers designed to muffle it.

A young committee member with fashionable side-whiskers leaned back in his chair. "I wasn't aware we had extended invitations to ladies' magazines," he drawled.

"The *Metropolitan Review* covers industrial affairs extensively," Amelia replied, her voice steady despite the heat rising in her cheeks. "Our readership includes many factory workers and their families. I believe their perspective merits consideration."

The committee member smirked up at the grille. "Perhaps she wishes to inquire about the proper height for sewing tables, gentlemen."

Subdued laughter rippled through the chamber. From her restricted position, Amelia could see Charles sitting seemingly impassively, his countenance betraying nothing, though his hands were in fists.

"Actually," she projected clearly, "I wish to inquire about the mortality rates in factories that have implemented safety guards versus those that haven't. The *Review* has compiled statistics suggesting a forty percent reduction in fatal incidents where such measures exist. Yet Lord Hereford suggests the cost would be prohibitive. I wonder if he has calculated the cost of dead workers?"

The chamber fell silent. The young parliamentarian who had mocked her leaned forward, peering up at the ladies' gallery.

"And your name, madam?" he asked, his tone dripping with condescension.

"Lady Hereford," she replied evenly.

The man's expression froze. His eyes darted to Charles, who was watching him with something dangerous in his gaze. The parliamentarian swallowed visibly.

"A most astute question, Lady Hereford," he managed, his tone suddenly respectful. "Perhaps Lord Hereford would care to address it directly."

Charles' eyes met Amelia's across the chamber. For a moment, something unreadable flickered in their depths.

"My wife raises an excellent point," he said, placing subtle emphasis on 'wife.' "Mortality rates are indeed lower in establishments with proper safeguards. However, implementation requires careful phasing to avoid sudden closure of operations that cannot immediately bear the cost. Better to have safer workplaces gradually than no workplaces at all."

It was a diplomatic answer, artfully threading between competing interests without fully committing to either. The committee moved on, but Amelia noted how Charles' gaze returned to her periodically throughout the remainder of the session.

When the committee adjourned, Amelia gathered her notes with quick, efficient movements. Her question had opened the door for others, and several male journalists were now freely interviewing committee members, including her husband.

"Lady Hereford."

She turned to find the young parliamentarian who had mocked her standing nearby, his expression now solicitous.

"Lord Waverley," she acknowledged coolly.

"I must apologize for my earlier remark," he said, glancing nervously toward where Charles stood across the room. "I had no idea—"

"That I was a marchioness?" Amelia interrupted. "Or that women might possess intellectual interests beyond sewing tables?"

Waverley reddened. "I only meant—"

"I'm quite aware of what you meant, Lord Waverley." She slipped her notebook into her reticule. "Good day."

She moved toward the exit, unwilling to wait for Charles. His tepid answers still rankled, despite the logic she reluctantly acknowledged might underpin them. Outside, a light rain had begun to fall, forcing her to seek shelter beneath Westminster's arched entrance while awaiting a hackney.

"You're angry with me," Charles' voice came from behind her, not a question but an observation.

She didn't turn. "I'm disappointed. You know better than

most the human cost of unsafe conditions, yet you continue to advocate for 'gradual change' that maintains your investors' profits."

"It's more complicated than that," he said, moving to stand beside her, close enough that she could detect the faint scent of sandalwood from his shaving soap. "Rigid things break, Amelia. I'm trying to mold, not shatter."

"While people die waiting for your molding to take effect," she countered, the bitter words escaping before she could temper them.

"And how many more would die if these factories closed because they couldn't afford immediate implementation?" His voice held no defensiveness, only a quiet intensity that made her finally look at him. "Change requires strategy, not just righteous indignation."

"You're giving those greedy men an excuse to evade investing in safety." Before she could elaborate on this accusation, a messenger boy approached, his cap pulled low against the rain.

"Lady Hereford? Message from Miss Bennett."

Amelia accepted the folded note, reading it quickly. "Miss Bennett is ill and cannot teach tonight," she said, more to herself than Charles. "Elisha is visiting Lancaster's family in Hampshire..."

She bit her lip, calculating her limited options. Thursday evenings meant the literacy program for factory children, but she was already behind on tomorrow's edition after spending the afternoon at Westminster.

"A difficulty with your charitable work?" Charles asked with sympathy in his voice.

"The children's literacy program," she explained reluctantly. "I must set the type for tomorrow's issue. We'll have to cancel the lesson portion, though the children can still receive their meal." She sighed. "Most come as much for the reading as for the food."

Charles studied her for a moment, his expression thoughtful.

"I will pay if you wish to hire extra hands to help you. I do not condone my wife returning home so late at night."

Amelia stared at him, caught off guard by this offer. "Truly? You will?"

"Of course."

A thought struck her then. "With the income from your salacious literature business?"

Charles' eyes widened, and for once, he appeared genuinely surprised. "I suppose I shouldn't be shocked. You likely heard from Elisha Lancaster."

"Yes. The duke passed it onto you when he tied the knot, didn't he? And yet, here you are, still operating the disreputable business as if you had no wife to consider."

Hereford's lips curved into that familiar smirk that both irritated and intrigued her. "Should you consider yourself my wife, I shall take due consideration about the literature business. You may wish to learn more about it before you hurt your neck looking down your nose at it."

"Next you'll tell me it's a secret charity," she retorted, though something in his expression gave her pause.

"It is," he replied simply. "I don't take a penny from it. The income earned is distributed to the writers, who are all women who have fallen on hard times or women who pleasure men but want to leave the profession." He crossed his arms and regarded her with unexpected seriousness. "Sometimes, Lady Hereford, you're as rigid as that leg of yours and just as pretentious."

Amelia felt heat rise to her cheeks, not from anger but from the shame of misjudging him yet again. She had rationalized her contribution to the salacious business by using the funds to invest in her literature program. It hadn't occurred to her that her husband might have a selfless motive.

"Since you have decided long ago I was useless except for entertaining the ladies, I hate to disappoint," he continued. "However, for those students who are determined to learn, I could teach the lesson."

Amelia's head snapped up to meet his eyes, her embarrassment forgotten. "You?"

"You needn't sound quite so incredulous," he said, a hint of amusement warming his eyes. "I read fluently on good days. I believe I can manage one class."

"It's not a question of capability," she said, a surprised laugh escaping her. "These are factory children, Charles. They come straight from work, unwashed, exhausted—"

"Children nonetheless," he interrupted gently. "Children who deserve the opportunity to lose themselves in adventure for an hour before returning to their labors."

"Adventure? Do you plan to reenact the book you read?"

"Perhaps. Rest assured, it need not be one of my salacious pamphlets," he said roguishly.

His kind offer pushed aside her frustration with his committee testimony, replacing it with a confusion that was becoming increasingly familiar. This man who navigated political waters with such calculated caution was the same one now offering to spend his evening with society's most vulnerable. He must have misinterpreted her silence as doubt rather than wonderment, because he added, "You need to prepare tomorrow's edition, the children need their lesson, and I find myself with an unexpectedly free evening. It seems a simple solution."

She offered him a smile then, genuine and warm. "Thank you, Charles. Truly."

Something flickered in his eyes at her sincere gratitude, a momentary vulnerability that vanished so quickly she might have imagined it. He offered his arm to escort her through the downpour to their waiting carriage. As they settled into the cushioned seats, Amelia found herself studying his profile, the strong line of his jaw, the contemplative set of his mouth.

Who was this man she had married? The calculating aristocrat who carefully maintained the status quo in committee rooms, or the man who distributed his profits to fallen women and volunteered to teach street children? Perhaps both were true, existing in a complicated harmony she had yet to fully comprehend. For the first time since their marriage began, Amelia felt a genuine curiosity about Charles Bartholomew Hereford that had nothing to do with their arrangement and everything to do with the enigma of his character.

"What are they reading?" he asked, apparently oblivious to her scrutiny.

"The beginners are working on simple primers. The advanced group is midway through *Robinson Crusoe*."

"Excellent choice," he nodded. "A tale of survival against all odds. I imagine they relate to Crusoe's ingenuity with limited resources."

His immediate understanding of why that particular book might resonate with factory children impressed her. "Yes, precisely."

"I happen to do a rather excellent Man Friday," he added, his expression lightening. "A talent I've rarely had occasion to demonstrate in Society drawing rooms."

Amelia found her lips twitching in response to his unexpected enthusiasm.

THE *METROPOLITAN REVIEW'S* back offices had been transformed for the evening. Desks pushed against walls, makeshift benches arranged in rows, and the scent of freshly baked bread mingling with printer's ink. As the children filed in—factory workers, chimney sweeps, scullery maids—they stared openly at the elegant gentleman who stood beside Miss Thornton's desk.

Charles had discarded his formal committee attire for a simpler shirt and waistcoat. He watched the children settle onto benches, his expression betraying none of the discomfort Amelia had half-expected. Instead, he scanned their faces with genuine interest.

"Good evening," he began, his voice carrying the easy authority of his station. "I understand you're studying the adventures of Robinson Crusoe. A personal favorite of mine. Who can tell me where we left our hero last week?"

Silence greeted his question. The children exchanged uncertain glances, none willing to speak first to this elegant stranger. Charles waited, his posture relaxed, his expression open. Finally, a small girl in a frayed pinafore raised her hand.

"Please, sir. He'd just found the footprint on the beach."

"Excellent!" Charles beamed at her. "And what did that footprint signify?"

As the discussion began, Amelia moved to the back of the room, supervising the preparation of the children's meal while working on her editorial. From her office, she could hear Charles guiding the conversation with gentle questions, drawing out even the shyest children. When they reached a passage for reading aloud, he assigned parts, taking the role of the cannibals himself with such theatrical growls that the children dissolved into giggles.

When one boy struggled with a difficult passage, Charles didn't correct him sharply or take over the reading as many tutors might. Instead, he broke the word into smaller pieces, guiding the child through it sound by sound until comprehension dawned on the young face.

"I've got it!" the boy exclaimed. "Pre-par-a-tions!"

"Brilliantly done, Master Frank," Charles praised. "Now, what do you think those preparations entailed?"

As the lesson continued, Amelia found herself watching Charles more than supervising the meal preparation or finishing her work. He had loosened further as the evening progressed—his hair slightly mussed where he'd run his hand through it in animated explanation, his waistcoat unbuttoned in the warm room, his expression more open than she'd ever seen it in ballrooms or dinner parties.

Here was yet another version of the man she'd married—

neither the aristocrat navigating political waters nor the surprisingly patient fencing instructor. This Charles spoke to these children with genuine respect, treating their questions and observations with the same seriousness he might afford a peer of the realm.

When the reading concluded, the children surrounded him, peppering him with questions about shipwrecks and desert islands. He answered each one thoughtfully, never talking down to them or dismissing their curiosity.

"Have you ever been shipwrecked, m'lord?" Freddy asked, wide-eyed with wonder.

"Not shipwrecked, precisely," Charles replied. "Though I was once stranded on a sandbar off the coast of Greece. Had to swim to shore with my valet clinging to my back, poor man. He never quite forgave me for ruining his best livery."

The children laughed delightedly at this image. As Charles described the incident in more detail, Amelia noticed how he subtly corrected their grammar while never making them feel ignorant or lesser. He met them where they were, gently elevating rather than condescending.

When the time came for the children to leave, Charles helped distribute the small parcels of leftover bread and cheese Amelia always prepared for them to take home. She watched as he knelt before a tiny girl, carefully wrapping her parcel in an extra handkerchief "to keep it warm."

The last child departed just before nine, leaving behind the familiar chaos of displaced furniture and crumb-scattered floors. Charles surveyed the scene, then quietly began helping Thompson return the desks to their proper positions.

"You needn't do that," Amelia said, still processing the evening's revelations. "The staff will manage."

"I don't mind," he replied simply. "Besides, I recall how back-breaking such work can be."

"You've rearranged furniture before?" She couldn't keep the skepticism from her voice.

His smile held a touch of self-deprecation. "My father believed in practical education. I spent every summer from age twelve to sixteen working alongside the estate staff—fields, stables, kitchens. Said I couldn't properly manage people whose work I didn't understand."

Another piece of the puzzle that was Charles Bartholomew Hereford slipped into place. "That explains your ease with everyone tonight."

"We all contain multitudes, Amelia."

"Thank you for stepping in tonight. The children adored you."

"They're remarkable little beings," he said, his expression softening. "So eager to learn despite everything working against them." He paused, seeming to consider his next words carefully. "I should like to come again, if you wouldn't object."

"You want to teach regularly?" The question emerged more incredulously than she'd intended.

"Is that so difficult to believe?" There was playfulness in his tone.

Amelia regarded him thoughtfully. "After your performance at the committee meeting today, yes. Now... I'm not so certain."

His expression sobered. "About that. There are complexities you may not fully appreciate. The committee members who seemed most opposed to immediate implementation are actually more likely to support gradual reform. Pressing too hard too quickly would only harden their resistance."

"So you play both sides?" she asked without her earlier heat.

"I navigate the middle ground," he corrected gently. "Fighting for what can actually be achieved rather than what should ideally exist." He gestured toward the empty benches where the children had sat. "Those children need better conditions now, not perfect conditions never."

Put that way, his approach made a certain pragmatic sense, even if it chafed against her idealism and patience.

"You continually surprise me, Charles," she admitted quietly.

"Good." He offered his arm with a slight bow. "A little mystery keeps a marriage interesting, wouldn't you agree?"

As they departed the *Review's* office, Amelia found herself contemplating the man beside her with new eyes. The Charles who patiently guided struggling readers, who knelt to speak to children at their level, who understood the value of education for those society overlooked—this was someone she hadn't anticipated when she'd agreed to their arrangement.

Maybe there was merit in his approach to reform as well—working within the system, molding rather than breaking. Perhaps there were more layers to the Marquess of Hereford than she had been willing to see. And perhaps, just perhaps, some of those layers might be worth discovering.

THE SALVE

T HE GRANDFATHER CLOCK in the hallway had just struck two when Amelia admitted defeat in her battle with sleep. Stump pain clawed at her missing limb tonight, a sensation both impossible and agonizingly real—as if the leg that had been taken thirteen years ago was being crushed anew with each heartbeat. She sat up, pushing tangled hair from her face, and reached for the small tin of medicinal salve she kept in her bedside drawer.

Grimacing, she lit the small bedside lamp and pushed back the covers. The polished wood of her prosthetic gleamed in the lamplight where it rested against the nightstand, a reminder of absence made tangible.

With a sigh, Amelia reached for the small pot of violet ink at her desk and withdrew a fresh sheet of cream paper. The first dip of her pen was always the most difficult, but once the ink touched paper, the words began to flow, and with them, a liberating sense of escape.

> Lady Caroline Westwood leaned against the library balcony, observing the room below where her husband, the imposing Earl of Westwood, had just sent another young candidate scurrying off with nothing more than a withering glance. His possessive nature had once vexed her beyond measure, yet tonight she found herself watching him with reluctant appreciation.
>
> "That's the third gentleman you've frightened off this even-

ing," she remarked when he joined her, his tall frame casting her in shadow.

"Merely the third you noticed," he replied, his hand settling at the small of her back with casual ownership. "There were two others whose intentions I found equally objectionable."

"I'm certain their only intention was to collect their hard-earned compensation," Caroline remarked.

"That's just it, my dear. I don't want them getting hard at all where you're concerned."

"You are scandalous!" Caroline swiped at his arm playfully as his arm wrapped around her waist. She could feel the evidence of his desire through the layers of her skirts. "You cannot keep me locked in a tower, my lord," she said, her face flushed, though the heat was not from anger.

His smile, that rare expression reserved solely for her, transformed his severe features. "That is rather unfortunate, my dear. I had hoped to discipline you in the tower for daring to disagree with me."

Amelia paused, her cheeks warm as she considered her next words. The scene was taking a decidedly improper turn, even by Snowflake's standards. Yet something compelled her to continue, to explore this territory of desire and liberation through the character's encounter.

She dipped her pen again, the violet ink glistening in the lamplight, and allowed her imagination to follow Lady and Lord Westwood into realms that the Marchioness of Hereford could never publicly acknowledge but that Snowflake could render in exquisite, scandalous detail.

As her pen scratched across the page, drawing Lady Westwood ever deeper into her husband's embrace, Amelia found her thoughts straying to her own husband. The way Charles had looked at her the other night, his eyes dark with want. The taste of him, the heat of his hands, and the hardness of him...

She shook her head, banishing such distracting thoughts.

Lady Westwood's fictional passions were far safer to explore than her own confusing feelings. With renewed focus, she returned to her tale of forbidden desire, where consequences remained safely confined to paper and violet ink.

A sudden worry crossed her mind. Did Charles suspect? Sometimes when he looked at her, particularly after returning from meetings with Patrick Adams, she caught a curious gleam in his eye. Did he recognize something in her writing style? Had she inadvertently included details only she would know? The thought of him reading her most intimate fantasies, perhaps even recognizing himself in her thinly disguised aristocratic characters, sent a thrill of both fear and forbidden excitement through her.

Stabbing pain in her injured leg diverted her attention. She unwrapped the bandages around her stump, wincing as the cool air hit sensitive skin rubbed raw by the day's activities. The flesh was red and angry tonight, a combination of overexertion and the damp weather that always made the ghost sensations worse.

As she began massaging the salve into tender flesh, a muffled oath from beyond her door caught her attention. Then a soft thud. Amelia froze, listening intently.

Silence stretched for several heartbeats before she heard it again—a quiet rustling from the sitting room, followed by the distinctive clink of crystal against crystal. Hereford was apparently also finding sleep elusive tonight.

She should ignore him. Return to her ministrations and wait for him to retreat to his own chambers. That would be the prudent course, the sensible choice that maintained their careful boundaries.

Instead, she found herself reaching for her robe. The decision was impulsive, born perhaps of too many sleepless nights spent alone with unrelenting pain.

She didn't bother with the prosthetic—it would only aggravate her already inflamed skin. Instead, she reached for the plain wooden crutch she kept for such situations, wrapped her stump carefully, and made her way to the sitting room door.

Hereford sat in one of the wingback chairs before the dying fire, a glass of amber liquid cradled in his long fingers, his usual immaculate appearance nowhere in evidence. His dark hair was disheveled, as if he'd been running his hands through it repeatedly, and he'd shed his formal attire for a simple banyan over loose trousers. The familiar mask of aristocratic indolence had slipped, revealing something rougher and more vulnerable beneath.

He looked up at the sound of the door opening, surprise flickering across his features as he took in her appearance—loose hair tumbling over her shoulders, the wooden crutch, the absence of her usual composure.

"Amelia." Her name emerged as barely more than a whisper. "I didn't mean to disturb you."

"You didn't," she replied, suddenly acutely conscious of her state of undress. The robe covered her adequately, but she rarely allowed anyone to see her without the wooden leg. "I was already awake."

His gaze dropped briefly to the crutch before returning to her face with cautious politeness. "Trouble sleeping?"

A different night, she might have offered some vague excuse. But something in his own evident restlessness, the shadows beneath his eyes, made her answer honestly.

"Ghost pain," she admitted, moving farther into the room. "Sometimes the leg that isn't there hurts worse than the existing leg with crushed nerves."

He nodded as if this made perfect sense to him. "The brain struggles to interpret the absence."

"Yes." She was oddly touched by his matter-of-fact response. No pity, no awkward attempt to change the subject. "I use a salve sometimes, but tonight it's particularly persistent."

"May I?" He gestured to the chair opposite his.

She hesitated only briefly before making her way across the room, settling into the offered seat.

"Would you like some?" He indicated the decanter of brandy on the small table between them.

"Please." She accepted the glass he poured, taking a sip and feeling the liquid warmth spread through her chest. "What's keeping you awake?"

A shadow crossed his face. "Old ghosts. Nothing of consequence."

"It must be significant to drive you from your bed at this hour," she observed.

He studied her for a moment, as if weighing something in his mind. Then he sighed, setting down his glass. "Have you ever met Carlisle's valet, David?"

The unexpected question caught her off guard. "I don't believe I've had the pleasure."

A smile tugged at Hereford's lips. "You'd remember if you had. The man is impossible to miss—dresses himself and, tragically, Carlisle in the most appalling color combinations imaginable. Purple waistcoats with orange trim, emerald cravats paired with yellow striping. The man has a positive genius for chromatic discord."

"And Lord Carlisle permits this?" Her eyes sparkled with intrigue.

"Permits it? He actively encourages it." Hereford's eyes crinkled at the corners, his expression warming with amusement. "Says he owes David whatever small pleasures he can provide."

"Owes him?"

"David saved Carlisle's life before he was an earl, back when he was working the docks." Hereford leaned forward slightly, his glass cradled between his hands. "A two-ton shipment came loose from its moorings—would have crushed Carlisle entirely if David hadn't pushed him clear."

"How heroic," Amelia said softly.

"Indeed. Though David paid a terrible price." Hereford's expression sobered. "The shipment caught his leg instead. It had to be amputated above the knee."

Understanding dawned in Amelia's eyes. "So, he suffers from ghost pains as well."

"Yes. When Carlisle received his earldom for providing ships during the war, he immediately made David his personal valet, though the man knew nothing about proper gentleman's dress." Hereford's smile returned. "Thus, the predilection for color combinations that would make a peacock weep with envy."

Despite her discomfort, Amelia found herself smiling. "This is all interesting," she said, "but I don't quite see how it relates to your sleeplessness."

Hereford's expression turned slightly sheepish. "Not my sleeplessness but yours. You see, David developed a method for managing his ghost pains—a particular type of massage that targets the muscles above the amputation site. He showed Carlisle, who—" He hesitated, slowly rubbing the stubble on his jaw. "After perhaps too much brandy one evening, Carlisle enthusiastically demonstrated it to me when I mentioned a hunting acquaintance with a similar affliction."

The image of the rugged Earl of Carlisle, tipsy on brandy, eagerly demonstrating massage techniques on Hereford was so incongruous that Amelia couldn't suppress a soft laugh. "That must have been quite the demonstration."

"Oh, it was theatrical in the extreme. David supervised, criticizing Carlisle's technique and his 'inadequate appreciation for the finer points of pressure application.'" Hereford's impression of what must have been David's haughty tone was remarkably good. "But the method itself proved effective for my acquaintance."

He hesitated, studying her with suddenly serious eyes. "I could try it, if you'd allow it. David was quite thorough in his instructions, and I have a decent memory."

The offer hung in the air between them, weighted with implications that extended far beyond a simple therapeutic gesture. It would require trust, vulnerability, physical contact outside the bounds of their careful arrangement. Well, they'd been there already, had they not?

"A valet with a missing leg who dresses his master in terrible colors taught you a massage technique while drunk?" She couldn't help the skepticism in her voice, though there was humor there too.

"When you put it that way, it does sound rather implausible," he acknowledged with a self-deprecating smile. "But I promise the method proved sound, even if its transmission was somewhat unorthodox."

She believed him, which was perhaps the most surprising realization of all. Despite their earlier argument, despite the walls she'd built around her heart, she found herself trusting the sincerity in his eyes.

"All right," she said quietly.

Charles set down his glass and moved to kneel before her chair, his movements deliberate and unhurried. "May I?" he asked, hands hovering near but not touching her wrapped stump.

Amelia nodded, unable to form words as he carefully unwrapped the bandages, exposing the scarred flesh beneath. She tensed, waiting for his reaction. But none came. He studied the limb with clinical interest, his expression never changing from one of focused concentration.

"The pain is here?" he asked, his fingers tracing the air just above the knotted scar tissue.

"Yes. And it feels as if the foot that isn't there is being crushed."

He nodded, as if this made perfect sense. "According to David, his brain still believes the limb exists." His hands moved to her thigh, just above where the amputation had occurred. "The muscles here contract, trying to protect a limb that's no longer present."

His hands were warm against her skin as he began a slow, methodical massage, starting well above the amputation site and working outward in careful circles. His touch was firm but gentle.

"Tell me if anything hurts," he said, focused entirely on his task.

"It's... actually helping," she admitted, surprised as the sensation began to recede under his ministrations. Or was she merely distracted by his hands on her intimate parts? "David knew what he was talking about."

"He claims it's the only thing that gave him relief after conventional medicine failed." Charles continued the careful, rhythmic pressure. "I admit I was skeptical until I saw how it helped my acquaintance."

As his hands worked their magic, Amelia felt the ghost pain gradually subsiding, replaced by a different sort of awareness—of his touch, his proximity, his competence and kindness. This was a side of Charles Bartholomew Hereford she'd never anticipated but was encountering more and more.

"Better?" he asked after several minutes.

"Much," she admitted. "Thank you."

He completed the treatment before carefully rewrapping her stump with a bandage.

When he finished, he returned to his chair rather than using the moment of intimacy to kiss her. Her husband simply poured them both another measure of brandy. This restraint disappointed her which, in turn, caught her off guard.

She gathered her thoughts, the brandy and lingering relief from pain making her more forthcoming than usual. "You surprise me, Charles." She studied him over the rim of her glass.

"Good." His eyes held hers, warm with mischief. "I would hate to be predictable." He surprised her again by not asking for an explanation—a feat achieved by only those with self-assurance.

A comfortable silence settled between them, broken only by the occasional pop from the dying fire. The ghost pain had receded to a dull ache, manageable now.

"It's late," he said finally, setting down his empty glass. "And you should rest while the pain is lessened."

"Yes." She hesitated, reluctant to break the peace between them. "Thank you, Charles. Truly."

He rose, offering her the crutch. "If the pain returns, don't hesitate to ask for assistance. David would be mortified if I failed to properly apply his technique."

"I wouldn't want to disappoint David," she said with a small smile. "Though I might request to meet him sometime. Anyone who can convince an earl to wear purple and orange together must be quite remarkable."

"He's a force of nature," Charles agreed with a warm chuckle. "And fiercely defensive of Carlisle. Rather like your Mrs. Pierce with you."

As she stood, steadying herself on the crutch, she found herself unexpectedly close to him—close enough to catch the faint scent of him, to see the light stubble shadowing his jaw, to notice how his eyes reflected the dying firelight.

For one breathless moment, she thought he might lean forward, might close the small distance between them. His gaze dropped briefly to her lips before returning to her eyes, a question in their depths she wasn't prepared to answer.

"Goodnight, Amelia," he said instead, stepping back.

"Goodnight, Charles," she replied, suddenly acutely aware of how his name felt on her lips.

As she made her way back to her chamber, she found herself replaying every moment of their encounter—the gentle competence of his hands, the compassion in his eyes, the restraint that spoke of respect rather than disinterest.

The man who had shared that quiet interlude was nothing like the rakish aristocrat she'd married. And that realization was perhaps more dangerous than any ghost pain could ever be.

CHARLES REMAINED IN the sitting room long after Amelia had retired, lingering amid the subtle traces of her presence—her scent, the impression of her body in the chair, the lip-marked brandy glass. His hands still tingled with the memory of her skin beneath his fingers.

Sleep had eluded him even before their unexpected encounter. He'd ached for her. Ever since he'd kissed her, felt her heat and tasted her, his body had refused to settle. He hadn't felt like pleasuring himself either. Hours of pacing had yielded nothing but frustration. But when he saw her, his hunger had been quelled by her suffering.

Something about tonight had shifted the foundations of their arrangement. The quiet dignity with which she'd revealed her vulnerability, trusting him despite every reason not to, had caught him entirely off guard. That rare, genuine laugh when he'd told her about David and Carlisle's sartorial disasters had been startlingly warm compared to her usual measured responses.

As he'd massaged her phantom pain in the dim light, he'd noticed something curious—a faint violet stain on her fingertips. The observation had triggered a fleeting thought about the manuscripts from Snowflake, always penned in distinctive violet ink. Surely it was coincidence; violet ink wasn't so uncommon among women writers. Yet... Amelia had surprised him so many times already. Could his sharp-tongued, principled wife possibly be the same woman who wrote those scandalously erotic tales that had captivated London's underground literary scene?

The possibility seemed absurd, but he filed the observation away.

"What are you doing, Bartholomew?" he whispered. This wasn't how their arrangement was supposed to progress, but did it matter? It did if he wished to guard his heart. His pulse shouldn't quicken at her rare smiles. He certainly shouldn't lie awake contemplating the many facets of her character with such fascination.

At her door, his hand rose halfway to knock before falling back to his side. "Idiot," he murmured, turning resolutely away.

As sleep finally claimed him, Charles resolved to make himself useful tomorrow—to show her he could be more than an inconvenient necessity in her life. Perhaps she might smile at him again, in that unguarded way that transformed her eyes from forest depths to spring meadow.

His final conscious thought wasn't of willing widows or past conquests, but of a brilliant, stubborn woman with chestnut hair and a smile that felt increasingly precious for its rarity.

THE JEALOUSY REVELATION

THE BANCROFT MASQUERADE ball transformed Lady Bancroft's already opulent ballroom into a fantastical dreamscape. Gold and silver decorations caught the candlelight, creating an ethereal glow, while masked figures in elaborate costumes moved through the space like creatures from myth and legend.

Amelia adjusted her Venetian mask, its emerald plumage matching her gown. She'd chosen the costume of Artemis, goddess of the hunt, with a silver bow slung across her back and a crown of delicate silver leaves woven through her upswept hair.

"You look magnificent," Charles murmured as they entered the grand ballroom.

Amelia's breath caught as he removed his cloak. He'd chosen to come as a Roman gladiator, the costume both elegant and imposing. A burnished bronze breastplate covered a fine white shirt, with decorative leather straps crossing over his shoulders. A short crimson cape was draped artfully from one shoulder, and leather arm guards adorned his forearms, leaving only a glimpse of his muscled arms exposed. A simple golden mask covered the upper half of his face, and a ceremonial sword hung at his hip. The overall effect was striking—suggesting the power and strength of a gladiator while maintaining the decorum expected of a marquess.

"As do you," she managed, her mouth going dry. "Though I wonder if your choice of costume isn't a touch theatrical?"

His grin flashed, white against his tanned skin. "A masquerade demands theatricality, my lady. Besides, the alternatives were worse. Patrick suggested I come as Bacchus, complete with grape vines and little else."

"Thank goodness you showed restraint," she replied dryly, though her eyes lingered on the defined muscles of his arms.

She had known, of course, that her husband kept himself in excellent condition—fencing required significant physical prowess—but seeing even this modest evidence in the strong line of his forearms and the way the breastplate accentuated his powerful chest made her cheeks warm beneath her mask and stirred something possessive beneath her ribs.

They made their way through the crowd, stopping occasionally to exchange greetings with acquaintances. Amelia noticed the appreciative glances directed at her husband from various ladies and found herself unconsciously moving closer to him. His hand settled at the small of her back, warm and steadying.

"There are the Lancasters and our brother," Charles observed, guiding her toward where Elisha and her husband stood conversing with Steven.

Elisha, costumed as Cleopatra, greeted them with a warm embrace. "You both look wonderful! Though Charles, I'm surprised Lady Bancroft hasn't swooned at the sight of your bold dress."

"She's made of sterner stuff," Charles replied with a laugh.

"The costume suits you," Steven acknowledged with a nod to Hereford before kissing his sister's cheek. "Though I'm sure half the ladies present will be scandalized."

"Only half?" Charles raised an eyebrow. "I must try harder."

"Let me fetch you both some champagne," Charles offered after a moment. "You'll want refreshment before the dancing begins in earnest."

As he moved away toward the refreshment table, Amelia seized the rare opportunity for a private word with her brother.

"Steven, while we have a moment alone—I've been meaning

to ask you about Crown Street Textiles. Do you know if Malcolm Phillips still maintains his law offices on Fleet Street?".

Steven's brows furrowed with concern. "Are you investigating your accident?" he asked, studying her face carefully. "After all these years?"

She met his gaze steadily. "I need to know who was responsible for such atrocious factory conditions, who was willing to risk my life and numerous others."

He nodded slowly, understanding darkening his features. "The ownership will be deliberately obscured," he said, his voice pitched for her ears alone. "These manufacturing concerns build labyrinths of management companies and investment trusts specifically to shield the true proprietors from liability."

"Which is precisely why I need Malcolm's expertise," Amelia said. "His understanding of corporate structures might help me navigate the maze."

Steven considered this for a moment. "Malcolm's office is still on Fleet Street. He would be a valuable ally in this pursuit. His practice has grown considerably since you last met—he's developed quite a specialty in untangling these corporate webs." He placed a reassuring hand on her arm. "I'll write to him tomorrow and arrange a meeting. Perhaps Wednesday next week?"

"Thank you," Amelia replied, gratitude softening her voice. "This means a great deal to me."

The Lancasters turned toward them after finishing their conversation. "I've received excellent news regarding our railway project. The final approvals were granted last week," the duke said smoothly.

"All thanks to your marriage," Steven added, offering Amelia a smile that held both gratitude and a touch of guilt.

Amelia nodded, allowing the shift in topic. It was comforting to know that her arrangement with Charles had yielded tangible benefits, although her personal price was yet to be fully realized.

"The railway will transform transportation throughout the

region," Lancaster continued, his enthusiasm evident. "Goods that once required weeks to move will arrive in days. The economic implications alone are staggering."

"Not to mention the humanitarian aspects," Elisha added, her eyes brightening. "Vulnerable women can be moved to safety with unprecedented speed and discretion."

"The investors are already projecting returns well above our initial estimates," Steven noted. "And the employment opportunities for local communities will be substantial—station masters, ticket agents, porters, not to mention the construction workers needed to build the lines."

As Amelia listened, she felt a momentary satisfaction warm her chest. Perhaps her unconventional marriage had served a greater purpose after all. Her gaze drifted across the ballroom, idly seeking Charles among the revelers.

She found him at the refreshment table, but he wasn't alone. A woman in an exquisite Cupid costume stood beside him, tiny wings of gossamer and gold attached to her shoulders, a miniature bow and quiver hanging decoratively at her hip. The woman's hand rested with casual intimacy on Charles' arm, her fingers lingering against his skin as she leaned close to whisper something that made him laugh—a genuine laugh that transformed his features with boyish delight.

Something sharp and unexpected twisted in Amelia's chest at the sight. The woman was stunning even behind her rose-gold mask, her costume modest by some standards yet perfectly designed to accentuate her figure and flawless complexion. The easy familiarity between them spoke of an established connection, one that predated Amelia's arrival in Charles' life.

As Amelia watched, Charles placed his hand at the small of the woman's back in a casual, intimate gesture.

"Amelia?" Elisha's voice broke through her distraction. "Are you all right? You seem miles away."

"I'm fine," she replied automatically, dragging her attention back to the conversation. "Just a touch warm."

Her eyes, however, kept returning to Charles and the mysterious Cupid. Their body language spoke of established familiarity—the easy way they leaned toward each other, the casual touches, the shared laughter. A knot formed in Amelia's stomach, tight and uncomfortable.

"Ah, there's Charles returning," Lancaster observed. "And with champagne, thank goodness. I'm parched."

Charles rejoined their group and distributed glasses. "My apologies for the delay. Margaret insisted I hear about her latest adventures in Bath."

"Most likely involving her hands straying to improper regions," Amelia mumbled before she could stop herself, the words emerging sharper than intended.

Charles glanced at her, a question in his eyes, but said nothing.

The orchestra began to play, signaling the start of the dancing. Lancaster immediately led Elisha toward the floor, and Steven excused himself to greet an acquaintance, leaving Amelia alone with her husband.

"Shall we?" Charles offered his arm, his expression unreadable behind his mask. "I believe this is a waltz."

Amelia accepted with a nod, allowing him to guide her to the dance floor. His hand settled at her waist, warm through the silk of her gown, as they joined the swirling couples.

"Is something troubling you?" he asked as they moved through the first turn.

"Not at all," she replied, her voice deliberately light. "Why do you ask?"

"Because your smile doesn't reach your eyes," he said softly. "And you've been watching something—or someone—across the room with remarkable intensity."

She kept her expression carefully neutral. "I'm merely observing the various costumes. Some are quite elaborate."

"Indeed." His voice held a hint of amusement now. "Any particular costume that caught your interest?"

Despite her best intentions, Amelia's eyes drifted to where the Cupid stood conversing with another couple. Charles followed her gaze and swallowed a smile.

"Ah," he said, "I see."

"I don't know what you mean," Amelia replied stiffly.

"Don't you?" His smile widened to a decidedly wicked grin. "Could it be that my wife of convenience is most inconveniently experiencing a touch of jealousy?"

"That's absurd," she protested, though heat rose in her cheeks. "I was merely noting the impropriety of her costume. Those wings are ridiculously impractical for dancing."

Charles laughed, the sound low and warm. "Of course. The wings. How thoughtless of me not to realize that your architectural interest in proper wing construction was the source of your fascination."

"You're being deliberately obtuse."

"And you're being deliberately evasive." His voice softened as he drew her slightly closer. "Tell me, Amelia, does it bother you to see me conversing with other women?"

"You're free to converse with whomever you please," she replied, lifting her chin. "Our arrangement doesn't preclude social interactions."

"Hmm." His eyes studied her face with unnerving intensity. "So, you wouldn't mind if I danced with her next? Perhaps even escorted her to the terrace for some air?"

The mere suggestion sent another sharp pang through Amelia's chest. "Of course not," she lied. "Though it might raise eyebrows, given that you arrived with me."

"Ah, so your concern is for appearances," he said, his tone making it clear he didn't believe her for a moment. "How considerate."

"Exactly," she agreed, relieved to have a plausible explanation. "We must maintain proper decorum."

"Indeed, we must." His thumb traced a small circle against her back, the gesture both distracting and intimate. "Though I must say, I find your concern for propriety remarkably selective. For instance, you don't seem at all troubled by my scandalous costume."

"That's different," she protested.

"Is it?" His voice dropped to a teasing murmur. "I could swear I caught you admiring my 'impropriety' earlier."

Amelia felt her cheeks flush hotter. "You're being insufferable."

"And you're being adorable," he countered, spinning her through a turn with effortless grace. "Particularly when you're jealous."

"I am not jealous," she insisted, though the protest sounded hollow even to her own ears.

"No?" His expression turned thoughtful. "Then you wouldn't mind meeting her? I should introduce you properly."

Alarm flashed through Amelia. "That's hardly necessary—"

"I insist," Charles said, his eyes dancing with mischief. "In fact, let's do so now. The dance is ending."

As the music concluded, he kept her hand firmly in his, leading her through the crowd toward where the Cupid stood by the refreshment table. Amelia tried to pull back, but his grip was gentle yet unyielding.

"Charles, really, this is ridiculous—"

"Nonsense," he replied cheerfully. "You'll like her immensely. She has a wicked sense of humor."

The Cupid turned as they approached, her face lighting with a brilliant smile. "There you are, Charles! I was beginning to think you'd forgotten me entirely."

"Never," he assured her. "I was simply dancing with my wife." He drew Amelia forward. "My dear, allow me to introduce Lady Margaret Sutton. My cousin, my mother's sister's daughter. Margaret, this is my wife, Lady Hereford."

Amelia felt the breath leave her lungs in a rush of relief and embarrassment. His cousin. The woman was his cousin.

Lady Margaret's laugh was warm and genuine as she extended her hand. "So, this is the woman who finally captured the elusive marquess! I've been dying to meet you. Charles has told me so much about your newspaper—it sounds absolutely fascinating."

"It's a pleasure to meet you, Lady Margaret," Amelia managed, taking the offered hand. "I wasn't aware Charles had family attending tonight."

"Oh, it was a last-minute decision," Margaret replied. "I've been in Bath for the Season, but I couldn't resist coming to town for Lady Bancroft's masquerade. They're always so deliciously scandalous!"

As the women conversed, Amelia became acutely aware of Charles watching her, his expression a mixture of amusement and something warmer, more tender. When Margaret was momentarily distracted by another acquaintance, he leaned close to whisper in Amelia's ear.

"Still not jealous?"

She turned to face him, finding him closer than expected. "You're enjoying this far too much."

"I am," he admitted without a trace of remorse. "Though not nearly as much as I'm enjoying the knowledge that you care whom I 'converse' with."

"I—" she began automatically, then stopped herself. "You're an arse."

"And yet you want me anyway," he murmured, his voice low enough that only she could hear. "Enough to glare daggers at any woman who dares touch me. Even my cousin."

The truth of his observation was mortifying, yet Amelia couldn't bring herself to deny it. Something had shifted between them in recent weeks—the careful boundaries of their arrangement blurring into something more complex, more emotional.

"Perhaps," she admitted finally, her voice barely audible, "I find I don't particularly enjoy sharing your attention."

His expression softened, triumph giving way to genuine warmth. "Then it may please you to know that my attention is entirely yours, Amelia. Regardless of whom I converse with or dance with, it always returns to you."

The simple admission made her heart race. Before she could formulate a response, Lady Margaret rejoined them, linking her arm through Amelia's with easy familiarity.

"Charles, you must allow me to steal your wife for a while," she declared. "I shall introduce her to the *ton*. Then I want to hear all about how she manages to run a newspaper while navigating Society as a marchioness. It sounds positively revolutionary!"

As Margaret led her away, Amelia glanced back at Charles. He was watching them with evident satisfaction, his posture relaxed and confident. When their eyes met, he winked, the gesture playful and flirtatious.

Perhaps, Amelia thought as she allowed Margaret to introduce her to other members of the *ton*, their "arrangement" had evolved into something that included the sharp sting of jealousy and the sweet warmth of belonging.

⇒⇒⇒⟨⟨⟨

CHARLES OBSERVED THE distant interaction between his cousin Margaret and Amelia with a mixture of amusement and something deeper—perhaps pride. Margaret had taken his wife under her wing, introducing her to various friends with the enthusiasm of someone who had found a new favorite. Amelia appeared reserved but receptive, her natural grace evident even from across the ballroom.

"Your wife seems to be making a favorable impression," Patrick Adams remarked, appearing at Charles' elbow with two glasses of champagne. "Lady Sutton has adopted her already."

Charles accepted the offered glass with a nod. "Cousin Margaret has excellent judgment of character. Always has."

"Speaking of character," Patrick lowered his voice, "our mysterious Snowflake has sent another manuscript. I have it with me."

Interest sparked immediately. "Here? You brought it to a Society function?"

"Where better to conceal such business than amid Society's gossip?" Patrick's eyes glinted with mischief. "Besides, I could not wait to show you."

Charles glanced toward where Amelia stood, now engaged in conversation with Lady Ardley. "Is it another Greek adventure?"

"No, something quite different this time." Patrick slipped a packet from his inner pocket. "A country house party. Rather detailed descriptions of what occurs after the candles are extinguished."

Charles took the packet, feeling the familiar weight of high-quality paper. "Let's find somewhere private."

They retreated to a small anteroom adjoining the ballroom. Charles unfolded the pages and began to read, his eyebrows arching appreciatively. The story opened innocently enough—a young widow attending a house party, a chance encounter in the library with a man described only as "the scholar." But as the narrative progressed, the tenor shifted dramatically.

"Good heavens," Charles murmured, his eyes widening at a particularly vivid passage. "Listen to this: 'Her fingers ventured boldly where no proper lady would admit knowledge, discovering the tender sac beneath his manhood, like twin plums ripe for harvest. As she caressed this secret garden, he took himself in hand, stroking with increasing urgency until—'"

He broke off, genuinely impressed by both the explicitness and the artful language. "She's outdone herself this time. The imagery is remarkably specific."

Patrick peered over his shoulder. "The garden metaphors are inspired. 'His seed spilled like spring rain upon fertile soil.' Poetic, yet unmistakable."

"This will sell extraordinarily well," Charles said, turning the page to continue reading. "The way she describes the physical sensations is unlike anything I've read before—it's as though she's combining scientific precision with artistic sensibility."

He continued reading, drawn deeper into Snowflake's narrative. As he read further, something about the phrasing caught his attention—an unusual turn of phrase: "like a scarecrow, only observed when the crows are already feasting on the crops." He paused, the words tugging at his memory.

"What is it?" Patrick asked, noting his hesitation.

"Nothing. Just… the writing style seems oddly familiar." Charles carefully refolded the manuscript. "Increase her payment by twenty percent. Talent like this deserves proper compensation."

"Do you think she might be someone we know?" Patrick asked cautiously.

Charles tapped the pages thoughtfully against his palm. "Perhaps. Though London is full of educated women with secret lives." He tucked the manuscript securely in his inner pocket. "The mystery is part of the appeal, is it not?"

"For the readers, certainly." Patrick gave him a searching look. "For the publishers, knowledge is sometimes preferable."

"Let her keep her anonymity," Charles said firmly. "It's clearly important to her, and honestly, I am uncertain if I wish to know."

As they prepared to return to the ballroom, Charles found himself dwelling on the particular phrases, the unexpected literary references. Whoever Snowflake was, she possessed not just a vivid imagination but an intellect—someone who could quote classics while describing acts that would make a courtesan blush.

They rejoined the festivities just as Margaret was leading Amelia toward a group of elderly relatives. Charles watched his wife's composed expressions, the careful way she navigated conversation with strangers, and felt a surge of pride. She belonged here, despite her own circumstances and doubts.

Their eyes met briefly across the room. Something in Amelia's expression suggested she had been tracking his movements. The realization sent a pleasant warmth through him.

When Amelia later returned to his side, there was a subtle shift in her demeanor—a slight softening, a new awareness. The territorial feelings that she displayed had surprised him earlier.

"Cousin Margaret has been most welcoming," she said, her voice carefully neutral though her eyes held questions about his absence.

"She recognizes quality when she sees it."

As the evening continued, Charles found himself increasingly attentive to his wife—not merely for appearance's sake, but from genuine inclination. The manuscript in his pocket seemed to burn with significance, a reminder that people—women especially—contained surprises and complexities beyond what Society permitted them to show.

UNWELCOME DISCOVERY

THE SWORDSMAN'S SOCIETY was nearly empty at this hour, most members having retired to their clubs or brothels. Hereford drummed his fingers against the polished table, irritation mounting with each passing minute. Patrick Adams was never late—except tonight, when Hereford's nerves were already frayed from another evening of wondering where his wife had disappeared to.

When Patrick finally arrived, the grim set of his mouth made Hereford's stomach tighten.

"What's happened?" Hereford demanded without preamble.

Patrick slid into the chair opposite him, signaling for port without meeting Hereford's eyes. "It's about Lady Hereford."

A cold weight settled in Hereford's chest. He'd known, hadn't he? Known something was wrong from those late returns, those vague explanations, the way she couldn't quite meet his gaze over breakfast.

"Tell me," he said.

Patrick swirled the port in his glass, staring into it as if seeking courage. "She's been seen meeting someone. After dark."

The cold in Hereford's chest crystallized into something sharp and painful. "Who?" The single word scraped his throat raw.

"No one can say for certain." Patrick leaned forward, lowering his voice. "Jenkins spotted her five nights ago near the Blind

Beggar tavern in Whitechapel. And again three nights ago, entering the Crimson Harp off Cheapside. She arrives around ten in the evening."

Hereford's mind raced through possibilities—newspaper business, reform meetings, charity work—each explanation more desperate than the last. "Perhaps—"

"At places no respectable woman would visit, Charles," Patrick cut him off gently. "Dressed in a way no marchioness would appear in public."

The room seemed to tilt slightly. "What do you mean?"

Patrick's hesitation only made the roaring in Hereford's ears grow louder. "Jenkins said she wore a gown that mimicked those of the working girls—cut low. Her hair down, face painted like…" He trailed off, clearly uncomfortable.

"Like a woman meeting a lover," Hereford finished, the words tasting like ash. Something fierce and primal clawed at his insides. Not just jealousy, though God knows that burned hot enough, but something deeper. Betrayal. Humiliation. And beneath it all, a bewildering sense of loss.

His fingers tightened around his glass until he feared it might shatter. With deliberate control, he set it down and spread his hands flat on the table to hide their trembling.

"She stays for about two hours," Patrick continued, watching him warily. "Always leaves around midnight."

Hereford surged to his feet, needing to move before the violence building inside him found release. He paced the length of their alcove, every step carefully controlled when what he wanted was to tear the room apart with his bare hands. The thought of Amelia—his Amelia—touching, baring herself to another man… It was an agony he'd never felt before.

And what of him? The notorious Marquess of Hereford, known for bedding other men's wives, now cuckolded by his own. The irony would delight Society's gossips.

"What will you do?" Patrick asked after a long silence.

The real question hung unspoken between them: would he

call her out? Lock her away in the country? All the usual remedies of betrayed husbands.

But beneath his rage, another emotion writhed like a wounded thing: desperation. The thought of losing her, even after this betrayal, created a hollow ache in his chest he couldn't name.

"Find out who she's meeting," he said finally, his voice rough with suppressed emotion. "And why my wife feels compelled to dress like a…" He couldn't bring himself to say the word, not about Amelia.

"Charles…" Patrick's warning tone cut through his thoughts.

"What?"

"Be careful. Don't jump to conclusions however it may look."

Hereford's jaw clenched as he reached for his coat. His mind flashed to the connecting door between their chambers, to the nights he'd stood listening to her move about her room, wanting nothing more than to cross that threshold. Had she been preparing for another man's touch those nights? The thought was a knife twisting in his gut.

"If someone is taking advantage of her," he said, his voice dropping to a dangerous whisper, "there won't be a corner of England where they can hide from me."

"And if it's not that?" Patrick asked quietly. "If she's chosen this?"

The question hung in the air between them. Hereford paused at the door, the mask of aristocratic indifference cracking just enough to reveal the wounded man beneath.

"Then I've already lost her, haven't I?"

He strode out before Patrick could respond, the roaring in his ears drowning out everything but the relentless, tormenting vision of Amelia in another man's arms.

AMELIA WAITED FOR the footsteps to disappear before slipping through the side door. It was likely a servant doing Hereford's bidding or the cook completing preparations for the next day. She paused in the entrance hall, removing her worn cloak and plain bonnet, attire chosen specifically to blend into London's poorer districts. Her shoulders ached from tension, and her wooden leg throbbed after hours of uneven cobblestones.

As she turned toward her quarters, a match flared in the darkness. Hereford sat in a wingback chair in an alcove, his face briefly illuminated as he lit a lamp.

"This is becoming quite the habit," he said, his voice deceptively calm though his eyes glittered dangerously in the lamplight.

Amelia froze. "I didn't realize you'd still be awake."

"Evidently." He rose, setting the lamp on a side table. Even in his disheveled state—cravat discarded, shirt partially unbuttoned—he maintained that aristocratic grace that both irritated and fascinated her. "Perhaps you expected me to be asleep. Conveniently unaware of my wife's late-night wanderings."

"I was working," she said automatically, the lie falling from her lips.

"Were you? How curious." He stepped closer, and she caught the scent of brandy on his breath. "Because I've been informed that you had left the office late afternoon."

Her blood ran cold. "You're still spying on me?"

"Like I said before, protecting," he said, his voice hardening. "Though it seems what you truly need protection from is your own reckless behavior."

"You don't understand—"

"Then enlighten me." He advanced until she was backed against the wall, his arms braced on either side of her. "Explain why my wife has been sneaking through London after dark." His fingers traced the low line of her décolletage, her mounds pushed up to reveal her abundance with the fabric stretched taut over her bosom. His lips parted and breathing stilled for a moment. Amelia's chest heaved under his intense scrutiny, her pulse racing with anticipation. When he spoke, his voice was hoarse. "Dressed in a manner no respectable woman would appear in public, entering a tavern…" He broke off, lifting his gaze to her face again, jaw clenching.

Humiliation and anger flooded her cheeks with heat. "You think I'm meeting someone? That I would betray our arrangement so blatantly?"

"What am I supposed to think?" His control slipped, revealing raw pain beneath his anger. "You disappear for hours, return in the dead of night, offer vague explanations that don't align with what my sources tell me—"

"Your sources are wrong!" Her hands balled into fists at her sides. "I wasn't there to entertain. I was investigating."

Doubt, or perhaps desperate hope flickered in his eyes. "Investigating what?"

Amelia exhaled, suddenly exhausted beyond words. "Crown Street Textiles. The owners. Their practices." She met his gaze steadily.

Disbelief warred with confusion on his face. "Why that factory specifically? Why risk your safety, your reputation?"

"Because they took my leg." The words escaped before she could stop them, hanging in the air between them.

Hereford went very still.

"My accident…" Her voice trembled, the word catching in her throat. "It happened there. The owners decided amputation was…cheaper than proper care." A bitter taste coated her tongue. "I've been tracking the current foreman, David Fardell, to discover who owns the factory." She forced the words out, each one a shard of glass. "I cultivated friendships with the women of the night there to approach Mr. Fardell… to discover how much he knows."

A dark line etched itself between his brows, deepening the intensity of his gaze. "And what price did you pay for such… access?"

Her gaze faltered, unable to hold the heat in his eyes. "Not what you're implying."

Skepticism clouded his features, hardening his jaw. "Then what, my lady wife? I find it difficult to believe a man would impart with secrets for merely pleasant conversation."

"He saw me as a harmless diversion," she retorted, a touch of defiance in her tone. "He wouldn't suspect a woman, especially one he believes to be a courtesan, of investigating the factory."

Hereford's eyes blazed, the air around him crackling with a barely suppressed fury. "He believes you to be a courtesan? And you expect me to accept that your interactions were entirely chaste?" He pushed away from the wall and walked away from her, his back rigid, raking a hand through his dark hair. The silence stretched, thick and heavy with unspoken accusations.

"I manipulated his vanity," she confessed, her voice barely a whisper. "I played upon his pride."

He turned toward her, stalking forward until she was pinned between his body and the cool plaster of the wall, his hands bracketing her head. The scent of him, sandalwood and something inherently masculine, filled her senses and stole her breath. Her heart hammered against her ribs, a frantic drumbeat against the sudden, desperate yearning that coursed through her. She wished he'd step closer, and, paradoxically, yearned for him to retreat.

"Prove it," he breathed, his voice a low, gravelly rasp that sent shivers down her spine.

"How could I...?"

He lowered his head, his breath warm against her neck as he pressed a soft, lingering kiss just below her ear. A jolt of pure sensation shot through her, setting her nerves alight.

"H-how would this...prove anything?" she managed, her voice a shaky, breathless plea.

His lips trailed a burning path along her jawline, pausing at the sensitive hollow beneath her ear, then moving to the other side of her neck.

"I'll know if another man has kissed you, has been inside you... if you've reached your peak recently," he murmured against her skin, each word a deliberate caress.

"Wh-what does it matter?" she protested, the heat of his mouth blurring her thoughts. "We lead entirely separate lives."

He pulled back just enough to look into her eyes, his gaze dark and possessive. His attention dropped to her mouth, then back to her eyes. "Are you saying you would find no consequence if I were to become intimate with another woman?"

The thought landed painfully in her chest, but she didn't want him to know that now. "I… I don't know, Charles," she managed, her voice a breathless whisper.

His gaze dropped, lingering on the curve of her lips as if he tasted them already. Slowly, deliberately, he leaned closer, his breath a warm caress against her ear. "Close your eyes, Amelia."

"Why?"

"Do it and you shall see."

Hesitantly, she did his bidding. She felt his warm body more acutely, his breath on her temple, and the heat of his hand on the small of her back.

"Imagine my mouth on another woman's breast…" His voice was a low, seductive murmur. "…tugging, suckling, exploring…"

A shiver traced its way down her spine, heat blossoming low in her belly. The image he painted was vivid, unsettlingly arousing.

"Then imagine my hand…" He punctuated the words by boldly cupping her bottom, his fingers kneading the soft flesh. A low groan rumbled in his chest, a primal sound that resonated deep within her. "…pulling her close, molding her against me as I slide inside her, deep and slow." He pressed against her, his arousal a hard ridge against her abdomen, a blatant and undeniable claim.

"Charles…" The name escaped her lips, a plea and a protest all in one.

"Tell me, Amelia. Would that truly mean nothing to you? Knowing another woman feels me inside her?" His breath was hot and ragged against her cheek, his grip on her hips tightening as he began to subtly grind against her, igniting a firestorm of sensation.

"No. I... I don't want you with another woman," she whispered, the words tumbling out in a rush, driven by a sudden, fierce possessiveness.

His mouth left her ear to trail scorching kisses down her throat. "Tell me then, Amelia. Where should I find my pleasure? With whom should I satisfy this... this aching that you've stirred?"

His fingers, no longer gentle, worked with practiced skill, loosening the ties of her bodice. The thin fabric parted, revealing the swell of her breasts, the dusky peaks straining against the confines of her thin chemise. He sucked in a sharp breath, his eyes devouring her.

Impatiently, he attacked the fastenings of her corset, reaching up to the bottom of her breastbone, his knuckles brushing against her sensitive skin. When the whalebone finally yielded and fell away, he exhaled on a strangled gasp. Her breasts, unbound, rose and fell with her quickened breaths, the cool air raising gooseflesh on her flushed skin. The raw hunger in his gaze sent a jolt of pure, untamed desire through her veins.

"Amelia... hellfire... I shall wither with longing if you deny me." His voice, roughened with desperation and edged with a hint of raw frustration, sent shivers dancing across her skin. "Tell me where, Amelia. Where should I seek release from this torment you have ignited?" He lifted his gaze, pinning her with an intensity that stalled her breath.

"Me," she said, her voice fueled by desire. "Your wife."

His mouth claimed hers then, a brutal, possessive assault that banished all hesitation, all restraint. This was a claiming, a demanding, a desperate plea disguised as a ruthless conquest.

Amelia met his onslaught with equal fervor, her fingers tangling in the thick silk of his hair, pulling him closer, arching her body against his. All the pent-up tension, the unspoken desires, the carefully constructed barriers they'd erected between them, shattered in that instant, igniting like dry tinder consumed by a raging inferno.

His arms tightened around her and lifted her effortlessly. He carried her to his quarters, his steps sure and steady, the only sound the soft rustle of their clothes and the frantic rhythm of their hearts.

⤜⟫⟩⟨⟨⤛

THE MOONLIGHT SPILLED through the tall windows, casting a silvery glow on Amelia's cheeks as Hereford's hands moved urgently over her. His fingers fumbled with the delicate lace of her chemise, his breathing ragged with desire. When she stiffened, her hand flying to cover her leg, he caught her fingers roughly, bringing them to his mouth. He pressed heated kisses to each one, his eyes dark with passion.

She lay before him in her chemise and stockings, a vision of pale skin and soft curves. Her waist was small, accentuating the generous flare of her hips that made his mouth go dry. Her shoulders were narrow and delicate, a stark contrast to the full, round breasts that strained against the thin fabric of her chemise.

Unable to resist, he cupped her breasts, feeling their weight in his palms. He squeezed gently, relishing the way she gasped, and felt his arousal grow even more insistent. "How did I not notice these before?" he murmured, awestruck. "They're impossible to miss."

She turned her head away, a blush creeping up her neck. Her shyness only inflamed his desire further, his manhood straining uncomfortably against his trousers.

"I usually bind them with linen," she said softly.

He raised an eyebrow.

"Easier to see and maintain my balance," she added.

Nodding, he loosened the straps of her wooden leg and set it carefully on the floor. When she hid the stump under the blanket, he gently massaged the sore flesh through the counterpane, wanting her to know he accepted every part of her.

"You are strikingly beautiful," he murmured, his voice thick with desire.

"Even my… injured leg?" she whispered, her eyes downcast.

"Especially your injured leg. It shows your strength," he said and pulled her in for a kiss.

He gathered her against him, reveling in the feel of her soft curves pressed against his hard planes. His hands roamed freely over her body, claiming what was rightfully his. He squeezed her taut flesh with one hand while the other tugged at her chemise, slowly revealing more of her creamy skin. His teeth grazed against her throat and earlobe, eliciting a soft moan that sent a jolt of desire straight through him. His mouth devoured hers hungrily, pouring all his pent-up passion and longing into the kiss.

As he explored her body with reverent hands, Hereford marveled at how right this felt, how perfectly she fit against him. He silently vowed to worship every inch of her, to make her forget any doubts or insecurities. Tonight, he would show Amelia just how beautiful and desirable she truly was.

His own clothes became an unbearable barrier, each button and fastening a maddening obstacle between them. Hereford tore at his cravat with clumsy fingers, yanking it free and casting it aside without care. His waistcoat followed, buttons scattering across the floor as he wrenched it open, his hands shaking with the force of his desire.

The fine linen of his shirt clung damply to his skin, and he pulled it over his head in one swift motion, desperate to feel nothing between himself and Amelia's touch. He managed to release her long enough to stand up and remove his breeches, which proved equally troublesome in his fevered state, and he cursed under his breath as he struggled with the fastenings, his usual composure completely abandoned in his urgent need to be free of every constraint.

He watched her eyes widen and lips part as his hard length

sprung free. The wonder and lust in her eyes had blood pooling in his groin.

She lay still, staring up at his chest, her eyes wide and luminous in the moonlight. He stood, bared to her gaze, his heart pounding in his chest. She swallowed, the delicate movement of her throat drawing his attention.

"I've heard rumors you're...beautiful," she breathed, her voice a husky whisper.

A wry smile touched his lips. "I hope I don't disappoint."

She shook her head, her gaze unwavering, and he finally allowed himself to succumb to the desire that had been building between them for weeks. He enveloped her frame in his arms, his hands instinctively finding the generous curves of her bottom, kneading the soft flesh. His other hand cupped one of her breasts through the thin chemise, feeling the taut nipple harden beneath his palm.

He lowered his head, taking one rosy peak into his mouth. He sucked, teasing and grazing the sensitive flesh with his teeth, delighting in the sharp intake of her breath, the soft moans that escaped her lips.

"Hell, Amelia, I had no idea..." he groaned, the pleasure of her almost unbearable. He shifted his attention to the other breast, pinching and nipping the nub with his lips, then soothing the ache with his tongue. Amelia arched her back, her hips rising to meet his, positioning her sex against his thigh and rubbing against the thick muscle. He could feel the heat radiating from her, the desperate need mirroring his own.

With a groan, he gently laid her back against the soft pillows, then rose to his knees, his eyes never leaving hers.

"Blazes, Amelia," he rasped. The compulsion to bury himself inside her was powerful but the need to savor this moment, to watch pleasure overwhelm her, was more so.

As she hesitantly parted her thighs, granting him access, he ran a delicate finger along the moist lips of her vulva, caressing the swollen flesh until he felt it swell even further beneath his touch.

"Oh…" she breathed, her voice barely audible, her expression a mixture of awe and apprehension.

"Are you… untested, Amelia?" he asked bluntly.

"Y-yes…"

The beast within him reveled in the knowledge, a primal satisfaction surging through his veins. And the part that longed to bury himself deep inside her regretted the pain he was about to inflict.

"I shall use my fingers first," he said, his voice low and rough with desire. "To prepare you for… my member." His gaze burned into hers, conveying the promise of the pleasure that would follow, the connection they were about to forge.

When her eyes closed and a soft gasp left her lips, he slipped a finger inside her. Amelia's back arched with a small cry. Hereford watched her rosy cheeks flush in the candlelight, a surge of possessiveness tightening his grip. He could scarcely believe his luck. The soft curve of her breast, the generous flare of her hips… Her body was made for him, a vision plucked straight from his most forbidden dreams.

He covered her body with his own, claiming her mouth in a deep, hungry kiss. Her small gasp was like music to his ears. His rod throbbed against her thigh, so hard he feared bruising her delicate skin.

Rising onto his knees, Charles pinned her thighs wide open with gentle grip, needing to bare her completely to him. Amelia's face turned crimson, her inner thigh muscles contracting.

He nudged her opening with his cockhead, his breathing becoming shallow, his body impossibly tense from fighting for control. His girth looked enormous against her delicate quim, and he forced himself to move slowly. He pushed against her entrance with a little more force.

"Amelia, this may hurt," he breathed before driving into her. Her cry mingled with his own scream as pleasure overwhelmed him. He closed his eyes, savoring the sensation, willing himself to suppress the rising tide.

With a deep breath, he plunged into her all the way with a groan, burying himself to the hilt. He began to move slowly, his engorged cock grinding against her tender flesh. He hugged her close, whispering, "Your cunny is so sweet, Amelia Hereford. Utterly incredible. And you're all mine now."

"Yes," she breathed, clinging to him, her body trembling. "I'm yours."

Her breathing grew shallow and rapid, and her moans became more consistent, a symphony of pleasure that fueled his own mounting desire. Rising back up, he moved his hand over to her bud again and began to massage the sensitive nerves, his gaze fixed on her full breasts.

"That's it, just like that. Swell for me, my darling," he murmured, his voice a low, seductive purr.

He fought to hold back the mounting pressure which threatened to burst from him. But the urge to climax was becoming irresistible. He moved faster and faster, both hands now gripping her hips as he drove into her willing heat that sucked him in with each push.

Then it all went quiet and still, until his body released the tension that had been building up for weeks. With a gasp, he leaned over her and rode the orgasm that overtook his mind and body. His cock pulsed again and again as her flesh squeezed and pumped his seed inside her, filling her completely. When at last he was finished, Charles collapsed over his wife, burying his face in her nape, enjoying the sensation of being inside her even as all tension left his body.

"Christ," he whispered against her neck. "So good. So responsive."

He sprinkled kisses on her throat, tasting the salt and breathing in the musky scent of sex. He then locked his gaze with hers.

"There will be no separation, Amelia," he declared, his voice rough with possessiveness.

She lifted her heavy-lidded gaze to meet his. "But you said

one year."

He smiled smugly. "I didn't want you to be miserable in my company. But I have a feeling we can remedy that."

"I'm still miserable," she said, a playful glint returning to her eyes.

"Is that so? I shall try harder next time."

As their breathing returned to normal, they lay together, both slick with perspiration. The sight of her, naked and vulnerable beneath him, aroused a fresh wave of desire, a faint stirring that quickly escalated into a fierce longing. It was going to be a long night, a night of chasing pleasure and exploring the depths of their newfound passion.

Later, after he had taken her twice more, driving her toward a shuddering climax with each possessive thrust, she lay curled against him in the pale gray light of pre-dawn. He felt the dampness of her tears from orgasms against his chest, as a silent storm of emotions he couldn't quite decipher overwhelmed him.

As the dawn broke and they lay tangled, Hereford broke the silence, his voice low and firm.

"No more, Amelia," he said quietly, his hand gently stroking her hair. "No more late-night investigations. No more disguises. No more risking yourself. Do you understand?" His tone was gentle but firm. This wasn't a request, but a command born of fear and a desperate need to shield her. "I cannot risk losing you."

The naked emotion in his voice seemed to still her.

He pressed a soft kiss to her forehead as she burrowed into his chest. Soon after, he felt her relax against him, the tension slowly bleeding out of her body as sleep began to claim her. As Amelia drifted off, Hereford felt a sense of purpose, a sense of belonging, that had been missing from his life for far too long. Perhaps, just perhaps, he had finally found something worth fighting for, something worth protecting with everything he had. And he would, even if it meant facing down the darkest corners of London and confronting the demons of her past.

MORNING AFTER

LIGHT FILTERED THROUGH the tall windows, casting a gentle glow over the unfamiliar bedchamber. Amelia stirred, momentarily disoriented by the weight of an arm draped across her waist and the warmth of another body pressed against her back. The memories of the previous night flooded back in a rush of sensation: Charles' hands on her skin, his mouth claiming hers, the tenderness in his eyes as he'd explored her body.

She tensed, suddenly acutely aware of her nakedness and vulnerability. This wasn't part of their arrangement. And yet she'd surrendered completely to this man who was still, in many ways, a stranger.

Behind her, Charles shifted, his arm tightening around her waist as he drew her closer against the solid warmth of his chest. His breathing remained deep and even. Still asleep, then. Amelia allowed herself a moment to simply feel: the steady rhythm of his heartbeat against her back, the gentle puff of his breath stirring her hair, the surprising comfort of being held.

How had they arrived here? From mutual animosity to… whatever this was now?

She needed to think, to regain control of the situation before he awoke. Carefully, she tried to extricate herself from his embrace, only to have his arm tighten instinctively around her waist.

"Where are you running to?" His voice was thick with sleep,

the words rumbling through his chest and into her back.

"I'm not running," she said, stilling her movements. "I simply need to… prepare for the day."

A soft grunt vibrated against her skin. "The day can wait."

Before she could form a response, he shifted, rolling her gently onto her back so he could look down at her. In the early morning light, his face appeared softer, unguarded, the aristocratic mask momentarily set aside. His dark hair fell across his forehead in tousled waves, and the shadow of stubble along his jaw made him look rougher, less polished.

"Good morning, Wife," he murmured, his voice low and intimate.

Amelia felt heat creep into her cheeks. "Good morning."

His gaze traveled over her face, lingering on her mouth before returning to her eyes. "You're overthinking this already, aren't you?"

"I don't know what you mean," she countered, though they both knew it was a lie.

Charles smiled, a genuine expression that transformed his features. "Yes, you do. I can practically hear the wheels turning." He brushed a stray lock of hair from her forehead, his touch impossibly gentle. "Stop analyzing, Amelia. At least for a few more minutes."

The casual use of her given name said with a gentle command sent an odd flutter through her chest. They'd crossed a threshold last night, moved from formal distance to a new, undefined territory. How were they meant to navigate this shift? What did it mean for their arrangement?

"Charles," she began, uncertain what she even wanted to say.

"Hmm?" His thumb traced the curve of her jawline, the gesture absent-minded and strangely intimate.

"Last night was…" She faltered, searching for the right words.

"Unexpected?" he supplied, a hint of amusement in his eyes. "Inevitable? Extraordinary? Masterful?"

"Complicated," she finished.

He chuckled, the sound warm and genuine. "Ever the prag-matist."

"One of us should be," she replied.

His expression sobered slightly as he studied her face. "Do you regret it?"

The question hung between them, weighted with possibili-ties. Amelia considered her answer carefully. Did she regret surrendering to the passion that had been building between them? Allowing herself to be vulnerable with a man she never thought worthy of her attentions?

"No," she said finally, opting for honesty.

He shifted, lying on his side and propping himself up on one elbow. "Excellent. I don't regret a moment."

Something in his tone made her heart swell with joy, but she carefully kept her voice neutral. "Even though this wasn't planned?"

"Especially because." He traced idle patterns on her shoulder, his touch raising gooseflesh on her skin. "Nothing about our marriage has proceeded according to plan. Why should this be any different?"

Before she could respond, he leaned down and pressed a soft kiss to her lips—brief but tender enough to momentarily silence the doubts swirling in her mind. When he pulled back, his expression had turned more serious.

"Now, about these late-night excursions of yours, tell me what you found. What have you discovered in your investiga-tion?"

She hesitated, weighing how much to reveal. Despite the intimacy they'd shared, trust and vulnerability were new between them.

"Mr. Fardell admitted there had been bribes to government inspectors, doctors paid to falsify reports, compensation to silence families of injured workers." She swallowed, her hand uncon-sciously moving to her leg beneath the sheet. "I've been piecing together who might lead me to the owners of the factory."

He rubbed his jaw pensively. "Crown Street most likely operates under multiple corporate entities, making it difficult to trace who actually owns it."

"Precisely. The financial records would be helpful, but I've no clue how I'd get access."

Charles was quiet for a long moment, his expression thoughtful. "If these men discover you are tracking them, they won't hesitate to protect themselves."

"Which is precisely why I need to expose them before they discover my objective," she insisted.

"I understand, but we must approach it differently. More strategically."

"We?"

"Yes, we." His lips curved into a slight smile. "I have connections, influence, things that could prove useful."

Amelia weighed his offer. Having his resources would undoubtedly make her investigation easier, potentially safer. But it would mean letting him in, trusting him with something deeply personal. Now that they'd consummated their marriage, she ought to think of him as a partner for life. They were one unit now regardless of her fears.

"I'm afraid," she blurted.

"Of what?" He reached out, stroking her hair. The casual intimacy of the gesture sent warmth through her.

"Of getting hurt. If I can't give you an heir when—"

"Shh..." Charles pressed her against his chest, stroking her back. "Now I am yours regardless of the heir."

Amelia looked into his eyes then.

"After all," he continued, "I have not bestowed spousal privilege onto other women."

Amelia arched her brows. "You cannot mean bedding."

His laugh was playful. "No, obviously not. I mean the fencing lessons. I don't give them away willy-nilly, you understand."

She rolled her eyes. "The Duchess of Rutland may disagree."

"Those were not real lessons."

"Yes, I've noticed," she said flatly.

"I believe you are jealous, Wife," he teased with a glint in his eyes.

"Of course, now that we've…" She trailed off, feeling shy about acknowledging she was his real wife in a real marriage.

"We've what?" he teased.

"You know what."

"Tell me."

She looked up at him with narrowed eyes. "Rutted."

Hereford's laugh was half shock and half delight.

"That'll teach you not to challenge me," she said.

"You never cease to surprise me, my sweet," he said with a chuckle, his hand roaming down her bottom, then her thigh as casually as if he was touching his own leg.

"I've been meaning to ask," he said with careful casualness. "Why don't you use a cane?"

Amelia stiffened slightly. "I don't need one."

"Maybe so." His voice was gentle. "I've watched you navigate uneven garden paths, crowded ballrooms. It can't be easy when you are fatigued."

She was quiet for a moment, weighing her response. "A cane draws attention," she said finally. "It makes the disability the first thing people notice. I prefer to be judged on my words, my work. Not by my limitations."

Understanding dawned in his eyes. "So, you endure the pain instead."

"It's not so bad," she shrugged, though they both knew she was understating her struggle. "I've grown accustomed to it."

Charles studied her face, something like admiration mingling with concern in his expression. "Your determination is remarkable, Amelia. But there's no shame in accepting help when it's needed."

The tenderness of his voice still surprised her. This was a side of Charles she was still struggling to reconcile with the rakish aristocrat she'd first met.

"I should go," she said, suddenly acutely aware of the time. "There's work to be done at the *Review*, and—"

"And you need space to think," he finished for her, releasing her hand. "I understand."

Amelia nodded, grateful for his understanding. She gathered the sheet around herself and moved to rise from the bed. It was only when her foot touched the cool floor that reality crashed back. Her wooden leg lay across the room where Charles had carefully placed it the night before.

She froze, suddenly exceedingly aware of her vulnerability. Walking across the room without her prosthetic would be impossible, yet asking for help felt like an admission of dependency she wasn't prepared to make. Had she been alone, she would have hopped or crawled, not caring how undignified she appeared.

Charles seemed to sense her dilemma. "Would you like me to bring it to you?" he asked quietly.

Pride warred with practicality. "Please," she said finally, the word barely audible as she pushed down the shame that had accompanied her disability since childhood.

But instead of retrieving her prosthetic, Charles moved closer, gathering her into his arms, sheet and all. Before she could protest, he was pulling her back against his chest, his arms encircling her waist.

"Charles, what are you—"

"Helping," he murmured against her ear, his voice low and warm. "Just not in the way you expected."

His lips found the sensitive spot beneath her ear, sending a shiver through her body that had nothing to do with the morning chill. One hand splayed across her stomach, holding her securely against him while the other traced a path from her knee upward, his touch both reverent and possessive.

"You'll need to retrieve my leg eventually," she managed, though her protest sounded weak even to her own ears.

"Eventually," he agreed, his breath warm against her neck.

"But not quite yet."

His hands continued their gentle exploration, retracing paths discovered the night before. "I want you to remember this today," he whispered, his voice roughening with desire. "When you're sitting at your desk, working on your articles, I want you to feel me with every movement."

His words sent heat spiraling through her, desire mixing with a strange, fierce tenderness that caught her off guard.

Charles pushed away the sheet separating them and flipped her onto her stomach. His warm skin pressed against her backside. The hard ridge of his cock nestled between the soft curves of her bottom as his hand cupped her breast, kneading gently.

"Confound it, Amelia," he breathed, his voice husky with desire. "You drive me mad with want."

He positioned himself at her entrance, then plunged into her with a low groan that reverberated through her body. Slowly, torturously, he withdrew completely, only to thrust back in with renewed fervor. His fingers found her sensitive bud, circling and rubbing as he established a rhythm of deep, measured strokes.

Amelia moved her hips in tandem, meeting each thrust with a forceful tilt of her pelvis. The friction was exquisite, sending waves of pleasure coursing through her body.

"Christ, you feel divine," he rumbled, his pace quickening. He slid in and out of her with increasing urgency, his breaths coming hard and fast against her neck. "Come for me, Amelia. I want to feel you squeeze my cock."

"Charles, I'm… Oh God…" As she cried out his name again, she began pulsing around him, pushing him over the threshold of ecstasy.

With a sharp intake of breath, Charles stiffened behind her. His body curled around hers, every muscle tightening and relaxing as his release washed over him. As the tremors subsided, he stilled, one hand still cupping her breast possessively.

"These are perfect," he breathed, gently squeezing the soft

mound. "You are perfect."

Afterward, as they lay tangled in the sheets once more, Charles pressed a tender kiss to her temple. "I'll fetch your leg now, if you still wish to leave."

She watched as he rose, moving across the room with a confident grace, unashamed of his nakedness.

"Thank you," she said softly as he returned to the bed, her prosthetic held with reverence in his hands, with the same careful attention he'd shown to her body.

"Would you like privacy?" he asked, setting it beside her.

She considered for a moment, then shook her head. "No. You've seen all of me now."

A smile touched his lips, warm and genuine. "So I have." He moved back, giving her space. "And I find myself wanting to see more."

His words, filled with pride and acceptance, warmed her heart.

"Seven o'clock?" he asked as she rose and tested her balance.

"For the fencing lesson?" she clarified, reaching for her discarded chemise, her movements deliberately unhurried, though her pulse hammered in her ears as his gaze followed her every movement.

"Unless you have other, more… persuasive… plans for us," he replied, his voice a low, suggestive murmur, his eyes alight with a teasing gleam.

Despite her best efforts, Amelia felt her lips curve into a smile, a flicker of warmth spreading through her at his audacity. "I admire your self-assurance, my lord, but I still prefer the fencing lessons… for now." She gathered her clothes, deliberately avoiding his gaze. "Seven o'clock it is."

His laughter, warm and resonant, echoed in his chamber as she slipped away to her own room. Once inside, she leaned back against the cool surface of the connecting door, closing her eyes and taking a slow, steadying breath.

HEREFORD LAY STILL, savoring the lingering warmth where Amelia's body had pressed against his, the scent of her hair still clinging to his pillow. A bone-deep satisfaction coursed through him—not merely physical, though God knew that had been extraordinary, but something far more profound. She was his now, truly his, in ways that transcended their original arrangement. Yet even as contentment settled over him like a warm blanket, unease prickled at the edges of his mind. This fierce, brilliant woman who had just surrendered so completely in his arms was the same one who prowled London's darkest corners without a thought for her safety, who demanded sword lessons with the determination of a warrior. The very qualities that made her magnificent—her courage, her relentless pursuit of justice, her refusal to be caged by Society's expectations—were precisely what would drive him to distraction with worry. How did one protect a woman who saw protection as imprisonment?

A soft knock interrupted his reverie.

"Enter," he called, assuming it was Amelia returning for something forgotten.

Instead, Barker appeared with fresh linens draped over his arm, his expression studiously neutral as he surveyed the thoroughly disheveled state of the bed.

"Good evening, my lord. I trust your... negotiations... with her ladyship concluded satisfactorily?"

Hereford felt heat creep up his neck. "Barker—"

"Quite right, my lord. No need for details." Barker began efficiently stripping the bed linens, forcing Hereford to leap from the bed while hastily wrapping himself in the nearest blanket. "I feel compelled to mention," Barker continued with perfect composure, as though he hadn't just displaced his master from comfort, "that Mrs. Hudson has taken the liberty of having the connecting door hinges oiled. Apparently, they've developed quite a persistent squeak."

"How thoughtful of her," Hereford managed.

"Indeed. She's remarkably practical about such matters." Barker shook out a fresh sheet with a crisp snap. "She also mentioned that Cook has prepared a rather substantial breakfast for this morning. Something about the importance of maintaining one's strength."

Hereford buried his face in his hands. "Does the entire household—?"

"Know that you've finally consummated your marriage? I'm afraid subtlety has never been your strongest suit, my lord." Barker tucked the corners of the sheet with military precision. "Though I must say, the staff is quite pleased. There was a betting pool, you see."

"A betting pool?"

"Mrs. Hudson wagered on Christmas. Cooper was optimistic about Michaelmas. I, having observed your growing distraction, placed my money on November." Barker straightened, looking smugly satisfied. "Two pounds richer, as it happens."

THE DANCE OF STEEL

AMELIA ARRIVED PRECISELY on time at the Swordsman's Society, dressed in the modified practice clothes Hereford had commissioned for her—trousers tailored to accommodate her prosthetic, a loose shirt that allowed for freedom of movement without the restriction of stays.

She found him already waiting, stripped down to shirtsleeves and waistcoat, foils laid out neatly on the side table. But there was also a long, narrow package resting beside them that hadn't been there during previous lessons. He turned upon her entrance, and the way his eyes swept over her sent tingling through her body. There was a new awareness in his gaze, a kind of heat that hadn't been present during their previous lessons.

"My lady," he said, voice pitched low enough that the single attendant couldn't overhear. "You look... rested."

The slight emphasis he placed on the word made color rise in her cheeks. "I managed some sleep," she replied, striving for her usual composure despite the images his simple greeting had evoked—tangled sheets, his hands on her skin, the weight of him above her.

A knowing smile touched his lips. "I'm pleased to hear it." He gestured to the package. "Before we begin, I have something for you. It arrived this morning."

Amelia regarded the long, narrow box with a mixture of surprise and wariness. "What is this?"

"Open it," he urged, unable to suppress his boyish excitement.

She unwrapped the package carefully, lifting the lid to reveal an elegant walking cane. The shaft was polished ebony, the silver handle crafted in the shape of a lioness' head, eyes glinting with small emeralds.

"It's beautiful," she said softly, lifting it from the box.

"There's more," Hereford said, stepping forward. "Twist the handle and pull."

Amelia did as instructed, her eyes widening as the cane separated, revealing a slender sword concealed within.

"A sword cane," Hereford explained, his smile growing. "Practical support when you need it and protection when circumstances demand. The blade is Sheffield steel, perfectly balanced for both defense and offense."

She tested the weight of the blade, finding it lighter than expected but perfectly balanced. "This must have cost a fortune."

"The cost is irrelevant. Your safety isn't." His voice softened. "I know you prefer not to use a cane, that you feel it draws attention. But perhaps something that serves a dual purpose... something that makes you more formidable rather than appearing vulnerable..."

Amelia swallowed the lump in her throat, hiding the tears pooling in her eyes by carefully reassembling the cane. She looked away as she ran her fingers over the intricate silver work of the lioness head. "You've been planning this for weeks."

"Since our first lesson," he admitted. "When I saw your determination despite the challenges. You deserve a weapon that matches your spirit—beautiful, practical, and unexpectedly dangerous."

The tenderness in his voice made her throat tight. This wasn't just a gift; it was an acknowledgment of her struggles, her strength, her refusal to be limited by her injury.

"Thank you," she said quietly, meeting his eyes finally. "It's perfect."

Something passed between them in that moment—not just the new intimacy from last night, but a deeper understanding. He saw her, truly saw her, not as someone to be pitied or protected, but as someone to be equipped for her own battles.

"Shall we test it?" he asked, gesturing to the practice floor. "See how it handles compared to the foils?"

"You want me to fence with a real sword?"

"Why not? In reality, you're more likely to have your cane than a proper foil if you need to defend yourself." He selected a practice foil for himself. "Besides, I'm curious to see how you adapt the techniques we've been working on."

They moved to the practice floor, and Amelia found the cane sword surprisingly natural in her hand. The weight distribution was different from a foil, but the lioness head provided an excellent grip.

"The principles remain the same," Hereford said, circling her with a professional eye. "But you have advantages now—the element of surprise, the dual functionality."

He moved behind her, his chest nearly touching her back as he adjusted her stance. His hands settled at her waist, warm and steady through the thin fabric of her shirt. The familiar proximity felt charged with new meaning after last night.

"Shift your weight here," he murmured, his voice close to her ear. "The cane's weight changes your center of balance slightly."

She followed his direction, acutely aware of his hands, of how different this felt from their previous lessons. Before last night, his touch had been instructive. Now, there was an intimacy to it that made concentration difficult.

"Better," he approved, though he didn't immediately step back. "Try a basic parry."

They worked through familiar sequences with the new weapon, Hereford guiding her through modifications needed for the cane sword's different balance and reach. Each correction brought them into contact—his hand covering hers to adjust her grip on the lioness head, his arm against hers to guide a parry, his body pressed against her back to demonstrate proper weight distribution.

"You're adapting quickly," he noted after she successfully completed a defensive sequence. "The cane suits you."

"It feels right," she admitted, looking down at the silver lioness. "Like it was made for me."

"It was," he said simply. "Every detail was chosen specifically for you. The height, the weight, even the lioness—fierce, protective, beautiful."

Color rose in her cheeks at the implications. "Charles…"

"Your form has improved considerably," he said, stepping closer, the heat in his eyes unmistakable. "Both with the foil and now this."

"I have a good teacher," she acknowledged.

His smile turned wry. "I'd suggest we celebrate your progress, but I fear my idea of celebration might scandalize the attendant."

The casual reference to intimacy sent heat through her. "Charles!"

"What?" His innocent expression didn't fool her at all. "I merely meant a glass of brandy. What were you thinking, my wanton one?"

Before she could formulate a response, he stepped closer, lowering his voice. "Though if you were thinking of something else… something involving significantly less clothing and perhaps that particularly interesting position we discovered this morning, I would be more than willing to indulge you."

"We're in public," she hissed, glancing toward the attendant.

"So we are," he agreed, looking unrepentant. "Though I find myself increasingly impatient for privacy." His gaze traveled over her. "You move beautifully with that cane, Amelia. Like you were born to wield it."

She carefully sheathed the blade back into the cane, using the motion to compose herself. "I should return to the *Review*. Tomorrow's edition…"

His expression shifted to concern. "Working late again? Alone?"

"Yes. The duke doesn't allow Elisha to stay past six."

"I wouldn't either if you were not the proprietor. Hire more staff so you can be home for dinner."

"We can't afford more staff quite yet."

Hereford sighed. "I shall pay for extra assistance, but for now, come. I shall take you there and assist."

Amelia regarded him skeptically. "Assist? With the printing press?"

He offered her a disarming smile. "I'm quite skilled at hiding behind one if you recall. Besides, I cannot possibly fall asleep knowing you are toiling alone."

She couldn't deny the warmth his concern generated. "Very well, but be warned, it's not a pretty sight and it will be quite strenuous."

"Not precisely the kind of labor I was hoping for," he said, withdrawing his pocket watch, "at nine o'clock at night."

As they prepared to leave, Amelia gripped her new cane, feeling its solid weight, its hidden danger. Charles had given her more than a weapon—he'd respected her wishes despite his reservation, had acknowledged her need for security. It was perhaps the most thoughtful gift she'd ever received.

"Thank you," she said again as he helped her with her cloak. "For the cane. For understanding."

His hands lingered on her shoulders. "You never need to thank me for seeing you as you truly are, Amelia. Fierce, brilliant, and absolutely magnificent."

The words, spoken with such quiet conviction, made her heart race. As they left for the *Review* offices, her new cane clicking confidently against the floor, Amelia realized that Charles had become more essential than silver and steel.

Over the next few hours, Hereford proved adept, as Amelia expected by now. He listened intently as she explained the intricacies of the press. He wasn't afraid to get his hands dirty, diligently cleaning type and helping to feed the massive machine. Amelia found herself both impressed and strangely touched by his willingness to immerse himself in her world.

"Remember when you corrected my leading?" Amelia asked, a teasing note in her voice as they worked side-by-side, the rhythmic clang of the press a steady backdrop to their conversation. "Or when you critiqued my margins? I assumed you wanted to drive me mad."

Hereford paused, wiping a smudge of ink from his cheek, his eyes crinkling at the corners. "Perhaps I did, a little," he admitted, a mischievous glint sparkling in his eyes. "But mostly I enjoyed seeing that flash of fire in your eyes when I vexed you. I find you exceedingly charming when you're provoked."

She shook her head, feigning indignation. "You are incorrigible."

"And you, my dear, are utterly captivating." He winked before returning to his task.

As the hours ticked by, the atmosphere in the printing office shifted. The initial awkwardness dissolved, replaced by a comfortable camaraderie. Amelia found herself explaining aspects of the printing process she found fascinating, and Hereford listened with genuine interest, asking insightful questions. He even started taking the lead in some of the steps, showing his competence that belied his usual devil-may-care demeanor.

Finally, as the first rays of dawn peeked through the grimy windows, the last page of the edition rolled off the press. A collective sigh of relief swept between them.

"Well," Amelia said, wiping her brow with a handkerchief, "I suppose that's that. Thank you for your assistance, my lord."

Hereford grinned, his face smudged with ink, his eyes sparkling with exhaustion and something else… something that made her heart flutter. "My pleasure, Lady Hereford. I must say, I found the experience enlightening."

"Please don't think you have to do that every night." She then started cleaning up, careful not to dirty her white shirt with ink.

He watched her for a moment, a thoughtful expression on his face, then stepped forward, reaching out to gently brush dust off her elbow beneath the rolled-up sleeve. "Nonsense. I wouldn't miss it for the world." He let his hand linger there for a moment, his fingers tracing the delicate skin. "Besides," he murmured, his voice dropping to a husky whisper that sent shivers down her spine, "I find I rather enjoy getting my hands dirty with you."

Before Amelia could respond, before she could even fully process the intimate gesture, Hereford stepped closer, backing her against the cool metal of the printing press. The clang of metal and the scent of ink, usually so familiar and mundane, suddenly took on a charged quality.

He braced his arms on either side of her, effectively trapping her. His gaze dropped to her lips, lingering there for a long, breathless moment.

"Do you know what I really enjoyed about tonight, Amelia?" he whispered, his breath warm against her cheek.

She swallowed hard, her pulse racing. "What?"

He leaned closer, his lips brushing against her ear, sending a jolt of electricity through her. "Watching you so passionate about your work, so meticulous. Your intense focus to achieve excellence. You are a force to be reckoned with, Wife, and I find that incredibly arousing."

A sudden, overwhelming wave of lust washed over her, erasing all thoughts of propriety. Before she could think, she kissed him, wrapping her arms around his neck. Their tongues swirled against each other, the dance now familiar and effortless. He tugged at her backside with his hand and turned her to face the printing machine. She moaned at the feeling of his hard ridge digging against the crevice of her arse.

"Let me show you how much..." He trailed off, teasing and tantalizing her with the unfulfilled promise.

While she watched over one shoulder, Hereford yanked down her trousers. He held her bottom firmly against his steely rod, the impropriety of it sending a jolt of pleasure through her.

Her breath hitched in her throat, her heart pounding against her ribs. She knew they shouldn't be doing this, not here. But the raw desire in his eyes, the heat of his body pressed against hers, banished all thoughts of resistance.

He stood behind her, the evidence of his lust undeniable, pressing insistently against the fabric of his trousers. Her gaze drifted downward, drawn to the tantalizing bulge, and a fresh wave of heat washed over her. She wanted him, wanted him now with a fierce, almost desperate intensity.

Hereford unfastened his falls and freed his engorged member. Then he positioned his cock between her thighs, the head pressing against her heat. She waited, anticipation holding her breath captive in her lungs.

"Tell me, Amelia," he murmured, his breath hot against her ear, his words a seductive command. "Tell me what you want me to do to you."

"Don't be so cruel," she begged. "You know precisely what I crave."

She closed her eyes, took a deep, shuddering breath, and surrendered to the desire that had been building within her. "I want you inside me, Charles. I want you to fill me completely."

With a guttural groan that vibrated against her spine, he swiftly drove into her, a powerful invasion that had her gasping.

Her hands gripped the edge of the printing press, her body instinctively trying to get closer to him, pushing against his cock, urging him to drive deeper.

"Amelia," he grunted suddenly, his control snapping, then with a surge of raw urgency, he gripped her hips firmly and plunged his cock into her to the hilt.

"Charles!" she cried out, the sound a raw, primal expression of pure sensation, as each thrust sent waves of heat coursing through her body, igniting a fire that threatened to consume her entirely. She clung to the edges of the printing press, her knuckles white, her head thrown back, her breath coming in ragged gasps.

He leaned forward, his hands sliding beneath her shirt to cup her breasts, his thumbs teasing her nipples into hard, aching peaks. She moaned, her bottom pounding against him, seeking more, needing more.

He continued to thrust, deeper and faster, his movements becoming increasingly frantic, until she was lost in a sea of sensation, her mind blank, her body on fire. Her body trembled, her muscles clenched, and she cried out his name, her voice barely audible above his own ragged breaths.

Then, with a final, earth-shattering thrust, he reached his climax, his body convulsing against hers. He held her tight, burying his face in her hair, his breath coming in rough gasps.

They stood entwined for a long moment before he withdrew, his body still trembling. He turned her around, his eyes filled with a tenderness that made her heart melt.

"Are you all right, Wife?" he whispered, his voice still husky with passion.

She nodded, unable to speak, her body still humming with the afterglow of their lovemaking. She had never felt so alive, so desired, so utterly and completely fulfilled.

He brushed his lips against hers, his fingers lingering against her skin. "That," he said, a slow smile spreading across his lips, "was a most productive use of our time, wouldn't you agree?"

Amelia couldn't help but laugh, the sound light and airy. "Indeed, husband," she said, her eyes sparkling. "Most productive indeed."

They held each other for several more minutes before Amelia reluctantly disentangled herself to fix her clothes. Hereford followed suit while watching her with a look of satisfaction that seemed to extend far deeper than mere physical pleasure.

A Most Peculiar Visit

THE *METROPOLITAN REVIEW'S* office hummed with the familiar rhythms of a newspaper in production—the clack of typesetters, the scratch of pens, and the occasional burst of excited conversation when a promising lead came in. Amelia sat at her desk, surrounded by stacks of papers, factory inspection reports, and letters from workers detailing unsafe conditions. She'd been working since dawn, determined to complete her exposé on industrial safety violations before the next edition went to print.

A knock on her office door interrupted her concentration. She looked up to find Thompson, her assistant editor, looking somewhat flustered.

"My lady, Lord Norwich is here to see you."

Amelia straightened in her chair, setting aside her pen. "Send him in, please."

Lord Norwich entered her office with the confident grace of a man accustomed to commanding rooms. His salt-and-pepper hair was impeccably styled, his attire refined without being ostentatious. He carried a leather portfolio under one arm, and his expression brightened when he saw her.

"Lady Hereford," he said, bowing slightly. "I hope I'm not interrupting your work."

"Not at all, Lord Norwich." Amelia gestured to the chair across from her desk. "I am curious about to what I owe this honor."

He settled into the chair and placed the portfolio on her desk. "Given your interest in factory working conditions, I took the liberty of gathering some documentation I thought might interest you."

He opened the portfolio to reveal several official-looking documents. "These are inspection reports from the Blackwell Mill in Southwark. The owner has been falsifying safety records for years."

Amelia leaned forward, her journalistic instincts immediately engaged. "How did you obtain these?"

"I sit on several industrial committees," Norwich explained, his tone modest. "In my position, one hears things, sees documents. When enough whispers point in the same direction, I've found it worthwhile to investigate."

He spread the papers before her. "Look here. The official inspector's signature is clearly forged on at least three of these reports."

Amelia's fingers traced the discrepancies he pointed out, her mind already formulating how this would strengthen her article. "This is exactly the sort of evidence I've been seeking, my lord. But why bring it to me? Surely the authorities—"

"The authorities?" Norwich's smile held a touch of bitterness. "They're often in the pockets of these factory owners. No, Lady Hereford, I've found that public exposure through reputable publications like yours is often the only way to force change."

He leaned forward slightly, his expression earnest. "I admire your courage in tackling these issues. Few would dare challenge such powerful interests, especially from your position in Society."

Amelia replied, still examining the documents. "These will be tremendously helpful, my lord."

"I have more," Norwich said, turning to another section of his portfolio. "Information about the Penridge Works in Whitechapel. Their record of accidents is appalling, and the owner—a man named Harrison—has been known to dismiss injured workers without compensation."

As he continued detailing various safety violations at different factories, Amelia took careful notes. His knowledge seemed impressively comprehensive, and his apparent dedication to exposing such abuses aligned perfectly with her own mission. The conversation flowed easily as they discussed various reform efforts and potential targets for investigation.

"You should focus particular attention on these three factories," he said, marking locations on a map he'd brought. "Their owners are particularly negligent, and I've heard rumors of children as young as six working the machinery."

"This is extraordinary information," Amelia said, genuinely grateful. "How can I possibly thank you?"

"By continuing your excellent work," Norwich replied with a warm smile. "Your voice carries weight, especially now that you're Lady Hereford. I am only happy to assist you in this worthy endeavor."

They were still deep in conversation when the knock on the door interrupted them. Thompson stood at the door, announcing Hereford's arrival. The man had an uncanny ability to show up when Norwich called on her.

Amelia quickly put away the confidential documents in her drawer. Soon, Hereford stood in the doorway, his tall frame filling the space. His eyes immediately locked on Norwich seated across from his wife, and his expression hardened.

"My lord," Amelia said, standing somewhat awkwardly. "I wasn't expecting you."

"Evidently," Hereford replied, his voice cool. His gaze shifted to the papers spread across Amelia's desk, then back to Norwich. "I see you're busy."

"Lord Norwich was kind enough to stop by to answer some of my questions regarding the industrial committee," Amelia explained, noting the tension radiating from her husband.

"Is that so?" Hereford stepped fully into the office, closing the door behind him. "How generous."

Norwich rose to his feet, his manner impeccably polite despite Hereford's hostility. "Merely supporting Lady Hereford's admirable efforts."

"And your sudden passion for workers' rights?" Hereford asked, his drawl more pronounced than usual—a sign, Amelia had learned, of carefully controlled anger. "When did that develop, Norwich? Between investments, perhaps?"

The atmosphere in the small office grew decidedly uncomfortable. Norwich's expression remained pleasant, though his eyes had cooled. He gathered his hat, his movements unhurried despite the tension. "I believe I should leave and give you some privacy," he said smoothly. "Lady Hereford, please feel free to contact me should you have further questions."

He turned to Hereford with a slight bow. "Your wife's work shall make a genuine difference, my lord. You should be proud rather than suspicious." His voice lowered slightly. "Unless, of course, your concern stems from something more personal than professional."

Hereford's jaw tightened visibly. "Be careful, Norwich."

"Always," the other man replied with a small smile. He turned back to Amelia. "Good day, Lady Hereford."

After Norwich departed, Amelia closed the door quietly behind him and rounded on her husband.

"What was that?" she demanded. "You were unforgivably rude to a man who is helping me."

"Helping?" Hereford's voice was sharp. "Amelia, the man is manipulating you. His sudden interest in your work, his private meetings—it's too convenient."

"Based on what evidence? Vague suspicions and personal dislike?"

"Perhaps he's covering his own guilt," Hereford said quietly. "He may be attempting to distract you."

"That is not evidence."

Hereford's expression darkened. "No, but I know men like Norwich. They present carefully crafted facades while hiding their true nature. Just be cautious. That's all I ask."

She gathered Norwich's papers. "I won't reject valuable information because you dislike the source."

They stared at each other across an impasse neither could breach.

"Very well," he said finally. "I can see your mind is made up."

As he turned to go, she felt a twinge of regret. "Charles—I understand your concern. But perhaps you're judging him unfairly."

He paused. "Perhaps. Or perhaps you're not judging him critically enough."

THE OFFICES OF Phillips & Sons, Solicitors, occupied a narrow but respectable building on Fleet Street, just around the corner from the Inns of Court. Malcolm Phillips had been her brother Steven's school friend and was now the *Review's* legal advisor. His willingness to meet with her without a male escort was just one of many reasons she had valued their association.

"Lady Hereford," Malcolm said, rising from behind his desk as she was shown in. "What a pleasant surprise. Though I suspect this isn't a social call?"

"I'm afraid not," Amelia replied, setting her portfolio on his desk. "I need to verify some information about factory ownerships before publication."

Malcolm's eyebrows rose slightly, but he merely nodded and examined the papers. "Penridge Works in Whitechapel... Harrison is listed as the owner here."

"Yes, but I have reason to believe the actual ownership may be more complex," Amelia said. "Is there any way to determine who truly controls these operations?"

Malcolm tapped his fingers on the desk, considering. "Not easily. Most manufacturing concerns are private arrangements, partnerships shielded by all manner of legal instruments. The information isn't publicly available."

"But not impossible to discover?" Amelia pressed.

A slight smile touched his lips. "For the sister of one of my oldest friends? I might have some resources." He stood. "Give me a day or two. I'll see what I can uncover about these particular factories."

"I'd be most grateful," Amelia said.

THE CLOCK HAD just struck midnight when Charles found Amelia still hunched over her desk in the small library, surrounded by stacks of documents related to Crown Street Textiles, some of which he'd obtained for her. The single lamp cast long shadows across her face as she made careful notes in the margins of what appeared to be factory inspection records.

"You should rest," he said, setting down two glasses and a decanter of brandy. "These documents will still be here in the morning."

Amelia looked up, blinking as if emerging from a trance. "I've found something," she said, ignoring his suggestion entirely. "Look at these inspection dates."

Charles moved behind her chair, leaning forward to study the paper she was indicating. Her finger traced a series of dates, each marked with an official-looking stamp.

"Four inspections in one month," she explained, "all signed by different inspectors, yet the handwriting is identical on all four reports. And look at the date." She pointed to one corner of the paper. "That's shortly after my accident."

Charles squinted at the signatures, his eyes widening at the revelation. "You're right. Someone's been falsifying inspection records. That's how they got away with the accident. They blamed worker error."

"Exactly," she said, a note of triumph in her voice. "And look at this." She pulled another document from a separate pile, placing it alongside the first. "The same handwriting appears on Crown Street's records from two years prior to my accident."

Their heads were close together now, his cheek nearly touching her hair as they both examined the evidence. The scent of her lavender soap mingled with ink and paper, an oddly intoxicating combination.

"How did you notice this?" he asked.

"Patterns," she replied, shuffling through more papers. "I've been studying handwriting variations in anonymous newspaper submissions for years. Certain people have distinctive ways of forming their letters, particularly when trying to disguise their hand."

Charles straightened, regarding her with new appreciation. "You're rather remarkable at this, you know."

She glanced up, surprise flitting across her features before she composed herself. "Years of investigative journalism teaches one to look beyond the obvious."

"I imagine so." He poured them each a measure of brandy, noting how she unconsciously shifted in her chair, trying to find a more comfortable position for her leg. Without commenting, he moved a footstool closer, positioning it where she could easily use it if she chose.

Their eyes met briefly—his offering, her acknowledgment—before they returned to the documents without a word about her discomfort. He'd learned that direct references to her leg were unwelcome, but subtle accommodations were accepted.

"What else have you found?" he asked, settling into the chair beside her.

For the next hour, they worked in companionable focus, sorting through financial records, inspection reports, and ownership documents. Amelia had devised an ingenious system for cross-referencing information, color-coding certain details and creating a timeline that revealed patterns he might never have noticed.

"Here," she said suddenly, extracting a document from near the bottom of a stack. "This might be significant."

Charles took the paper, studying the faded ink. It was a partial list of shareholders in Northern Industrial Management, the company that ostensibly controlled Crown Street Textiles, from sixteen years ago.

"I don't recognize any names here," he observed.

"No," she agreed, "but look at the third entry."

His eyes found the name she indicated: C.N. Holdings, Ltd.

"Cynthia Norwich, perhaps?" he whispered with a frown. "He could be hiding his ownership behind a shell company named after his then wife."

Amelia nodded, her eyes bright. "The same holding company appears on other old documents as well. And if we cross-reference this with the land registry documents…" She rifled through another pile, wincing slightly as she twisted to reach it.

Without a word, Charles rose and retrieved the stack for her, placing it within easy reach. Their fingers brushed as she accepted the papers, the brief contact sending warmth through his hand.

"Thank you," she said softly, her eyes meeting his for a moment longer than necessary before returning to the documents. Then, without warning, she gasped, her hand flying to her leg.

"What is it?" Charles asked, alarmed.

"Just a cramp," she said through gritted teeth. "It happens sometimes when I sit too long."

Charles knelt beside her chair. "May I?" he asked, his hands hovering near but not touching her leg.

She hesitated before giving a short nod.

With gentle hands, he removed the wooden leg. He could feel the stump through the fabric of her dress. He carefully massaged the spasmic muscles.

"Better?" he asked after a while.

"Yes," she admitted, color rising in her cheeks. "Thank you."

He rose, returning to his seat without making her endure further acknowledgment of the moment of weakness.

Thank you. It was a simple statement, but it carried the weight of a transformation. The words hung in the air, soft but steady. He hadn't expected her to say it—not in such a way, not with such quiet tenderness and sincerity.

Her expression was open, unguarded in a way he rarely saw.

"You're welcome," he replied softly. His voice was just as gentle, as though acknowledging the shift between them, as if he feared breaking the fragile thread weaving its way into their tenuous connection.

THE PAPER TRAIL

A MELIA RETURNED TO find Malcolm looking considerably more serious than usual. He closed his office door firmly behind her.

"What I'm about to show you required calling in several favors," he said without preamble. "And I would appreciate discretion regarding my involvement."

"Of course," Amelia agreed, settling into the chair he offered.

He placed several documents before her. "Regarding Penridge Works and the other factories you've identified—I've found something rather surprising."

Amelia leaned forward, examining the papers. They appeared to be partial copies of investment agreements and banking records.

"These are confidential banking transactions from Coutts," she said, surprised. "How did you obtain these?"

"Best not to ask," Malcolm interrupted. "But look at the investing party."

There, listed as the primary investor in a consortium that had recently acquired controlling interest in Penridge Works, was a name that made her breath catch: Charles Eldem Bartholomew Hereford, Marquess of Hereford.

"This can't be right," she whispered, scanning further down the document. But there was no mistake. Similar records showed Charles had acquired interests in three other factories Norwich had specifically mentioned—all within the past year.

"When exactly did my husband begin acquiring these factory interests?" Amelia asked, her voice tight.

Malcolm consulted his notes. "The first transaction appears to be last May."

That would have been shortly after her editorial series on "The Children of London's Shadows" had been published—her investigation into how poverty forced families to send even their youngest into dangerous trades. She had written about children fainting from exhaustion beside massive looms, their small fingers valued precisely for the dangerous spaces they could reach between moving parts.

Her research had revealed there to have been only marginal improvements in working conditions at those factories. Penridge Works installed some rudimentary guards on a few machines, but workers reported the most dangerous equipment remained unchanged. The accident rate had decreased by perhaps five percent at most.

Amelia's heart sank. A mere five percent in a full year of ownership. If Charles had truly purchased these factories with reform in mind, surely he would have implemented more substantial changes. The alternative explanation turned her blood cold—that he had recognized the profit potential in operations known for cutting costs at the workers' expense.

"Did he purchase controlling interests in all of them?" she asked, desperately seeking some explanation that didn't paint her husband as a hypocrite.

"Only in two cases," Malcolm replied. "The others, he's acquired substantial minority stakes—enough to influence boardroom decisions, though not enough to dictate policy outright."

Conflicting explanations warred in her mind. Had Charles invested to change these factories from within, only to find himself constrained by other shareholders? Or had he simply seen an opportunity to expand his fortune through businesses regardless of her sentiment? The Charles who massaged her phantom pains with such tenderness seemed incapable of such calculated exploitation, yet the man who'd concealed these investments from her certainly might be. Wealth made people unpredictable, after all.

"Malcolm, is there anything in these documents indicating his intentions? Any notes on improvement plans or reform initiatives?"

"Nothing explicit," he admitted. "Though there are records of some heated board meetings where safety measures were discussed. The minutes don't attribute specific positions to individual shareholders."

So, Charles could have been fighting for reforms behind closed doors—or blocking them. The documents offered no clarity, only the damning fact that he had kept these investments from her while professing to support her work.

As she gazed at the papers before her, Amelia felt the ground shifting beneath her feet. The carefully constructed trust she'd begun to build with her husband now seemed built on quicksand.

"Thank you, Malcolm," she said, her voice sounding distant to her own ears. "May I take copies of these?"

His expression was sympathetic. "I've prepared duplicates for you. The originals must remain secure." He hesitated. "Lady Hereford, please be careful. These matters involve powerful interests."

She nodded, carefully placing the copies in her portfolio. "I understand. And I appreciate your discretion in this matter."

As she left the solicitor's office, stepping into the busy London street, Amelia felt as though she were moving through a dream. The revelation churned in her mind, disturbing and inexplicable.

Troubling still was the fact that Norwich had specifically directed her attention to these factories. Was this somehow a calculated move against Charles?

She boarded her carriage, her mind racing with questions that had no clear answers.

As the carriage rattled over the cobblestones, the documents in her portfolio seemed to burn against her side. No explanation could fully erase the fact that Charles had concealed these investments from her.

THE PRIVATE ROOMS at White's club offered quiet amid London's bustle. Hereford sat surrounded by financial records while Steven Thornton studied banking figures by the window, his expression grim.

"The ownership structure is deliberately convoluted," Hereford muttered. "Holding companies within holding companies, all leading nowhere."

"By design," Patrick replied. "To shield the true owners from liability."

The door opened, admitting Carlisle, his normally cheerful countenance replaced by urgency. "This couldn't wait," he said, placing a portfolio on the table. "My bank discovered something significant about Crown Street Textiles."

He opened the portfolio, revealing documents bearing the London Bank's seal. "The quarterly profits have been consistently directed to a single beneficiary." His finger tapped a name that made Hereford's blood run cold: Robert Benson Brydges, Viscount Norwich.

"You're certain?" Steven asked.

"Entirely. Norwich has been sole owner since 1829—six years before Lady Hereford's accident."

Hereford began to pace, cold fury building. "He's been manipulating her. Feeding her information about other factories to distract from his own operations."

"There's more," Carlisle continued. "He personally reviews all expenses above twenty pounds. An extended medical treatment would have crossed his desk." He extracted another document. "And he's been systematically acquiring competing textile operations—often after tragic accidents depress their share prices."

"Building an empire from others' misfortunes," Steven said with disgust.

"We need to speak with someone who was there," Hereford said. "The foreman—Peter Moore."

"Then it's time we paid him a visit," Steven agreed.

As they gathered the damning evidence, Hereford felt something shift inside him. The careful distance he'd maintained from his wife's crusade had burned away, replaced by a fierce and immediate need for justice.

DANCING WITH THE DEVIL

PETER MOORE'S MODEST terraced house sat wedged between identical dwellings on Turnmill Street, their brick facades darkened by years of soot and grime. Amelia adjusted her plain wool cloak and gripped her cane more tightly. The silver lioness head felt cool beneath her palm, a reminder of Charles' faith in her strength.

The house was respectable by local standards, with clean windows and a well-maintained front step. A few hardy flowers struggled against the smoky air in the small patch of ground before the door.

She lifted the brass door knocker and rapped firmly. From within came the sounds of domestic life—children's voices, the clatter of crockery, a woman's voice attempting to impose order on chaos.

The door opened to reveal a neat woman with her hair arranged beneath a modest cap. Her eyes widened at Amelia's refined bearing and the quality of her dress visible beneath the plain cloak.

"Good evening," Amelia said. "I need to speak with Mr. Peter Moore. It concerns Crown Street Textiles."

A shadow crossed Mrs. Moore's features. "And you are, my lady?"

"Someone with questions about an incident from thirteen years past."

The woman paled but stepped aside. "Please, come in. Peter's just finished his dinner."

The front parlor was small but scrupulously clean, walls papered in a pattern that showed signs of age. Children's voices grew louder from the back room.

"I'll fetch him directly." Mrs. Moore hurried toward the rear of the house, calling, "Peter! There's a lady here to see you."

Heavy footsteps approached, and Peter Moore appeared in the doorway, wiping his hands on a cloth napkin. His face, marked by years of factory dust and worry, showed immediate confusion at the sight of a well-dressed lady in his home.

Before he could speak, three children peered around their father—a boy of perhaps twelve, a girl slightly younger, and a small child of six or seven who clung to her father's leg. The sight of them made something twist in Amelia's chest. These children could run, could dance, had all their limbs intact.

"Back to the kitchen with you," Mrs. Moore said, reappearing to shepherd them away. "Let Papa speak with the lady."

"But Mama—" the youngest protested.

"Now, Alice." Mrs. Moore's tone brooked no argument, though she cast worried glances between her husband and Amelia.

Once the children's voices receded to the kitchen, Moore gestured awkwardly to a chair. "I'm Peter Moore, my lady. How may I help you?"

He took the chair nearest the door—positioned to flee, Amelia noted.

"I am the Marchioness of Hereford. You were foreman at Crown Street Textiles thirteen years ago," she stated.

His brows furrowed as he answered cautiously, "Yes, my lady. That was many years past."

"There was an accident. A girl named Amelia Thornton."

Color drained from his face and his whole body seemed to crumple. "That poor child." His voice broke. "I've never forgotten. Such a young thing, barely fourteen."

From the kitchen came the sound of children laughing, quickly hushed by their mother. The domesticity of it all—this man who had been complicit in destroying her future, surrounded by his intact, happy family—made Amelia's chest tight with complicated emotions.

"Tell me what you remember," she said quietly.

Moore's eyes filled with tears. "Everything. I remember everything. The sound when the machine caught her. Her screams. So much blood." He buried his face in his hands. "I carried her out myself. She was so small in my arms, so frightened. Her eyes... the way she looked at me, begging for help."

"What did you do?"

"I held her hand while we waited for the doctor. Tried to keep her conscious. I didn't know what else to do." Tears pooled in his eyes. "When they said they'd have to take the leg, I begged them to reconsider. Dr. Morrison, he said it could be saved with time and proper care, but..."

"But?"

"Mr. Bigham had orders. From the owner. He didn't know which one. The letter demanded economies. No extended treatments, nothing that would cost more than quick solutions." Moore rubbed his weathered face with shaky hands. "I had to... I was forced to hold her down while the doctor..." Amelia thought he might break down and start sobbing, but he suddenly looked up, awareness dawning. "Why are you asking about her? How are you related to Amelia Thornton?"

Amelia lifted her chin, perhaps to erase that pitiful girl from his memory. "I am Amelia Thornton."

His mouth fell open as his eyes roamed over her regal stature. "Dear Lord, you're... you're a lady."

Amelia nodded once and watched the man process her new station. He abruptly stood on shaking legs, moving to a secretary desk. "I kept these. Don't know why. Guilt, maybe. Or knowing someday someone would come asking."

He withdrew a folder with trembling hands, offering it to her.

"Another little girl was deemed disposable eight months after your accident. Their orders. Still unsigned. Still no identity of the owners."

Amelia opened the folder, seeing flowing ink on documents that had sealed another poor creature's fate. When she looked up, Moore was covering his mouth with his hand as if he was going to be sick.

Moore's knees buckled then. He fell to the floor, sobbing. "Forgive me. Please, Lord, forgive me. I have children—I understand what I took from you and the others. Every day I see them run and play, and I remember."

"Peter?" Mrs. Moore appeared in the doorway, alarm on her face. "What's happening?"

"This lady," Moore choked out, "she's the girl from the factory. The one whose leg…"

Mrs. Moore's hand flew to her mouth. "Oh, Peter."

"You held my hand," Amelia said softly, her own voice unsteady now. "When I was screaming, you stayed with me. You sang that song about spring."

"You remember," he whispered.

"I remember the kindness mixed with the horror." She moved toward him and offered her hand. "You were following orders you couldn't refuse without destroying your own family. I understand that."

From the kitchen, children's voices rose again—an argument over the last piece of pudding. Such normal, beautiful sounds of childhood.

"I'm sorry," Moore said as he took her hand and rose to his feet. "I'm so, so sorry."

"I know," she said softly as she stepped toward the door, documents clutched in her hand. "Thank you for keeping these."

With Moore's and his wife's voices faint in the background, Amelia emerged from the house just as a familiar carriage pulled up to the curb. Charles stepped out, followed by Carlisle, Patrick, and Steven. They stopped short at seeing her.

"Amelia?" Steven's shock was evident. "What are you doing here?"

"The same thing you intended, apparently." Her voice turned cool as she looked at Charles, the afternoon's discoveries about his factory ownership fresh in her mind. "Though I've already obtained what we need." She held up the folder. "The direct orders. Their identities are still hidden."

"You confronted Moore alone?" Charles moved toward her, concern evident despite her coldness.

"I confronted the man who carried me, bleeding, from that factory floor." She stepped back from his reach. "Just as I confront anyone who profits from workers' suffering."

Charles' expression shuttered at her pointed tone, clearly catching the accusation beneath her words. The other men exchanged uncertain glances.

"Perhaps we should return home," Charles said carefully. Without a word, she stepped onto the carriage with a footman's help.

The carriage ride was thick with tension. Amelia sat rigidly apart from Charles, while Steven kept shooting confused looks between them. Patrick and Carlisle maintained diplomatic silence, though their discomfort was palpable.

"Did Moore admit to—" Steven began.

"He admitted to following orders he couldn't refuse," Amelia said tersely.

"Did you have to use the cane?" Hereford asked. She shook her head brusquely, catching his meaning. Her husband turned his gaze toward the window.

When they reached the townhouse, the others quickly excused themselves, sensing the storm brewing between husband and wife.

CHARLES FOLLOWED AMELIA to the study, closing the door behind them with quiet deliberation. He sensed her rage, so much so that it seemed to vibrate out of her and ripple in the air.

Amelia moved to the desk where several documents lay spread out—the evidence of his own planning to confront Moore.

"I made some interesting discoveries today," she said, her voice carefully controlled. "About Penridge Works and several other factories with poor safety records."

A chill ran through Hereford, but he managed to keep his voice steady. "What sort of discoveries?"

She turned to face him, her expression hardening. "That you own them, Charles. Or at least, you've acquired interests in them over the past year."

The unspoken accusation hung in the air between them. Hereford had known this conversation might come eventually, but he'd hoped to have more time.

"I can explain," he began.

"Please do," she said, folding her arms across her chest. "Explain how my husband has secretly been acquiring factories known for their appalling safety conditions and worker mistreatment."

"It's not what you think, Amelia."

"No? Do you admit you've been deliberately concealing these investments from me?"

Hereford ran a hand through his hair. "Yes, I admit it. But I haven't acquired these factories for profit."

"Then why?"

"For leverage," he said, meeting her gaze directly. "To force through reforms from the inside. Sometimes the only way to change a system is to control it."

"Then why the secrecy, Charles? Why not tell me what you were doing?"

"Because I knew how it would appear. I knew you would doubt my motives, just as you're doing now."

"How did you expect me to react?" Her voice rose with indignation. "You've been warning me against Norwich while secretly owning the very factories you claim to oppose. These shares have been yours for a year, yet their safety records show only marginal improvement."

"Meaningful change requires both time and money, Amelia." His tone held forced patience. "I'm dealing with several major shareholders who resist every reform. I've been working to persuade them gradually—push too hard, too fast, and they'll dig in their heels out of spite."

Silence stretched between them, thick with tension, before Hereford finally asked, "How did you discover this? These ownership structures are deliberately obscured."

"Lord Norwich directed my attention to these particular factories," she said coolly.

Hereford's jaw tightened. "Of course he did. During your meeting at the *Review* last week."

"Yes. He's been providing documentation about safety violations at various operations. It was only when I verified ownership that your connection emerged."

"Don't you see what he's doing?" Hereford moved closer, urgency bleeding into his voice. "He deliberately led you to my holdings. This wasn't coincidence—it was calculated manipulation."

"Perhaps," she conceded, though her voice remained tight with suspicion. "But his manipulation doesn't prove your innocence."

Hereford drew a sharp breath, visibly struggling to contain his frustration. "I know how this appears, but surely you realize I would never sacrifice workers' lives for profit."

"Your explanations always seem so convenient," she observed with cutting coolness.

"How dare you!" The words exploded from him before he could stop them.

Amelia's eyes blazed. "How dare I? Yes, I dare! A factory girl dares to question her husband's business dealings when workers are losing limbs at his factories—factories he never bothered to mention!"

"Don't diminish everything we've built on one unproven assumption!" His voice cracked with genuine anguish. "Is our marriage worth so little that you'd discard it at the first doubt?"

Her voice turned arctic. "I'm prepared to sever ties with anyone who betrays my trust."

"I haven't betrayed you—I was trying to protect what we have!" Hereford's composure shattered completely. "Norwich has been poisoning you against me from the beginning, and you're letting him succeed!"

She exhaled slowly, as if summoning patience for a petulant child. "I base my judgments on actions, not suspicions. Your actions, not his."

"Then let me give you evidence," Hereford said, his voice dropping to barely controlled intensity. "Norwich was the sole owner of Crown Street Textiles when you were injured there, and he still is."

The color drained from Amelia's face. For a moment, she seemed unable to speak. "What?"

"Norwich was the sole owner thirteen years ago." Hereford moved to his satchel, withdrawing the documents they'd gathered. "That's where I've been today, gathering and confirming evidence."

Her hand trembled slightly as she took the papers, scanning them with growing horror. There at the bottom of a bank document was Norwich's signature. She reached into her reticule and withdrew the letter Moore had given her. Her lungs seized as her mind registered the extravagant bow-shaped swirl under capital *N's* and *O's* that were shaped like *U's*. "How did you discover this?" she asked after inhaling deeply.

"Carlisle's bank," Hereford said quietly.

Amelia sank back into her chair, the documents clutched in her hands. For a long moment, she simply stared at them, her face unreadable.

"And you think he's directing my attention toward your acquisitions because...?"

"Because you're getting too close to the truth," Hereford said, kneeling beside her chair. "He's manipulating you, Amelia. To distract you from his own culpability."

She looked up, her eyes full of pain as they met his. "He's invited me to tour one of his factories tomorrow. Not Crown Street—another operation he claims is a model of modern safety practices."

Alarm coursed through Hereford. "You can't go alone."

As Amelia fell silent, Hereford felt his chest tighten with anticipation. Her fingers traced the edge of the papers, the evidence of Norwich's deception laid bare between them. The lamplight caught the planes of her face, highlighting the furrow between her brows as she weighed his words.

Say something, he urged silently, his muscles coiled with the need to act, to protect, to somehow shield her from the dangerous game they were both forced into. His hands clenched involuntarily, then relaxed as he forced himself to remain still, to let her process what she'd learned.

THE EVIDENCE WAS incontrovertible—Norwich was responsible for her amputation. Amelia stared at the documents, the words blurring as tears she refused to shed pricked at her eyes.

The phantom pain in her missing limb flared with sudden, vicious intensity, as if her body recognized the proximity of its slayer. She pressed her lips together, fighting the wave of nausea that threatened to overwhelm her. How many times had she smiled at him? Thanked him for his assistance? She'd been dancing with her own devil, completely unaware.

Fool, she thought, the word echoing in her mind with bitter self-recrimination. *Stupid, trusting fool.*

Her hands began to shake, the papers rustling as tremors she couldn't control seized her fingers. The room tilted slightly, and she gripped the edge of the desk, her knuckles white against the dark wood.

"Amelia?" Charles' voice seemed to come from very far away. "Are you all right?"

She couldn't answer immediately. The magnitude of Norwich's deception crashed over her in waves—not just the factory decision, but every conversation, every sympathetic look, every carefully crafted manipulation. He had been *studying* her, learning her weaknesses, positioning himself as her ally while knowing exactly what he had stolen from her.

"I need…" she began, then stopped, unsure what she needed. To scream? To weep? To somehow go back in time and see through his mask?

Charles moved closer, his presence steady and grounding. "Take your time."

She drew a shuddering breath, then another. Slowly, the world steadied around her. "I trusted him," she whispered, the words scraping her throat raw. "All this time, I defended him against your warnings. I let him into my office, into my confidence. God, Charles, what if he had—" She couldn't finish the thought.

"But he didn't," Charles said firmly. "You're safe. And now we know the truth."

She swallowed hard, forcing herself to meet his eyes. "Perhaps we could work together on this."

Surprise flickered across Hereford's face, quickly replaced by relief. "Yes," he said, leading her by the elbow. "I have some thoughts on how we might approach this."

He spread the documents on the desk, his shoulder pressed lightly against hers as they bent over the papers. The warmth of his body was comforting, and she leaned against him, drawing strength from his steadiness.

"If we confront him directly, he'll deny everything," Charles said, his finger tracing a line of evidence. "But if you appear to be gathering information innocently…"

"I could still tour his factory," Amelia finished his thought, surprised by how clearly her mind was working despite the emotional turmoil. "Then catch him off guard."

"Exactly."

As they worked through the details—possible routes through Norwich's factory, positions where Steven and Patrick could station themselves, what questions she should ask about "safety innovations"—Amelia found herself watching Charles with growing wonder. How easily they worked together now, his mind complementing hers, anticipating her thoughts, building on her ideas without any of the calculated manipulation Norwich had employed.

When she suggested looking for connections between Norwich's current operation and Crown Street, Charles immediately understood and began mapping potential witnesses among the workers. When she shifted her weight uncomfortably, her leg aching from standing too long, he simply pulled a chair close, guiding her gently into it while continuing their conversation without pause.

The simple gesture made her throat tighten with unshed tears. Here was a man who noticed her discomfort without making her feel diminished by it, who anticipated her needs without making her feel weak.

"We'll need signals," Charles said, his voice dropping to a low murmur as his hand found hers. "Ways for you to alert me if you're in danger."

"You'll be nearby?" Her voice betrayed immense relief.

"Every moment." His eyes met hers, the intensity almost too much to bear. "I'll have Patrick and your brother positioned strategically. You won't be truly alone."

"How will you get in?"

His countenance brightened with a grin. "The same way we always obtain access. With charm, authority, and disguise."

They continued planning, but with each passing moment, Amelia felt the shame building in her chest like a physical weight. *God, what had I been thinking?* The guilt crashed over her in waves. She'd dismissed Charles' warnings as mere jealousy, had defended the monster who had destroyed her life. Her husband—her husband—had seen through Norwich's mask when she, with all her supposed insight, had been completely blind.

"Charles," she said suddenly, her voice barely above a whisper.

He looked up from the map they'd been studying, immediately attentive to the change in her tone.

"I owe you an apology." The words felt like broken glass in her throat. "I should have heeded your advice. I was wrong about Norwich."

Charles' expression softened, his free hand coming up to cup her face with exquisite gentleness.

"You tried to warn me, and I..." Her eyes filled with tears she could no longer hold back. "I accused you of jealousy. I defended him against your concerns. While you were protecting me, I was foolishly trusting the man who destroyed my life."

She could barely speak around the tightness in her throat. "I'm so sorry, Charles. I'm so achingly sorry."

He was quiet for a long moment, his thumb brushing away the tear that escaped down her cheek. When he spoke, his voice was infinitely tender.

"You had no way of knowing. Norwich's been playing this game for decades—he's a master at deception." His hands framed her face now, his touch compassionate. "Amelia... you owe me nothing except your safety tomorrow."

The complete absence of recrimination in his statement only made her tears fall harder. She leaned into his touch, feeling something fundamental shift between them. The dam burst then—all the fear, shame, and relief she'd been holding back poured out in broken sobs. Charles gathered her close, stroking her hair and murmuring soft reassurances until her cries gradually became hiccups.

Amelia dried her tears and took a fortifying breath. They continued planning in quieter tones, their heads close together as they refined their strategy. Charles' patient explanations, his careful attention to her safety, his absolute faith in her ability to carry out their plan despite the danger—it all combined to create a warmth in her chest that recognized the truth.

This was partnership. This was trust. This was what she'd been searching for without knowing it.

When he reached across her to adjust the factory layout map, positioning it so she could see better, when he automatically steadied her elbow as she leaned forward, when he anticipated her questions before she could voice them—she realized she was seeing the man she'd fallen in love with without even knowing it was happening.

"I love you," she whispered, the admission escaping before she could stop it.

Charles went very still, his eyes searching hers as if ensuring he hadn't misheard.

"I think I've been falling in love with you for months," she continued, the words tumbling out now that the dam had broken. "All those times you surprised me, challenged me, protected me when I was too stubborn to see I needed protecting…"

His breath caught, wonder spreading across his features. Then he was kissing her—soft, reverent, full of everything he couldn't say. When they broke apart, his forehead rested against hers.

"I love you too," he murmured. "God help me, Amelia, I've been lost to you since the day you gave me away to that angry gentleman with the walking stick."

A laugh escaped her despite her tears. "That seems like a lifetime ago."

"It was a lifetime ago. We're different people now."

"Better people," she agreed, holding onto him as if he might vanish. "Together."

"Always together," he promised, and in his voice she heard a vow that went far beyond their temporary arrangement. "Now, shall we finish planning how to catch your demon?"

Amelia nodded, feeling centered for the first time in months.

THE MONSTER UNMASKED

THE NORWICH MILL presented a stark contrast to Crown Street Textiles. Tall windows allowed natural light to flood the spacious work floor, ventilation systems whisked away the worst of the cotton dust, and the machinery appeared well-maintained and properly guarded. Workers—including children who looked no younger than twelve—moved with purpose rather than desperate haste, their faces tired but not haunted.

Amelia moved carefully through the factory at Lord Norwich's side, leaning lightly on her new cane. Its weight felt reassuring in her hand, the silver lioness head a reminder of her husband's devotion.

"As you can see, Lady Hereford," Norwich said, gesturing proudly at the operations, "proper conditions need not come at the expense of profitability. These improvements have reduced accidents by nearly forty percent while increasing production by fifteen."

"Impressive," Amelia replied, her tone genuinely appreciative despite reeling with anger inside. "Your commitment to reform is commendable." She paused, studying his face carefully. "Why do you suppose other factory owners refuse to implement such obvious improvements?"

Norwich's smile flickered almost imperceptibly. "Change requires vision, my dear. Many owners find themselves trapped by their initial economies."

Trapped by their economies, Amelia thought bitterly. The same excuse that had cost her a leg.

"Perhaps we could continue this discussion somewhere quieter?" Norwich suggested, his tone shifting slightly. "My office offers documents that might interest you—detailed records of our improvements."

Something in his eagerness set off warning bells but retreat now would arouse suspicion. "Of course," she said lightly. "How thoughtful."

As they moved toward his office, Norwich's hand touched her elbow—a gesture that now felt disturbingly possessive. She cataloged every exit, every potential weapon, every escape route.

Norwich's private office overlooked the factory floor, its elegant appointments incongruous against the industrial backdrop. A tea service awaited them, and once seated, he regarded her with apparent concern.

"I trust you've had opportunity to investigate those other operations I mentioned? Penridge Works, in particular?"

Amelia allowed reluctance to color her expression. "I have, yes. Though I discovered something rather unexpected."

"Oh?"

She met his gaze directly. "The factories you directed me toward are owned by my husband."

Norwich's posture relaxed, his expression shifting to calculated sympathy. "My dear Lady Hereford, how distressing. Though not entirely surprising, I'm afraid."

"What do you mean?"

"Men like Hereford seldom allow sentiment to interfere with profit." His voice carried concern, but something colder flickered beneath. "His reputation for moral flexibility is well-established."

"He tried to justify it as reform strategy," Amelia continued, watching him carefully. "Claiming he intended to improve conditions from within."

Norwich's laugh was sharp. "Reform? Hereford?" The vehemence revealed more than casual disdain. "The man has never shown the slightest interest in workers' welfare. No, Lady Hereford, you've married someone who values currency far more than conscience."

"I find myself torn," Amelia said, allowing vulnerability into her voice. "As a journalist dedicated to exposing unsafe conditions, yet married to a man who perpetuates them."

"What will you do?" Norwich leaned forward, his interest suddenly intense. "Will you write about these discoveries?"

"I'm considering it, though it would create quite the scandal."

"Sometimes scandals are necessary." His eyes gleamed with an emotion that sent chills down her spine. "Your voice carries considerable weight now. An exposé from you could force significant change."

He leaned closer, his voice dropping to something almost intimate. "A woman of your intelligence deserves better than a temporary alliance with such a man. When your arrangement concludes, you might consider more... advantageous partnerships."

Now, Amelia thought. Time to spring the trap.

She lowered her eyes as if considering his words, then looked up with apparent decision. "Perhaps you're right. This discovery has made me reflect on my own accident as well. How different things might have been if Crown Street had maintained standards like your mill."

For the first time, alarm entered Norwich's expression. "A tragic circumstance. Though medical decisions in such cases are complex."

"True." Amelia kept her tone conversational despite her hammering heart. "I've often wondered who made the final determination about my treatment. The factory doctor initially thought the leg could heal properly, you know."

"Did he?" The words came too quickly.

"Yes. Few were aware of that detail." She watched him intently. "The recommendation was changed rather suddenly. Only those directly involved would know the original prognosis."

Norwich rose abruptly, moving to pour himself a drink. "Medical records can be quite... thorough."

"Not in this instance. The final determination wasn't properly documented—merely a notation that amputation was deemed 'most economical.'" She let the phrase hang in the air. "An odd choice of words for a medical decision."

His hand stilled on the decanter. "Business considerations inevitably factor into such decisions, Lady Hereford. Particularly in industrial settings."

"Business considerations," she repeated softly. "Such as the fact that I suffered only a minor fracture? That proper treatment would have restored full function?"

When he turned, his mask had slipped further. "That can't be accurate. No physician would amputate over a simple fracture."

"But it is accurate. Dr. Morrison told me so before he passed."

The crystal stopper clattered to the floor. "You spoke to him?"

"I did. He was quite lucid, despite his illness." Amelia's voice hardened. "He remembered every detail about the pressure to choose the 'economical' option."

Norwich attempted his genial smile, but it came out strained. "The man was dying. Likely confused, speaking nonsense."

"So, you don't deny knowing him." Her tone sharpened. "He said the owner decided amputation was more practical than treating a 'dispensable worker.'"

Something dangerous flashed in Norwich's eyes—recognition that she was no longer the naive woman he'd been manipulating. His carefully constructed persona began cracking like thin ice.

"He was not of sound mind," Norwich said, but his voice had lost its warmth.

"He was adamant about the details. A simple fracture that—"

"It wasn't simple!" The words exploded from him. "Your leg was broken in three places! The muscles and arteries were damaged!"

The silence that followed was deafening. Amelia felt time

slow as she watched comprehension dawn on his face—the horrified realization of what he'd revealed. His lips parted as if to retract the words, but they both knew it was too late.

A strange calm settled over her, replacing the nervous tension. This was the moment she'd unknowingly worked toward for thirteen years.

"The only way you could know the extent of my injury," she said quietly, "is if you'd seen Dr. Morrison's medical assessment. The one he was ordered to ignore."

Norwich's face went ashen. For a long moment, he simply stared at her, his careful facade crumbling entirely. When he spoke again, all pretense was gone.

"You were an unskilled child laborer," he said flatly. "The economic calculation was straightforward."

The casual confirmation struck Amelia to the core. She had expected denials, rationalizations—not this cold acknowledgment.

"You destroyed my life for profit," she whispered.

"I made a sensible business decision. One of dozens required in industrial management." His voice had turned clinical, matter-of-fact. "It kept the factory operational and provided employment for hundreds."

Fury surged through her, hot and pure. "Is that how you justify it? All those lives you've ruined?"

"I didn't anticipate you'd discover Hereford's involvement so quickly," he continued, as if she hadn't spoken. "You're more capable than I credited."

"I'm going to expose you," Amelia said, her voice trembling with rage. "Everything—Crown Street, my amputation, your manipulation."

"Hereford's factories have deplorable conditions too," Norwich replied smoothly. "Exposing me will only make you a hypocrite. Think carefully. Do you believe Society will embrace accusations from a crippled woman against a respected peer?"

"They will with evidence. And with the Marquess of Hereford supporting me."

Norwich's expression darkened completely. "Evidence can disappear. As can troublesome journalists."

The naked threat hung between them. Amelia rose carefully, her hand finding the head of her cane. With practiced ease, she twisted and drew the concealed blade.

"Is that how you silence critics?" she asked, backing toward the door. "Through violence?"

"When necessary." He advanced with predatory grace. "Your husband has been inconvenient, acquiring interests in operations I've controlled for years. Perhaps your tragic accident will distract him sufficiently."

Amelia's wooden leg caught on a chair, sending her stumbling backward with a clatter. Norwich lunged forward, his hands seizing what he thought was her injured limb and her left arm.

Shock registered in his eyes as his grip met wood instead of flesh. The prosthetic detached, sending him staggering backward still clutching the wooden leg, his face a mask of horror and confusion.

Taking advantage of his shock, Amelia struck. She drove the sword downward through his polished boot with savage satisfaction.

Blood welled through the fine leather as Norwich collapsed with a howl. Amelia gripped her sword firmly, struggling to maintain balance on her remaining leg.

"You vicious little cripple!" he screamed, clutching his impaled foot.

Before she could respond, the door crashed open. Hereford's strong hands caught her, pulling her against his chest as Patrick Adams and Steven Thornton moved to flank the wounded Norwich.

"You're trespassing!" Norwich snarled, trying to rise but falling back. "This is assault!"

"With what witnesses?" Adams asked mildly.

"I witnessed you attacking the marchioness, Norwich," came

a deep voice from the side door.

The Duke of Lancaster straightened from where he'd been leaning against the desk, his expression coldly aristocratic.

Color drained from Norwich's face as he took in the four men surrounding him, then looked at Amelia standing defiant despite her ordeal.

"I need a doctor…" he said through gritted teeth, still clutching his bleeding foot.

Hereford's smile was cold. "Indeed. A surgeon has been summoned and shall arrive presently to relieve you of your limb, Norwich. More expedient, would you not agree?"

Norwich's face went pale, but his eyes blazed with impotent fury. "You wouldn't dare. I'm a peer of the realm."

"And you tried to harm a marchioness. My wife!" Hereford closed his eyes briefly and gathered his composure. "Though I suspect public opinion will find poetic justice rather satisfying."

Norwich looked around at the four men, then at Amelia, his expression shifting from rage to calculating assessment. Even wounded and trapped, he was already planning his next move.

"Impeccable timing," Amelia said, looking up at her husband fondly.

"Indeed," Hereford replied, his eyes crinkling. "Though it appears you were managing quite admirably on your own, my sweet."

SNOWFLAKE

THE EARLY MORNING sun cast dappled shadows through the leaves as Amelia adjusted her position in the saddle. Persephone, the gentle chestnut mare Charles had chosen for her lessons, stood patiently beneath her, occasionally twitching an ear but otherwise remaining still. Charles walked beside them, one hand resting reassuringly on the bridle while the other hovered near Amelia's waist, ready to steady her if needed.

"You're doing splendidly," he encouraged, his normally rakish grin replaced by something gentler. "Your confidence has improved remarkably in just three weeks."

Amelia couldn't help the flush of pleasure that warmed her cheeks at his praise. "It's all thanks to your patience," she admitted. "And Persephone's gentle temperament."

Charles nodded thoughtfully. "She's one of our most reliable mares. Perfect for building confidence."

They continued along the wooded path that wound through the private section of Richmond Park that the Hereford family had access to. It was their fourth riding lesson, and the first time Charles had suggested venturing beyond the paddock near the stables. The solitude was welcome after weeks of curious stares from stable hands who had never seen the Marquess of Hereford personally teaching anyone to ride, let alone his unconventional wife.

"Any word from your solicitor about Norwich's transportation?" Amelia asked, her voice carefully neutral despite the satisfaction that warmed her at the thought.

"Seven years in Van Diemen's Land," Charles replied with grim pleasure. "The Crown was quite receptive to our evidence of fraud and assault once presented properly. His noble connections couldn't save him from such overwhelming testimony." He squeezed her hand gently. "Justice, my dear. Finally."

Amelia was quiet for a moment, her fingers unconsciously tightening on the reins. "I confess I feel more relief than satisfaction," she said softly. "For so many years, I carried the weight of not knowing who was responsible. Now that burden is lifted, and perhaps other workers will be safer for it."

"They already are," Charles said with quiet pride. "The Parliamentary committee has implemented the safety standards we proposed across all textile operations. Your exposé changed everything, Amelia. No more thirteen-year-old girls will lose their limbs to men like Norwich."

"Thanks to you," Amelia said, her voice thick with emotion as she looked at her husband with profound gratitude.

"No, my sweet." Charles' voice was tender as he reached to pat her shoulder, his touch gentle. "It was your courage and persistence that made this possible. Your refusal to let injustice stand unchallenged." His eyes held hers, bright with pride and something deeper. "I am so very proud of you."

The tenderness of the contact, even through the glove, sent a familiar flutter through her chest. How far they had come from that first night when he'd hidden behind her printing press—two strangers bound by convenience, now partners in every sense that mattered.

They continued in companionable silence, the soft clip-clop of Persephone's hooves on the earthen path the only sound save for the birdsong filtering through the canopy above. Amelia found herself marveling at the strange turns life could take—how a marriage of necessity had blossomed into something neither of them had dared hope for.

"There's a clearing ahead," Charles said eventually, his voice carrying a note of anticipation as he guided Persephone around a bend in the path. "Perfect place for a rest."

As they emerged from the trees, Amelia gasped softly. A small meadow stretched before them, carpeted with wildflowers and bordered by ancient oaks. Near the center, beneath the sprawling branches of a particularly magnificent tree, sat a blanket laden with a picnic basket, cushions, and what appeared to be a bottle of champagne nestled in ice.

"You planned this," she said, unable to keep the wonder from her voice.

Charles' smile was almost boyish in its eagerness. "Cooper may have received instructions to have everything prepared. Do you approve?"

"It's beautiful," she admitted. Then, with a touch of the teasing that had become natural between them, "Though I'm suspicious of your motives, my lord. Such elaborate seduction seems unnecessary when I'm already your wife."

His laugh rang out, startling a nearby bird into flight. "Perhaps I simply enjoy surprising you." He reached up to help her dismount, his hands strong and steady at her waist. "Or perhaps," he added, his voice dropping to that intimate register that never failed to send shivers down her spine, "I find that anticipation enhances the experience."

Once safely on the ground, Amelia smoothed her riding habit, acutely aware of his nearness. He tethered Persephone to a low branch where the mare could graze comfortably, then offered Amelia his arm.

"Shall we? I'm told Cook has outdone herself."

The picnic was indeed magnificent—cold chicken, freshly baked bread still warm from being wrapped in linen, strawberries from the Hereford greenhouse, and tiny custard tarts that melted on the tongue. The champagne sparkled in crystal glasses that caught the sunlight, casting prisms across the blanket.

As they ate, conversation flowed easily between them.

Charles described his latest meeting with the factory reform committee, where several more owners had agreed to implement safety measures based on the standards they'd established. Amelia shared the response to her most recent editorial on educational opportunities for working-class children.

"Your readership has doubled yet again in the past month," Charles observed, refilling their glasses. "The *Review* is becoming quite influential."

"Yes, though I suspect some buy it merely to see what scandalous opinions the Marchioness of Hereford might express next." She smiled, leaning back against one of the cushions. "The novelty of an aristocrat championing workers' rights continues to sell papers regardless of their opinions of me."

Amelia reached for her champagne and took a sip. She then fixed Charles with a deliberately innocent expression. "I've been wondering, my lord, what is your favorite story from your salacious literature business? Any particular narrative that... captivates you?"

Charles, who had just taken a generous swallow of champagne, choked spectacularly. He coughed, eyes watering.

"I beg your pardon?" he managed once he'd recovered his breath, his voice hoarse.

Amelia maintained her innocuous mien, though mischief danced in her eyes. "Your publishing venture. I was simply curious which stories you found most... stimulating."

"Um... Why do you ask?" His voice was rough from coughing.

She tilted her head, studying his flushed face, the way his eyes had darkened despite his apparent confusion. "I was merely curious about your... preferences. Whether our encounters satisfy you as thoroughly as your fictional adventures."

The effect was immediate. His expression shifted, suspicion melting into something far more heated. He set down his glass and moved across the blanket until he was beside her, close enough that she could feel the warmth radiating from him.

"My darling wife," he rasped low, "I find each of our encounters more intoxicating than any fiction."

His fingers came up to trace the line of her jaw with exquisite gentleness. "Each time I learn something new about you—what makes you sigh, what makes you tremble." His thumb brushed across her lower lip. "What makes you whisper my name in that way that drives me half mad with wanting you."

Amelia felt heat bloom in her cheeks, spreading down her neck and across her chest. Despite their months of marriage and increasing intimacy, his words still had the power to affect her profoundly.

"Truly?" she whispered.

"Truly." His eyes held hers, all pretense and artifice stripped away, leaving only raw honesty. "I've had many lovers in my misspent youth, Amelia, but none have captivated me the way you do. None have challenged me, surprised me, or satisfied me as completely."

As he spoke, his fingers traced her jaw, and Amelia felt her own boldness growing. The strawberries, the champagne, the privacy of their secluded meadow—it all combined to make her feel deliciously wicked. When he fed her another strawberry, watching her lips with such intensity, she made her decision.

CHARLES WATCHED AS Amelia lay her head on his lap and closed her eyes. The sunlight danced across her face, highlighting the expressive contours and the copper highlights he'd come to adore. Her eyes, those intelligent eyes that had first challenged him across a printing press, opened and now regarded him with a softness that made his heart swell.

He stroked her hair, allowing himself to fully appreciate the moment before reaching for the bowl of strawberries. He selected a particularly plump specimen, its surface glistening with dew.

With deliberate slowness, he brought it to her lips, watching intently as they parted to receive the offering. The stark contrast of the bright red fruit against her pale skin fascinated him.

Her teeth sank into the strawberry, juice beading at the corner of her mouth. She closed her eyes, clearly savoring the sweetness. His breath hitched as a small, appreciative sound escaped her throat—not quite a moan, but something equally stirring.

"Good?" he asked, his voice hoarse.

She nodded, eyes still closed. "Simply perfect."

He selected another, trailing it lightly across her bottom lip before allowing her to take a bite. This time, he couldn't resist swiping at the tiny droplet of juice with his thumb.

Amelia's eyes opened, their depths darkened with an awareness that matched his own. Her tongue darted out to catch a drop of juice, inadvertently brushing against his thumb. The contact sent a current of desire through him that was far from simple.

"More?" he asked softly, offering her the remainder of the strawberry.

As she took it from his fingers, her lips closed briefly around them—a seemingly innocent gesture made provocative by the intensity between them. Charles found himself entranced by her mouth, by the sensual pleasure she took in something so ordinary as eating fruit.

He fed her another, then another, each exchange becoming increasingly intimate. The ritual transformed into something primal—the act of providing nourishment, of watching her receive it with such evident enjoyment, stirred his ardor.

Then he felt her hands reach for his falls, opening them with surprising efficiency.

"What do you think you're doing, Lady Hereford?" he asked with half shock and half hope.

"I thought I'd help you decide on your favorite salacious story, my lord," she whispered as his erection sprung to life, her warm breath tickling the exposed skin.

A low rumble escaped his throat, his rod twitching at his wife's attention. "What did you have in mind, Wife?" he asked, closing his eyes, not daring to dream. Then he felt her dainty fingers wrap around his girth and squeeze gently, the delicious pressure sending a jolt of pure pleasure through his body.

"Amelia…"

Her hand gently tugged on his member until he was on his knees, bracketing her head. With his breeches pulled down to his knees, Hereford gazed down at his wife, her eyes glazed with lust, and her hand gathering her skirts to reach her bud.

"Amelia… Christ…"

Her fingers moved to tug on his testicles, stroking and examining. The wickedness of the act had blood pooling in his cock. Hereford bit his bottom lip as the sight nearly pushed him over the edge.

Then the damnable woman brushed the sensitive skin of his bollocks with her tongue. A jolt of arousal thundered through his groin at the shocking sensation. A beastly groan escaped his throat as Hereford gripped his cock and began to stroke. His gaze fixed on his wife as her tongue swirled and stroked as if they were the sweetest plums.

"Sweetheart… bloody hell…"

Another thunderbolt of lust crashed through him as his eyes captured the hand that was rubbing her bud. Her moans vibrated through his balls even as his mind wandered between the reality and his heightened senses. A recognition erupted in his mind.

"Snowflake…" he muttered, his eyes flying open and sharpening on Amelia's flushed face. His wife… the innocent who had cried out in pain when he took her virginity, looked up at him with half-hooded eyes, glazed with lust as she continued to lick his bollocks.

A laugh escaped his mouth while the knowledge of his wife's mischief and her ministration drove him to his peak. With a sharp intake of his breath, Hereford exploded in his hand against the hem of his shirt, his body shuddering as it transformed every ounce of pleasure from his wife into a mind-shattering orgasm. Her tongue slowed and gentled, soothing the rawness that accompanied such a climax.

"Minx, you've been fooling me all this time," he murmured, his voice muffled while he removed his shirt.

Her smile was slow and sweet. "Yes," she agreed. "And drawing inspiration from you."

They lay together as their breathing returned to normal, bodies still intertwined, the remnants of their picnic scattered around them. Charles brushed a strand of hair from Amelia's flushed face, his expression caught between amusement and adoration.

"Snowflake," he said again, testing the name on his tongue. "I should have known when all the noblemen in her stories were foolish rakes being debauched by bluestockings."

Amelia's eyes sparkled with mischief. "I must say, my lord, I'm quite impressed that you had the presence of mind to recognize the scenario while in such a compromised position."

"I've always been able to maintain a clear head during diffi-cult situations," he replied with mock pride. "A skill that serves me well in many circumstances."

"It's no wonder you've been able to escape all those angry papas and husbands," she said, chuckling at the memory.

"I'd wondered, what with your violet ink and certain phrasings, but didn't dare to dream…"

Amelia's voice was contemplative when she replied, "I thought of you often, you know, while writing those provocative stories."

"Thank heavens for that," he murmured. "And here I thought I'd married a proper bluestocking editor."

"You did," she said, the tips of her fingers trailing down his chest. "You also married Snowflake. I contain multitudes, my lord."

"So you do." His heart swelled as he studied the tiny flutter-ing of her thick eyelashes. "A crusading journalist, a brilliant author of forbidden literature, and a marchioness who continues to surprise her husband at every turn.

Amelia reached up to trace the line of his jaw. "And you, Lord Hereford. There is more to you as well than merely a reformed rake."

"I shall deny it until the very end," he said, capturing her hand in his and kissing her knuckle.

"Is there an aspect of you I have yet to discover?"

"I suppose you'll have to keep investigating," he suggested, his smile turning wicked. "I hear you're quite talented at uncovering secrets."

"A lifelong pursuit," she declared solemnly.

"A most peculiar courtship we've had," he observed, linking his fingers through hers. "From arrangement to animosity to… this."

Amelia laughed, the sound carrying across the meadow. "And what is 'this' exactly?"

Charles considered her question. "I can't find the right words befitting the discovery of love in our forced marriage, uncovering corruption, and publishing scandalous literature. Together."

"I believe," she began, her hand playing with the hair on his chest, "that our own story might be the most scandalous one to date if I may say so myself."

His answering laugh was as warm as the summer sun. "Then by all means, my darling Snowflake, let us not stop being wonderfully scandalous."

The End

Wow, you made it to the end. Well done, you. Do me a favour if you can. Please leave me a review on Amazon, Bookbub or Goodreads.

If you want more of this goodness, please join Team Mihwa at dragonbladepublishing.com/team/mihwa-lee

Keep in touch! Sign up for my newsletter at mihwawrites.com

Want to hear about my writing process and inappropriate thoughts? Join Mihwa's Den of TMI on FB: facebook.com/groups/2110002726016346

Thank you.

About the Author

Mihwa Lee is NOT a New York Times, USA Today, or Amazon Best Selling Author. But what she is not, she makes up for with her sense of humour, unusual life experiences, and imagination. The combination of these qualities can yield entertaining stories and parties. As a result, she is a sought-after guest at all parties and karaoke except those that have banned her.

Mihwa became a writer after retiring as a medical expert witness in brain injury (like Law & Order but boring) because she hates disposable income and thought it would be fun to piss off her teenagers. She has bookmarked her favourite steamy scenes in her books for her children in case they need her advice once she's gone. Her children are mortified but tolerate her legacy because of the potential for a passive income.

Mihwa is passionate about equalising the world population through education. She has set up a scholarship in Costa Rica (where she used to live) to send underprivileged Latin American youths to university and/or fund their entrepreneurial ventures.

Mihwa believes in living life to the fullest. Therefore, she writes steamy historical romance like a woman possessed.

linktr.ee/mihwawrites
FB reader group: Mihwa's Den of TMI
TikTok: @mihwa.lee
IG: mihwawrites
YouTube: @DesireDialogue